D0435976

BLOOD IN
THE WATER

BLOOD IN THE WATER

A Gregor Demarkian Novel

JANE HADDAM

MINOTAUR BOOKS
NEW YORK

This is a work of fiction.

All of the characters, organizations, and events portrayed in this novel are either products

of the author's imagination or are used fictitiously.

BLOOD IN THE WATER.

Copyright © 2012 by Jane Haddam.

For information address St. Martin's Press, 175 Fifth Avenue, New York, N.Y. 10010.

Library of Congress Cataloging-in-Publication Data

Haddam, Jane, 1951–

Blood in the water / Jane Haddam. — 1st ed.

p. cm.

ISBN 978-0-312-64434-5 (hardcover)

ISBN 978-1-4299-5131-9 (e-book)

1. Demarkian, Gregor (Fictitious character)—Fiction.   2. Private investigators—Pennsylvania—

Philadelphia—Fiction.   3. Rich people—Fiction.   4. Women—Crimes against—Fiction.

I. Title.

PS3566.A613B58 2012

813'.54—dc23

2011041006

First Edition: March 2012

10   9   8   7   6   5   4   3   2   1

PROLOGUE

1

It was seven o'clock on the morning of Friday, October fifth, and Arthur Heydreich was at peace. "At peace" might not be exactly the phrase he was looking for. He'd been thinking about it the entire twenty-six minutes he'd spent in the shower. It was a wonderful shower, the best he'd ever had in his life. The shower stall was big enough for at least two people. It would have reminded him of the shower stall at school where everybody had to shower together after practice, except here the floor and walls were made of marble. The showerhead was huge, too. You could get two people in there comfortably, with both of them getting wet. He never showered with anybody else. He liked the feel of the water stinging his skin, especially when it was nearly hot enough to make him bleed. It was the hot that was the final nail, the nail that nailed it all together. He'd had enough of cold showers when he was growing up, and not because he needed to cool off from some hot fantasy on the Internet. There hadn't even been an Internet. No, he'd had enough of cold showers because his mother was always forgetting to pay the gas bill.

Either that, or she wasn't able to pay it. One way or another, the small, cramped apartment in South Philly had been cold.

Arthur stepped out into the middle of his bathroom and looked around. He'd bought this house because of this bathroom—or almost, sort of. He'd bought this house because it was in Waldorf Pines, but he could have bought any house in Waldorf Pines. He'd been only the second person to sign a contract. He'd looked at all the houses and then he'd seen this bathroom and that had been it. It was bigger than his bedroom at home had been. It had extra-large terracotta tiles on the floor and marble everything else. There was a whirlpool. There was a bidet nobody ever used. There were his-and-hers sinks and his-and-hers vanities. He could have played handball in there without feeling cramped.

He stepped naked from the bathroom into the even larger dressing room and headed for his own walk-in closet, because this house had his-and-hers walk-in closets in the master bedroom. The closet was also bigger than his bedroom at home. On one wall there were built-in drawers for things like underwear and socks. His shirts and ties were hung up next to his suits. The maid did it when she was finished cleaning up downstairs.

Arthur got a good black suit and a cream-colored shirt and one of the ties Martha had matched up for him. It amazed him that he could have spent the last few weeks in such an agony of depression—such an agony of something. He hadn't paid attention to the house or the suits or his car or anything at all, not for days. It was crazy. Ever since he'd started climbing his way out of the mess he'd been born into, he'd made it a point to note and appreciate every increase in his circumstances on a regular basis. He wanted to appreciate those things over and over again. He wanted never to forget, and he wanted never to get used to it. That was how people fell off the map. They got used to it. They took it for granted. They got sloppy. Arthur Heydreich was anything but sloppy.

He stepped into the bedroom proper and looked at his wife's side of the bed, ruffled and mussed and every which way, as if she'd been murdered there during the night and struggled so hard she'd pulled the bed sheets off. Martha always slept like that. It drove Arthur a little crazy. She tossed and turned at night and she left her clothes in a trail on the floor and she left dirty dishes on the kitchen table. This was apparently the way you behaved if you'd had maids all your life. It was also the way you behaved if you were dirt poor and didn't give a damn. Sometimes Arthur wanted to grab her by the shoulders and shake her.

On the other hand, the bed was something called a "California king." It was bigger than most beds. Arthur wondered why it wasn't called a "Texas king." Whatever it was called, he didn't need to worry about Martha tossing. She was far enough away that she might have been in a different room.

He got his wallet off the nightstand next to his side of the bed and put it in his pocket. Then he headed downstairs. "At peace" was not the phrase he wanted, but there had to be one out there. "Resolved" was wrong. It sounded as if he had made up his mind to do something, or come to some kind of decision. There were no more decisions to be made. He understood everything now. He had nothing more to worry about. All the problems had been . . . resolved.

Whatever.

The staircase to the ground floor was a big sweeping thing that came off a balcony. All the ceilings were very high. A chandelier hung down from the ceiling into the curve. The front door was actually a double door and had windows all around it. Arthur took note of each and every thing, cataloging it in his head, as if he were a real estate agent getting ready to show the place.

He went down across the foyer, then through the living room. The living room had a massive fieldstone fireplace that took up one entire wall. There were two conversational groupings of couches and love seats and chairs. Martha had done a very good job with all of it. She did a very good job at all the things he had married her for, except one.

Arthur went through the dining room—another chandelier, a table with chairs to seat twenty-four; they gave dinner parties here—and then through the butler's pantry into the kitchen. The kitchen was part of a big open space that included an octagonal sunroom for a breakfast nook and the family room. You really had to be careful going through this house. The lists alone could make you dizzy.

There was one place set at the kitchen table, a place mat with a stemmed crystal bowl full of melon balls on it. There was a silver spoon next to the bowl. There was a coffee cup and saucer next to the place mat. There was a linen napkin next to that. Arthur sat down, put the napkin on his lap, and said,

"Cortina?"

Cortina was the maid. She was very small and very Latina and probably, Arthur suspected, illegal. At first, he'd objected to that. He was very careful about the things he did in his life. He'd gotten all the way to Waldorf Pines and he intended to stay there. He didn't want to get fired one day because he'd been employing illegal immigrants and not paying their Social Security taxes. Martha had explained all that to him. It was a big world out there, one he'd never suspected.

"Cortina?" he said again.

Cortina stuck her head out of the walk-in pantry and grunted. "I am coming," she said. "Do you know how late Mrs. Heydreich is going to sleep? I need to have a time for the housecleaning or I get behind."

"Mrs. Heydreich isn't asleep," Arthur said. "She was up and out before I even woke up this morning. She must have one of her committees."

"Her car is in the garage. I saw it when I came in."

Arthur stood up and walked across, past the pantry door, to the mudroom. He went through the mudroom and then opened the door to the garage. It was a heated garage. Cars never failed to start just because of the weather. If you had good cars, you had to make sure to take care of them.

He had good cars. His own was a Mercedes S-Class sedan, a good dark blue, sober and responsible and establishment. Martha's was a

Mercedes, too, but one of those little two-seaters, and painted bright pink. It was sitting where it was supposed to be, in the bay farthest from the pantry door.

Arthur closed up and thought about it. Then he went back to the kitchen.

"Huh," he said. "Maybe she walked. It's only across the golf course. It's a nice day."

"Does that sound like Mrs. Heydreich to you? That she would walk?"

"It's a nice day," Arthur said. "Martha does walk. She walks all the time."

"She drives that car all the time. Everywhere. She's famous for it. You should hear the other maids talk about it. And it isn't just the maids."

"I'm not sure what you want out of me," Arthur said. "If she isn't here and she didn't take her car, she must have walked."

"Things happen," Cortina said. "People are kidnapped. People disappear. People are murdered and found in ditches."

"Are you saying you think my wife was kidnapped and murdered? Out of her own bed? With me in it?"

"I'm saying you don't know what happens. You never know. Things happen."

Arthur sat down at his place at the table again. Then he reached into his pocket and brought out his cell phone. "This is crazy. You do know that, don't you?"

"Things happen," Cortina said. "I don't live here. Maybe you sleep like the dead. Things happen all the time where I come from."

Arthur wanted to say that where she came from there was a drug war going on, and people killed their local government officials if they couldn't get a job in the post office for their uncles. He didn't say it because he didn't know it was true, and because that wasn't the way you talked to maids.

He punched Martha's speed dial number into the phone and waited. She had a million committees. She was on the admissions committee for the Waldorf Pines golf club and the cotillion committee, too, and she did volunteer work at the Waldorf Pines library. She had so many things to do, it almost didn't matter that she didn't get paid for them. She was busier than he was.

He let the phone ring for a moment and then, just when he was about to put it down and give up, he heard the ringtone on Martha's phone, sounding muffled but oddly close. He closed his phone and looked up.

"Ah," Cortina said.

"Don't be ridiculous," Arthur said.

He opened his phone and punched in the speed dial number again. This time, Martha's phone started ringing almost immediately, crashing its way through a tinny rendition of "I Enjoy Being a Girl."

Arthur got up and followed the sounds into the family room.

Martha's big Coach handbag was sitting on the coffee table in front of the couch, closed up tight and looking like she'd put it down there half a minute ago.

2

Caroline Stanford-Pyrie was at the end of her rope, and her ropes were never very long to begin with. It just went to show, really, that it was always a bad idea to sign yourself up for organized hospitality. Organized camaraderie might be more like what this was supposed to be—oh, she didn't know what it was supposed to be. She didn't even care anymore. She just wished the world would go back to being what she remembered it being, and then she'd be able to sit down and relax for a little while. As it was, she kept herself up at night, worrying that things were going to go wrong and it was somehow going to be all her fault.

Right now what was going wrong was this meeting, and it was going to go on going wrong as long as everybody insisted on showing up late. That was one of the ways you could tell the right people from the wrong ones. The right people were always absolutely punctual, even if they'd had a snootful the night before and felt like death warmed up. Caroline felt that way quite a lot of the time, but that didn't stop her from doing what she'd promised to do. Character, that was what mattered. Character and breeding.

Caroline made her way from the foyer of the Waldorf Pines country club to the big dining room at the back. There were no cars coming down that absurd circular drive. There was nobody at all arriving for this meeting, and she had set it for seven o'clock precisely to escape all those lame excuses everybody had for needing to be into work early. To hear these women talk, every business in America expected its junior executives to be at their desks and hard at it before dawn. It was nonsense, and she knew it. She knew that they knew she knew it.

She went through the big double doors into the dining room proper and looked around. Little Susan Carstairs was sitting at one of the tables near the big wall of windows looking out on the terrace. Susan was a mouse. It made Caroline crazy. It didn't matter who had done what or when or why, Susan apologized.

"Well, that's it," Caroline said. "Not a sign of anybody. And I'll bet there won't be a sign of anybody. They all say they want to be on committees. They all say they want to be part of things. Then when it comes time to do the work—well."

Susan sniffled. "Well," she said. "Maybe it really is the time, Caroline. Maybe we should hold meetings in the evenings."

"Don't be ridiculous," Caroline said. She went up to the big wall of windows and looked out. The swimming pool was blocked off by what looked like crime scene tape. It was just a yellow caution bar, because there were repairs going on in the cabana and the pool house. Repairs were supposed to be going on, but they weren't. Nobody was there working on anything. Nobody would be there working on anything today. The job would wait and wait and wait, just as it had waited and waited and waited since Labor Day. Then they'd bring somebody in at the last minute in the middle of the winter, and everything would cost more than twenty times what it would have if they'd managed to get it all done at the right time.

"Honestly," Caroline said.

Susan made a strangled little noise.

Caroline ignored her. "Can you imagine," Caroline said, "what our mothers would have thought of this place if they'd ever seen it? Do you remember what it was like, growing up on the Main Line when we did? Waldorf Pines. My God. It sounds like the kind of thing some backstreet hooker would make up for the name of her fantasy estate. It's a cotillion committee, for God's sake. It's not rocket science. They all want cotillions and they want their daughters to 'come out' and get their names in the newspapers, even if it isn't in the right part of the newspapers, except they don't know that, either. They don't know anything. It's enough to make you scream."

"I think they just want things to be nice," Susan said. "I know it isn't like what we had when we grew up—"

"I came out at the Assemblies. You did, too. You know what a cotillion is supposed to be about."

"Yes," Susan said. "Yes, I know, but—"

"There aren't any buts," Caroline said. "There are ways you do things and ways you don't. These people get jobs in brokerage firms and they think they've—oh, I don't know what they think they've done. A gated community. Can you honestly believe that? My mother would have died of embarrassment."

"It's good for privacy," Susan said.

Caroline shot her a look, but it was useless. Susan was looking at her hands. They had made a promise, when they first moved out here, that they would never even hint at any of the things that had made them decide to make the move, but Susan wasn't good at it. Susan thought about it all the time. Caroline could tell.

She moved away from the windows and sat down at the other side of Susan's table. "The Platte boy isn't on duty, either," she said. "He's supposed to be over there at six, making sure nothing gets messed about, but there's no sign of him. People have no sense of responsibility these days. Do you know that? They've got no sense of responsibility. Maybe these people never had. God only knows where they started out from."

"I do think they mean well," Susan said.

Caroline shrugged. There would be coffee in the kitchen. She could go out to find it and pour herself a cup. The dining room wasn't open at this time of the morning on a Friday. They only opened it for breakfast on weekends. She was enormously tired, and she was absolutely sure that she had made a mistake. She shouldn't have volunteered for this committee. She shouldn't have volunteered for any committee. She didn't belong here, and pretending to care if stockbrokers' daughters made fake debuts in overdesigned ball gowns did not change a thing about her life.

"You know what's really odd?" she said. "Even that awful woman didn't show up. She always shows up."

"Martha Heydreich," Susan said.

"Oh, I remember the name," Caroline said. "I could hardly forget the name, could I? She's the absolute symbol of what's wrong with this place and everything in it. That pink car. And that hair. And let's don't forget the makeup. You'd think she had stock in Max Factor."

"Maybe she does," Susan said, "except I think she wears Clinique. Something like that. She does have beautiful hands. I don't think I've ever seen such delicate hands."

"Well, yes, but she makes sure you notice them, doesn't she? That ring of hers is ridiculous, and she's always holding it out so that you see it. And the nails."

"She gets them done," Susan said. "But I wish I had hands like that. They're so long—do you remember what our mothers used to say about hands? You could always tell a lady by her hands. She's got a lady's hands."

"She's got a stevedore's backside."

Susan sniffed. "She's a very hard worker," she said.

"Yes, and very reliable most of the time. Wouldn't she be, though?

I mean, the one person you don't want to see show up, and there she is, looking like a circus clown and acting like—I don't know what. Even the nitwits who live in this place know there's something completely awful about her. That trilling voice. Those enormous bags. And the jewelry. Oh, never mind. I shouldn't go on like this. But it's indicative, don't you see? It's indicative of everything that goes on in this place."

"Of course I see," Susan said.

Caroline gave her a look. Susan did not see. Susan never could see. She sighed and got up. She might as well go get that coffee. At least that way the morning wouldn't be completely wasted. She wasted far too many mornings these days.

"I miss it," she said suddenly. "I know I'm breaking our rule, but I miss it."

"I miss it, too," Susan said.

"It's funny how things work out. If you'd told me just three years ago that I'd be living at a place called Waldorf Pines and refusing to watch the evening news in case—well, in case. I wouldn't have believed it. I really wouldn't have believed it."

"I know," Susan said.

"And then there are the boys," Caroline said.

She stood still where she was, contemplating her two sons. They were in New York now, she was pretty sure. She hadn't talked to either one of them in three years, and when she had talked to them she'd still been living in the Bryn Mawr house. She'd loved the Bryn Mawr house. There had been a topiary maze in the back garden, and the kind of staff it took to keep it all up. There had been committees that knew how to run like committees, where everybody showed up on time.

"Never have children," Caroline told Susan. "They'll just turn on you."

Susan looked at her hands again. She was fifty-nine years old, just two years younger than Caroline herself. Neither one of them was going to have any more children.

Caroline walked back to the wall of windows and looked out again. The yellow caution tape was blowing in the wind. The trees were all bright with color. The fairways were not quite green enough. It wouldn't be a bad landscape if it hadn't been so pretentious, so self-conscious, so uncomfortable. There was mock Tudor everywhere, and odd Gothic arches where they didn't belong. The whole place look like an Olde Tea Shoppe set up by somebody with no taste, no knowledge of history, and far too much money.

She wondered where Michael Platte was this morning, and then she wondered why she bothered to wonder. They were all off in the same places, these people. They were shopping, endlessly. Or they were at expensive restaurants where the food tasted like sawdust. Or they were at "charity" events where no charity was ever done but everybody got their pictures in the paper the next morning. They probably got their pictures on the Internet instantaneously. Waldorf Pines had a Facebook page these days. It was as if they thought nothing was really real unless people they didn't know could witness it.

"They don't even do affairs right," Caroline said.

Susan made another little squeak. "I never believed that," she said. "Did you? Did you believe it?"

"That Martha Heydreich was having an affair with Michael Platte? Is having, I suppose. I don't know. Everybody says so."

"But people say things," Susan said. "You know that."

"I do know that," Caroline said. "I'll admit, it seems completely impossible. The woman is—well. 'Sexy' isn't the word for it, anyway. Not that men won't have sex with women who aren't sexy. It's always astounded me what men will have sex with. At least she doesn't seem to be ruining her marriage over it, if it's true."

"Oh, no," Susan agreed. "He's very fond of her. It's nice, isn't it, to see a couple devoted to each other that way? That's not usual. Especially around here."

"That's not usual anywhere," Caroline said. "Oh, well. I still think it's peculiar. And you're right. Maybe it's all just something people made up. But they do spend a lot of time together. You see them everywhere around here. And you can't miss them. Not with that car of hers."

"Maybe we should give them a few more minutes," Susan said. "You know how it is early in the morning. People have a hard time getting started."

"They don't have a hard time getting started when they're doing something they really want to do," Caroline said—and then she just gave it up.

It was a nice day. She could think of things to do. She could work out the invitation design and settle on a list of possible favors by herself. Then she could call a meeting for something on a Saturday and they'd all be more than willing to troop in and okay her decisions. They were always willing to okay her decisions. They only wanted to be named as members of the committee and have their pictures taken when the time came.

She'd once thought that all that mattered to them was money, but this wasn't true. All that mattered to them was to be seen by other people to have money. They had not learned—if they were lucky they would never learn—that money is never enough if that is all you have.

Caroline went out the side door and down the narrow hallway to the kitchen. The smell of coffee was strong and insistent. They did do very good coffee in this dining room, although you could opt for the designer variety if you wanted to. Designer coffee. Designer tea at three hundred dollars a cup. Back in the Bryn Mawr house, she'd had Red Rose every morning and loved it. She had Red Rose every morning now.

She wondered what the boys were doing, out there somewhere, having jobs, loving women, maybe even getting married.

She wondered if they thought about the day she told them she would never see or speak to them again.

3

If there was one thing LizaAnne Marsh knew was absolutely pie-assed *retarded*—just first rate crapuscular *gay*—it had to be this thing about school starting at eight fifteen in the morning. Eight fifteen. Really. Even people who had to go to work to get money didn't have to be there at eight fifteen. Not unless they had a really crappy job that was just mopping up after people or working at McDonald's or doing something lame like being a cop. And that hardly counted. Real people didn't have jobs like that. Real people had careers.

LizaAnne put her tray of eye shadows back on her vanity table and looked at her lashes in the mirror. LizaAnne liked to wear really thick eye shadow and then a line of black right under her lashes, but that was something else that was wrong with eight fifteen in the morning. You couldn't get yourself up like that at eight fifteen in the morning without looking like somebody really stupid, like Martha Heydreich, and then people started making fun of you in the halls and in the gym and then . . . well, then. LizaAnne had never been on the wrong side of that "then," and she didn't intend to start now.

She got up from the vanity and went to the big bow windows that overlooked the golf course. This was only the second-best bedroom in the house, but LizaAnne knew a lot of houses where the first-best bedroom wouldn't be as good. It was all so stupid, it really was. Even her father, who would give her anything she wanted, she only had to pout a little—God, how he hated to see her pout, and he knew she was kidding, it was really amazing—but even her father went on and on and on about being a good community citizen and not kicking people when they were down and all the rest of that nonsense. It was like one of those stupid mantras people said when they did yoga or whatever it was. LizaAnne didn't know why anybody bothered.

Now she looked up and down the golf course, to the club building, to the pool house. There were two cars parked at the club building. That would belong to Mrs. Stanford-Pyrie and Mrs. Carstairs. It just went to show that LizaAnne's mother was always right. A man would take anything if he couldn't get laid. Those two must have met a couple of desperate losers to be Mrs. anybody at all. Mrs. Carstairs was a mouse. Mrs. Stanford-Pyrie looked like a horse. LizaAnne was more than half convinced that the two of them screwed each other when nobody else was looking.

Ewww.

LizaAnne had no problem with gay guys. She couldn't really imagine what they did to have sex with each other anyway. Gay women were something else. She could imagine that. It was disgusting. It was worse than disgusting. It was retarded.

LizaAnne looked back at the pool house. The yellow tape was still up. Michael was probably inside somewhere, walking around the pool, making sure everything was safe. Sarah Lefton's mother said that he hadn't just dropped out of Penn State, he'd been kicked out, right on his ass, for running around naked on the tennis courts. LizaAnne didn't know if she believed that. Running around naked on some tennis courts didn't sound like such a bad thing, not even if they were outdoor tennis courts. Stewie Edland had been caught actually burning down the teeter-totters at the municipal park last spring, setting them on fire with a pipe he was doing some drugs with, and all that had happened to him was rehab and five hundred hours of community service. People got too worked up about things. They really did. Nobody cared about kids fooling around, as long as that was all they were. Nobody cared about anything.

She checked the pool house again. It was still deserted. Maybe Michael was late this morning. He usually wasn't. She went back to the vanity and put her phone in the little stand that let her talk on speaker. The little stand was blue. So was the phone. So were the walls of the room. So was the brand-new BMW she'd gotten for her sixteenth birthday, the one that had featured so prominently when they'd filmed her episode of *My Super Sweet 16*. She had a dozen copies of the DVD of that episode sitting right on the shelf in the family room, in case anybody came over who wanted to see.

She punched in Heather's number with one hand and started going through her jewelry box with the other. She had some really nice jewelry. She didn't do fake stones, either. She'd explained that to her father. Her father had understood. And besides, why shouldn't he buy her nice things? He was rich. He owned the three biggest car dealerships in this part of Pennsylvania.

Heather's voice came over the speakers as a squawk. "LizaAnne? LizaAnne, is that you?"

"Of course it's me," LizaAnne said. "Who else would it be? You've got me on caller ID."

"I know I do," Heather said, "but you know what they're like. I mean, maybe it was really your mother trying to see if I could get you in trouble if I didn't know it was her. Or, you know. That kind of thing."

"Don't be ridiculous," LizaAnne said. "My mother doesn't have time for that kind of thing. Have you been watching this morning?"

"I've been watching a little," Heather said. "You know. I had to get dressed. I had to get my makeup on."

"Did you see anything?"

"No," Heather said. "It's been really weird. There's been nothing going on all morning. Oh, except Mr. Heydreich left to go to work. In his car. You know."

"Are you sure she didn't go with him?"

"Of course I'm not sure," Heather said. "I couldn't see into the car. He's got those tinted windows. Do you like tinted windows? I'd think they'd make the car dark. And nobody would know it was you."

"Maybe you wouldn't want anybody to know it was you. If you were famous, you know," Liza Anne said. "I think that's retarded, though. I mean, why would you be famous in the first place if you didn't want people to recognize who you were?"

"Maybe it's when you get death threats and that kind of thing," Heather said. "People who are famous are always getting death threats. Doesn't that sound sucky? You go to all that trouble to get famous and then you have to skulk around because people are trying to kill you. Do you think people are trying to kill Taylor Swift? I bet they are."

"Taylor Swift is retarded."

"I know. I know Taylor Swift is retarded."

"I want to go see Michael before the day gets started," LizaAnne said. "But I can't do it as long as I don't know if he's there. I mean, if I go over there and go wandering around in the pool house and there's nobody there, I'm going to look retarded."

"I don't think he's there," Heather said. "I'm practically right on top of the pool house and I haven't seen a thing all morning. And you know what she's like. As soon as she knows he's there, she comes right in, and in that car of hers, too. It's not like you can miss it."

LizaAnne looked at her jewelry. She had tiny sapphire studs for her ears. She had a ring of white gold with sapphires and diamonds in it. Heather had had a super sweet sixteen party, too, but the people from the show said they never did two in the same neighborhood, so they'd had to choose. Heather had gotten a car for her party, but it had only been a Ford. LizaAnne's father said that nobody with any sense bought Fords, because the names stood for "Fix or Repair Daily."

"Do you think I'm like her?" LizaAnne said. "The way everybody says?"

"Everybody doesn't say that," Heather said. "It's just a couple of people."

"It's a couple of people here."

"Well, it would have to be here, wouldn't it?" Heather said. "I mean, they wouldn't know who she was if they didn't live here. It's not like she's famous, or any of that kind of thing. Nobody knows her but the people around here."

"She hates me," LizaAnne said.

"Of course she doesn't hate you," Heather said. "Well. You know."

"She hates me," LizaAnne said again. "She hates me because she knows Michael likes me better than he likes her. He really likes me. He's just putting up with her because she gets him laid. She thinks she's going to make some big thing out of it, but she isn't. I mean, what would he want with her anyway, except, you know, her junk?"

"She's really ugly," Heather said. "And she's old."

"She's really thin." LizaAnne looked down at her very rounded arms.

"She's probably got an eating disorder," Heather said. "She probably throws up in the bathroom all the time. It's really disgusting."

"It's retarded."

"It's worse than retarded," Heather said. "It's really gay."

"Maybe she's got some kind of thing on him," LizaAnne said. "Maybe she's blackmailing him. Maybe he's hiding out from the law or something and that's why he came home."

"Maybe she's one of those sick people who can't stand to be with anybody her own age," Heather said. "Maybe she'll have a psychotic breakdown and end up in an insane asylum. Then when people come to see her her hair will hang down in front of her face and she'll scream."

LizaAnne picked up more of her jewelry. She had dangling earrings with little emeralds in them. She had whole sets for each of the four piercings on each of her ears, each in a different color.

"I wish she wasn't on that committee," she said finally.

And then, because that was the thing they had both been trying very hard not to say, they both fell silent.

LizaAnne looked around her room. She liked her room. She thought anybody would like it. She looked past the vanity at the clothes hanging in the walk-in closet. She put all her jewelry back in her box.

"There's an arrangement," she said. "My father said so. Every girl who's going to be eighteen and out of high school in the spring is going to be invited. The committee has to."

"That makes sense," Heather said. "It's not her who's paying for it. It's our fathers who are paying for it."

"He said even if she did try to pull something, we wouldn't have to put up with it," LizaAnne said. "We could sue the committee, and the membership board of the club, and that kind of thing."

"She won't try anything," Heather said. "It's not like people want her here. That's the thing. It's not like she's Stanford-Pyrie or somebody that everybody sucks up to. Nobody can stand her."

"Those breasts of hers are fake, don't you think?" Liza Anne said.

"Of course they're fake."

"Nobody could have breasts that really look like that. And if they do have them, they don't keep them."

"They don't keep them?" Heather sounded confused.

"They get them reduced. My mother said. She thinks she's so perfect, hanging around the pool in a bikini the size of a postage stamp, and she's what? Forty? I think there ought to be a law against people wearing little tiny bikinis when they're forty," LizaAnne said.

Suddenly, talking to Heather was just making her tired. She got up and got the phone out of its stand. It really was retarded, this whole stupid thing. And it was boring.

"I'm going to hang up," she said. "I'll pick you up in ten minutes."

"Okay," Heather said. "Ten minutes would be fine."

LizaAnne made a face at the phone. With Heather, ten minutes would be fine, and so would be two, or sixty. It could be any time at all.

"I'll be ten minutes," LizaAnne said again. Then she shut off the phone, so she wouldn't have to hear Heather's stupid boring voice any more. Heather was a stupid boring person with a stupid boring voice.

In fact, everything about Waldorf Pines was stupid and boring, but at least it wasn't retarded.

4

Eileen Platte had been up all night, all twenty-four hours of it, waiting. It was not the first time she had done this, and her greatest hope this morning was that it would not be the last. She'd been waiting for the last night for a long time now. There had been the day she had finally got up her courage to go through Michael's drawers when he was at school. He'd been twelve that year, in sixth grade, and they had still been living in Wayne. She had been thinking about it for weeks, watching Michael when he came through the door off the school bus, watching him at dinner. He would lock himself in the bathroom for hours at a time, and she would sit there, just a few feet away, waiting.

In the end, she hadn't found anything she hadn't expected to find. She had gone through his drawers one by one. She had pushed his socks around just the way she did when she was putting them away when she'd done the laundry. Then she'd gone through the drawers of his desk. Finally, she'd done something she'd promised herself she wouldn't do. She'd lain down on the floor and pushed herself under his bed. The marijuana was in a clear plastic bag taped to one of the wooden slats.

It was almost eight o'clock in the morning now, and there had been no sign of him since four yesterday afternoon. He'd been headed over to the Heydreichs' house then, which is where he always went these days. The job guarding the pool didn't give him enough to do. She couldn't blame the club board. With Michael's record, she wouldn't have given him anything else to do, either. He was barely managing to handle this. Still, it was true. It wasn't enough. It gave him too much time to think.

"I don't understand what you see in her," she'd told him, as he was pulling on his windbreaker and heading out back. He'd walk, of course. He couldn't take the car. His license was suspended, and everybody at Waldorf Pines knew that.

"She's such an unpleasant person," she'd said, although she knew this was the worst possible tack to take. You couldn't tell your nearly grown-up son that the woman he was spending his time with was an unpleasant person. That was not going to get him away from her and it wasn't going to get him back to you.

"I'm sorry," she'd said. "I don't mean to criticize. But I don't like her."

"I don't like her much, either."

"Then I don't see the point."

"She's good for me," Michael had said. "You have no idea just how good she is for me."

It was one of those conversations that left Eileen feeling a little strangled. She'd had a lot of them over the years, and not just with Michael. Her father had been like that, in the worst periods of his drinking. Her husband was still like that, and, as far as she could tell, he had neither drinking nor drugs to blame anything on. There were times she wished that she could just turn off the conversation and then turn off her mind as well, letting everything go.

This morning, she was so tired, the air felt like it had patterns. She thought she could reach out and touch it, and it would feel like a quilt. She had a headache. She had a feeling in her limbs as if all the blood had been drained out of them.

Michael had stayed out all night before. He stayed out all night often. Once or twice he'd disappeared for a day or two. For some reason, this time did not feel like all the others. She could not make herself do anything but sit here, in this vast kitchen, wondering how she had ever thought it was the answer to her prayers. She prayed a lot. She even got down on her knees and said the rosary, although she did it in her own bedroom, when Stephen was off at work, so that he wouldn't see her and start railing about religion. Maybe that was why her life had turned out this way. Didn't St. Paul say something about it in the Bible? It was wrong of believers to marry nonbelievers. It didn't work out well. Maybe it was the other way around. Maybe believers were supposed to stay married to unbelievers, because that would change their minds. She had not changed Stephen's mind. Stephen had not changed hers, but that hardly counted for anything. She hadn't stayed true to God out of conviction. She'd only done it because she was afraid to do anything else.

She had coffee on the stove, but she didn't want to drink it. She had muffins from the bakery in the refrigerator. She didn't want to eat them. Michael ate almost nothing these days, and when he did eat what he ate was full of sugar.

"Listen," she'd told him once—it was only a week ago now. She couldn't believe it had been that recent. "Listen," she'd said, thinking she was desperate. "There's always one thing I can do. I can always go to the police."

"Go to the police about what? The drugs? You've already gone to the police about the drugs. What good do you think it did?"

"I could go to the police about her," Eileen said. She'd felt as if she were swimming through molasses. Sometimes she found it very hard to remember things. She remembered this from some kind of television program she'd watched, and she was desperately afraid that she'd got it all mixed up.

She'd gone on with it anyway. She'd had to go on with it. She couldn't let her son disappear into the awful woman's fantasies.

"I could go to the police," she'd said again, piecing it together slowly. "I could make them charge her with rape. Because of the age difference."

"You want to charge Martha Heydreich with rape?" Michael said. "Rape takes an unwilling partner. Hell, it takes a partner."

"No, not unwilling," Eileen had insisted. "It can be—it's the age difference. I heard about it on television. If there's enough of an age difference, the older person can be charged with rape. Something rape. There was a word for it."

"Statutory," Michael said. He'd sounded amused. "You're talking about statutory rape."

"Maybe," Eileen had gone on. "If there's enough of an age difference, the older person can be charged with statutory rape. Or some kind of rape. And they can be put in jail. And they can be put on the sex offender's registry."

"Only if the younger party is under eighteen," Michael said. "And I'm not under eighteen."

"She's using you," Eileen said. "You've got to see that. She's using you. She's got that silly husband of hers who'll buy her anything she wants, and she's got you to—she's got you to—"

"To what?"

Eileen had turned her face away, to the wall. They were in the living room. It was a plain blank wall, without wallpaper. She had had nothing to take her mind off it.

"If you think she's using me for sex," Michael had said, "you're out of your mind. I told you before about me and sex."

Eileen had kept her face to the wall. That was a discussion she was not going to have again. Besides, she didn't think he'd been telling the truth. It was the kind of thing he said when he was angry with her.

"I could go to the police," she'd said, thinking only that if she said it often enough it would sink it, it would scare him somehow.

But nothing ever scared Michael. He had always thought of himself as invincible. He'd thought it when he was climbing trees and hanging down off them from his knees. He'd thought it when he was smoking marijuana and taking pills out of the medicine cabinet and going down into Philadelphia to buy things from people who looked like somebody's worst nightmare on *Law & Order*.

"If you went to the police," he'd said, "you'd look like a prime ass, and they wouldn't be able to do anything anyway. It's like I said. The younger party has to be under eighteen. But honestly, Mother, you don't make any sense. One minute you're insane because I'm gay, and the next minute you're insane because you think I'm sleeping with a woman."

"She's not a nice woman," Eileen had said. "And it's not like—it's not like you don't have other opportunities. There's that Marsh girl. She's always mooning around after you. She's always asking me about you. She'd go out with you if you asked her."

"LizaAnne Marsh is a first-rate bitch and a tenth-rate everything else. I wouldn't go out with her if she were made of gold and gave platinum when she came. You've got to be desperate if you're trying to sic me on LizaAnne Marsh."

"I'm not trying to sic you on anybody," she'd said. She'd still had her back to him, but she'd known the conversation was over. He'd already started to sound bored. She kept looking at the paint as she listened to his footsteps walking away, walking across the carpet, walking across the tile of the foyer, opening the front door.

He'd stopped there and waited for a bit. Then he'd said, "I really am gay, you know. And it isn't Martha Heydreich who's using me."

Now she sat in the kitchen and tried to make sense of it. If Michael and Martha Heydreich had been out all night together, Arthur would know about it. He would at least know that his wife had been out. Would he know that his wife had been spending time with Michael? Eileen had no idea how these things worked. Stephen could have been having affairs with every other woman at the club, and she wouldn't have been able to tell.

The kitchen was a cavern. It echoed. Copper pots hung from the ceiling. A stove big enough to cook for a restaurant took up most of one wall. How had she imagined that she would be able to work in here, cook in here, feel at home in here?

It had been so long since she had felt at home anywhere—ah, but that was a cliché. Michael would hate the sound of it.

She took a very deep breath. She sucked up all the air in the room. She could always do the most obvious thing. She could always walk herself right over there and ring the doorbell. She wondered what the house was like. She'd never been in it. Maybe there were pink carpets on the floors. Maybe there were pink wallpapers on the walls. Arthur Heydreich was somebody she saw around once in a while. He was so normal. He did something professional in Philadelphia.

She would not go over to that house. She would not ring the doorbell. She had no idea what she would say if she did. Michael was nineteen. He could do what he wanted to do. He could do everything except buy alcohol. Did that make even the least amount of sense?

She thought about calling her sister-in-law, but she didn't. Stephen's sisters thought it was all her fault. No other Platte had ever turned out like Michael. She must have done something to him. She thought about calling her own sister, and didn't. Her sister was one of those people for whom bad luck is a myth, a rumor—the kind of thing that happened to other people, and was probably an excuse for their own fault. She thought about calling one of those advice programs she sometimes listened to on the radio, and then she felt like an idiot.

Michael was out there, somewhere. He was either dead or dying, lying in a ditch, on the side of the road, in an alley somewhere where he'd gone to buy drugs and ended up getting robbed and murdered instead. He was with a prostitute, who would make him ill. He was with Martha Heydreich, who was making him crazy. He had told her the truth when he told her he was gay. He had lied when he told her he was gay. She had lost him, utterly and completely, before he was ten years old.

And she didn't know why.

5

Horace Wingard knew for a certainty that everybody who lived at Waldorf Pines knew that his name was a fake, just as they knew his accent was a fake. Fake was not an issue at Waldorf Pines. He knew it wouldn't be as soon as he saw the place. That was why he had felt it was so important to get the job here when he first thought about it. It was all well and good to say that you should be yourself. What if yourself was not what you really were? Not everybody had the good luck to be born into exactly the right circumstances. Some people didn't have the luck to be born into even approximately the right circumstances. Horace himself had bombed out completely in the luck department, being born, but he thought he'd won the sweepstakes on substance. Horace was exactly the person he wanted himself to be. He only needed to tweak the ornamentation a little bit to make it all perfect.

Or nearly perfect. There was nothing Horace Wingard could do about time, and that meant he was living in the twenty-first century instead of the nineteenth. He would have done much better in the Philadelphia of the 1890s, when people knew how they were supposed to live.

Horace looked across his desk and frowned a little at the computer. The computer always looked out of place. Then he got the big ledger book out of the desk's center drawer and opened it at the computer's side. He liked the ledger book better than anything else he had to work with managing Waldorf Pines.

"Miss Vaile?" he said.

Miss Vaile put her head through the door at the far end of the room. Horace had hired her the way men usually hired secretaries, for her looks—but not for the kind of looks most men would have gone in for. Horace did not care one way or the other about a large chest or a face like Marilyn Monroe's. He had no idea if he was gay or straight and didn't want to find out. The whole idea of sex had always seemed to him to be more than a little insulting. No, he wanted Miss Vaile because she was the picture of the sort of woman who would have been secretary at a golf club in a novel by Henry James, except that in a novel by Henry James she would have come to her job through a distress in her circumstances.

Miss Vaile was actually from Paoli, and had gone to a very good secretarial school.

She came into the room with her steno pad in her hand. The steno pad was useless—Miss Vaile did her work on a computer, too, and she was good at it—but Horace liked the effect it made, and he insisted on it. She came across the carpet to his desk, glancing just a moment at the fire burning in the fireplace. Horace had heard her complain that he acted as if he thought the club's furnace was going to destruct at any moment.

She stopped by the desk and waited, patiently. That was also something Horace had taught her to do. He was not unaware that the job at the club was a very good one, and that he made it better in a thousand different ways that added up over time. Horace was one of those people who expected to get what he paid for.

"The cotillion," he said now. "I was supposed to have the paperwork on my desk this morning. How many tables in the dining room, how many girls to be introduced, everything. We have to have the paperwork or we don't know what to do next."

"I quite agree with you."

"And?"

Miss Vaile did not shrug. Horace did not like people who shrugged. Instead, she looked up out of the great tall windows that gave a view over the eighteenth hole and pinched her nose ever so slightly. When Miss Vaile pinched her nose, you knew that something truly impossible was happening.

"We don't have the paperwork," she said. "At least, it hasn't come to my attention, and that's where it should have come. There's no sign of it anywhere."

"And this is—who? Who was supposed to bring it in? Caroline Stanford-Pyrie?"

"No," Miss Vaile said. "Mrs. Stanford-Pyrie is the head of the committee, but it's Mrs. Heydreich who has charge of the paperwork. I did talk to Mrs. Stanford-Pyrie, of course, but she told me to talk to Mrs. Heydreich."

"And?"

There was the pinch of the nose again. "I haven't been able to reach her."

"What do you mean, you haven't been able to reach her?"

"I've called several times," Miss Vaile said, "but there's been no answer. She was supposed to be at a meeting in the dining room this morning, but she did not show up. I've talked to both Mrs. Stanford-Pyrie and Mrs. Carstairs. There's been no sign of her. I called her house. The maid said she was out."

"Extraordinary."

"If you don't mind my saying so," Miss Vaile said, "there have been other things to attend to this morning. There's been that business with the security cameras. I thought it was going to be a fairly simple sort of thing, but the more I look into it, the more complicated it gets. I know you told me to handle it myself, but I'm not sure I can."

"You're not sure you can handle a broken security camera by yourself," Horace said. "What can there possibly be to handle? You call the repair company and they come right out and fix it."

"I did call the repair company."

"And they haven't come out?"

"They have come out," Miss Vaile said. "They came out immediately. We would expect them to. We pay them a significant bonus to make sure that they always come out immediately."

"Then I don't understand what the problem is. They've come out, they should fix it. Or is it very badly damaged? Do we need a new one? That shouldn't be a problem."

It was Miss Vaile's turn to look somewhere else. She looked into the fire. "It's not damaged," she said finally. "In fact, at the moment, it's working perfectly normally."

Horace frowned slightly. "That can't be right," he said. "There was dead time this morning. I saw it."

"Yes, I know." Miss Vaile sighed. "The gentleman from the security company saw it, too. I saw it. But the fact is that there is nothing wrong with it. With the equipment, I mean. The equipment is functioning normally. It's just that, last night, between ten forty-five and twelve thirty, it stopped functioning normally, and nobody knows why."

Horace stared at her, amazed. "And that's it?" he said. "That's all anybody's going to say about it? It stopped functioning normally and nobody knows why? There has to be a reason for these things. They don't just sort of happen out of nowhere, for no reason."

"I do understand that," Miss Vaile said. "And the man from the security company also understands it. That's why he's still here. But it's all we've got at the moment, except for the fact that it wasn't the only camera that malfunctioned last night. They all did."

Horace Wingard put his hands down flat on his desk. He thoroughly hated computers and everything that went with them, but that was not the same thing as saying that he didn't understand them.

"Are you saying the entire security system went down? For nearly two hours in the middle of the night?"

"I don't know," Miss Vaile said. "I don't think so. He didn't mention anything about the alarms. I think he would have if they had malfunctioned. What he said was that it looked as if somebody had turned the system off and then turned it back on again."

"Turned it off and then turned it on again," Horace Wingard said.

"It could have been done," Miss Vaile pointed out. "It was only necessary to flip the switch in this office. It might have been an accident."

"If you mean I might have had an accident, Miss Vaile, I can assure you I didn't. And what's left after that? Possibly one of the residents just waltzed in here when I wasn't looking—"

"It really isn't out of the question," Miss Vaile said. "Especially at that time of night. There are always a lot of people in the club house, playing bridge, that kind of thing. And if you're here at all, you're out and around, not sitting at your desk. And I, of course, am not here at all. And I do think the man would have mentioned if something had gone wrong with the alarms."

"I don't think he would have," Horace said. "He'd be scared to death we'd move to another company on the spot. We can't have things like this. The whole point of Waldorf Pines is that we provide security twenty-four/seven. There aren't going to be any home invasions here. There aren't going to be any incidents, either, where your ex-wife shows up ready to blow your head off. We can't afford to have a system in place that goes down and leaves us vulnerable for two hours in the middle of the night. Can you get that man up here to talk to me right away?"

"Of course," Miss Vaile said.

"This is terrible," Horace said. "This is worse than terrible. Have you heard anything? Was there any kind of break-in? I don't believe a system just went on the glitch like that for no reason. Has there been a robbery?"

"Not that I've heard about."

"Has there been anything else?" Horace shuddered. "I hate to think of what else we could have had last night. But somebody must have done it deliberately. It's the only explanation. And if that isn't the explanation, we'll be in court with a suit in five minutes. We may be there even if somebody did it deliberately. Go get him, Miss Vaile. Go get him. I have to think."

Miss Vaile pinched her nose again, then turned on her heel and was gone. Horace got up and walked to his windows, looking out on what seemed to him to be a perfectly tranquil scene. None of the houses that ringed the golf course had burned down. There was no sign of vandalism on the tennis courts. The caution tape was still up in front of the pool house. Best of all, there was no sign of little clutches of women with their heads together, gossiping about everything.

If there had been an incident overnight, those women would know about it. Those women would talk about it. Those women would get him into an enormous amount of trouble with the governing board.

Horace Wingard had no use at all for the governing board, or for any governing board anywhere. They were all alike, these things. Everybody was convinced that democracy was the answer. Everybody was always wrong. You couldn't leave the governing of a place like Waldorf Pines up to people who cared only that they got to say they lived here.

Horace went back to his desk, sat down, and brought up his file on the security company on the computer. People thought he was a silly little man, but they underestimated him. He hadn't gotten this job because he'd changed his name or bought his suits at J. Press, custom tailored so that he looked as much like Clifton Webb as possible. He'd managed three other luxury developments before he'd landed at this one, and he was very good at his work.

If it turned out that somebody who shouldn't have been was on the grounds of Waldorf Pines last night, he'd find him, he'd get hold of him, and he'd make his life not worth living.

Horace Wingard knew a lot about making people's lives not worth living.

Walter Dunbar did not rely on the Waldorf Pines security system to keep himself and his family safe. Walter Dunbar did not rely on anybody for anything, if he could help it, and he could usually help it. It was the army that had made him that way, back when the army was something everybody had to put up with, whether they wanted to or not. If it had been up to him, they would have reinstituted the draft years ago, and sent young idiots like that Michael Platte off to South Carolina to march with packs on their backs. That was what was wrong with these kids these days. They didn't have any sense of discipline. They didn't have any sense of purpose. They didn't have anything to hate to the very bone, and that was why they didn't have any motivation.

Walter's motivation, at the moment, was "doing something" about the Waldorf Pines governing board. He was never more explicit than that, even inside his own head, but he had no doubt that anybody who heard him would know exactly what he meant. Walter had been on the governing boards of every gated community he'd ever lived in, and every country club he'd ever belonged to, and every professional association he'd ever decided was worth his while. He'd been on every one of them, but he'd never been on any of them more than once. That was because people didn't like reality anymore, even if they said they did. They liked fairy tales. They liked anything but to hear the truth spoken without fear or favor.

At the moment, what none of these people wanted to hear was that there was something wrong with their vaunted manager, although Walter didn't know how they could miss it when they looked at him. Horace Wingard, for God's sake. Walter had spoken to a very discreet private detective he knew—you had to get discreet ones; you never knew what you could be sued for. Walter had spoken to the man, at any rate, and it turned out that Horace Wingard had started his life as Bobby Testaverde in Levittown. Levittown. It was practically the symbol of post-War lower-middle-class blight, full of little houses made of ticky tacky that all looked just the same. Walter had grown up on the Main Line and gone to good private schools before being packed off to Colgate by a father who knew better. Walter thought anybody ought to know better. It was almost stunning how ignorant most people were.

Unfortunately, even the very discreet private detective couldn't perform miracles. Walter had asked him to look into the background of that Martha Heydreich, but he hadn't been able to come up with anything at all. It was, he wanted Walter to know, very unusual. People left traces of themselves around. They left trails.

If it had been up to Walter Dunbar, he would have required a full background check for anybody who wanted to buy a house in Waldorf Pines. What was the point in having a security system, with having cameras and locks and guards, if you were harboring a snake within your own bosom? That's what they were, these people like Michael Platte. Snakes. That's what that woman was, too.

Walter was standing on his deck, looking down at a garden hose. It was not his garden hose, and he had no idea where it had come from. He might even have thought it was his own if he hadn't been able to see his own, still coiled up properly around the outdoor faucet. This one was just lying around, as if somebody had tossed it there as he walked by on the golf course. Except, of course, that nobody ever walked along the golf course with a garden hose in his hand. Most of these idiots could barely handle their own clubs.

Walter looked up the fairway, into the blank distance that was the course unoccupied by a single questing golfer.

Then he turned around and went through the sliding glass doors to his own family room. It wasn't much of a family room. He had one of the smallest houses in Waldorf Pines. That was because his family was himself and his wife, Jessica. They had never had any children. Jessica had wanted them, the way women always did, but Walter had been smarter than that.

The family room was empty. It consisted of a cramped little room divided from the kitchen by a curving countertop. The countertop hid the sink, just in case the lady of the house didn't feel like doing the dishes and wanted to hide the mess. Jessica would never do that, because she knew he'd pitch a fit.

Sometimes you had to yell and scream to get what you wanted. Sometimes you had to threaten. Sometimes you had to call the lawyers and be done with it. Walter thought he was at the lawyer stage.

"Jessie," he shouted, pointing into the house and hoping he wouldn't have to call out more than once. That almost never worked. He didn't know where Jessie disappeared to, but she disappeared. "Jessie," he shouted again.

There was a faint little squeaking noise, coming from back there somewhere. Jessie was over in the part of the house with the two extra bedrooms. Walter had no idea what she thought she was doing there. They didn't have children, or grandchildren, or guests. They only had the extra bedrooms because it was always better for the resale value to have three bedrooms rather than one.

He walked off into the house. The walls were painted green. The floors were thick matte terra-cotta tile. He never really noticed where he was living, unless something went wrong with it.

Jessica was in the larger of the two extra bedrooms, changing the sheets. Walter didn't understand why she had to change sheets in this bedroom. It wasn't as if they had to worry about somebody complaining about the dirt.

Jessica looked up when he came into the room and then sat down on the side of the bed.

"I'm sorry," she said. "I just thought I'd get some work done while I had a free morning. Didn't you want to go out to the farmer's market this afternoon? It's the last of the sweet corn we're going to get this year."

"There's a garden hose on our deck," Walter said.

Jessica blinked. Jessica was something of an idiot. Walter had known that for years.

"Not our garden hose," Walter said, in the voice he thought of as "patient." "Our garden hose is where it's always been. There's a strange garden hose on our deck, just thrown there willy-nilly. Just lying there."

Jessica blinked again. "Why?" she said finally.

Walter sighed. "I don't know why, do I? I just found it there this morning. This minute, really. A garden hose, plain as day, when it's obvious no garden hose belongs there. Somebody was on our deck last night. Either that, or somebody was on the course, and they threw the garden hose up from there."

"But why would they?" Jessica said. "Why would anybody want to throw a garden hose onto our deck? And does it really matter, Walter? I can't imagine a garden hose did us any harm."

"That isn't the point, is it? It's not if the garden hose did us any harm, this time. It's the fact that anybody can get into this place and do anything he wants. Or else he's already here. This is supposed to be a secure place. It's supposed to provide us all with peace of mind. That's what we paid for. It's not living up to its part of the bargain."

Jessica twisted her hands in her lap. "I wish you wouldn't do these things," she said. "You just get everybody all angry, and it never changes things anyway. Except that they don't like us anymore, and we don't get invited to things."

"I paid for my house to be secure, I want it to be secure," Walter said. "You're too easy on people, Jessie. You let them walk all over you."

"Just once I'd like to move to a place and settle in," Jessie said. "I'd like to be just like everybody else. I'd like to have friends."

"People just won't listen," Walter said. "They like to live in their illusions. I tried to tell them we were in for trouble, and here we are."

"A garden hose isn't trouble," Jessica said desperately.

"It's just the beginning," Walter said. "That Michael Platte is a criminal, plain and simple, and I'd be willing to bet everything I have that Martha Heydreich isn't the housewife she pretends to be. Well, we already know that. She's hiding something. She has to be. What good does it do to have security cameras and security locks and guards and all the rest of it when you've got the danger living

35

right here in your own backyard? We're not protected from *them,* Jessie. We've got nothing to protect us from *them.*"

"Martha Heydreich seems like a very nice woman," Jessica said. "She's a little extreme, you know, in the way she dresses, and her mannerisms, and that kind of thing, but she still seems like a very nice woman. And she has such beautiful hands."

"She has small hands," Walter said. "I never trust anyone with small hands. They don't know how to work, that's what that is. They don't do honest work."

Jessica ignored him. "As for Michael Platte," she said.

"He was arrested for possession of cocaine," Walter said. "If his father hadn't been willing to pay through the nose to get him off, he'd be sitting in prison right now."

Jessica sighed. "Yes, Walter, I know. But it was never a secret, was it? They weren't trying to hide it. And what does it matter, anyway? He's had a little trouble. He's young. Maybe he'll grow out of it—"

"Maybe he's been wandering around this place all night throwing garden hoses on our deck. I'm telling you, Jessie. There's a problem out there. There's a very big problem. And pretending it isn't there isn't going to make it go away."

"Yes," Jessica said. "I understand."

"They're going to regret it," Walter said. "They're going to see this mess they've gotten themselves into, and they're going to regret it. It's going to be too late then. They're going to be murdered in their beds, and that's if they're lucky."

"Yes," Jessica said again.

She wasn't twisting her hands anymore. She wasn't looking at him, either. She was just sitting on the bed, looking at the floor, doing nothing and saying nothing and showing no emotion.

Walter felt a wave of dislike hit him, a huge tsunami of rage that went all the way down to the soles of his feet. Why had he married this woman? What had possessed him, all those years ago, to first propose to her and then to walk her down the aisle? Maybe it had been nothing more than the need to appear mature and responsible, the way you'd had to do in the days before all the nonsense started. Maybe it had been nothing at all. He really couldn't remember. There were just times when he wanted to put the heel of his shoe onto this woman's face and grind it and grind it and grind it until the blood spurted out or she started to say something.

He turned away and went back into the hall. They'd voted him off the governing board this last set of elections, and now they were reaping what they sowed. It served every last one of them right.

7

Fanny Bullman had a problem. It was not the kind of problem she would have talked to her friends about, or to her husband about. It was not the kind of problem most other people would think of as a "problem" at all. Problems were hard and material and intractable. They were not having enough money to pay the bills, or having an incurable disease, or losing your job. Sometimes they were smaller things, like having the car in the shop on a day you had to use it to go to your daughter's dance rehearsal, or having to find a way to make three hundred cupcakes for the Brownie Christmas party when you only had two cupcake pans that cooked six cupcakes each. Problems were like puzzles. You took all the elements of them and stretched them out in front of you. Then you put the elements together in different ways until you came up with either a solution, or a course of action. This problem was nothing like that, and Fanny didn't know what a solution would look like if she found it.

It didn't help, of course, that the house felt more than empty. It felt hollowed out. It felt as if nobody was in it, not even herself. And Charlie hadn't even been gone that long, this time.

The children were all wrapped up in their barn jackets now. Their backpacks were packed and zipped up and ready to go. Now it was only necessary to walk them out to the bus stop and wait until the school bus came along. Fanny did this every day, because she didn't trust the Marsh girl from across the golf course. Whoever had decided to give that girl an automobile must have been crazy. She zipped around as if she were on a racetrack, and then came to screeching halts for no reason Fanny could see.

Sometimes Fanny tried to think her way back to what it had been like in high school, but she couldn't really remember it. She couldn't really remember college, either. It was all out in back there in the mist. It was not about things that had happened, but about the way she had been. And that, of course, was the problem.

Mindy's backpack was pink and had Strawberry Shortcake on it. Josh's backpack was black and had Darth Vader on it. Some of their friends were surprised that she allowed Josh to have Darth Vader on his backpack when he was only seven. She just couldn't see the point in fighting the inevitable. Kids got the backpacks they wanted in the end. They got the video games they wanted, too. You could talk all you wanted about how it was a parent's responsibility to choose what her children ate and watched and read, but the real world didn't work that way.

She opened each of the backpacks in turn and carefully checked the contents of the brown paper bags she'd wrapped their lunches in. There were all kinds of rules for lunches these days, even though Josh and Mindy went to a public school. They were not allowed to have anything with peanuts, because one of the other children might be allergic. They were not allowed to have "junk food," like bags of chips or candy. They were not allowed to have soda. Fanny was fairly sure that wasn't the way it had been in her time, but all she could remember of her school lunches were the few times her mother had sent her in with sandwiches of cream cheese and jelly. She had really loved cream cheese and jelly. She had really hated peanut butter.

The lunch bags had bottles of Frutopia in them, and oranges, and bologna sandwiches with mustard on whole wheat bread. The school didn't like bologna sandwiches, but there was a point where you had to make compromises. Josh and Mindy wouldn't eat sandwiches made out of nothing but vegetables, and they wouldn't eat the multigrain everybody was supposed to prefer these days to keep them from getting fat.

Fanny zipped the backpacks up again and went into the family room. Josh and Mindy had turned the television on and were watching some kind of cartoon. The cartoon looked depressing and dull, but the children seemed riveted.

"Come on," Fanny said. "If we don't hurry, we'll miss the bus. I don't want to have to drive you to school today."

She went over to the television set and turned it off. It was the only way she could get them to listen.

"Come on now," she said.

The children got up off the floor, slowly, rolling a little and looking back at the dead black screen as if it were about to burst back into animation.

Fanny held out the backpacks and they took them, making some halfhearted whining complaints in the process. The complaints were so halfhearted, Fanny couldn't figure out if they were about school or each other.

"Let's go," she said again. Then she double-checked to make sure their jackets were buttoned.

They would look, today, like every other child at the bus stop. That's what elementary school was all about. Everybody wore the same clothes, and ate the same food, and played the same games. Everybody had the same birthday parties, too, and gave the same presents.

Fanny stopped for a moment and considered the possibility that she was going insane. The odd thing was, she didn't think so. Her days drifted past her, one after the other, and nothing happened in them, but that did not make her insane. It couldn't be insane to wonder about Charlie, or to wonder if the children would start asking where he had gone.

Mindy was looking through her jacket pockets, pulling out bits and pieces of Kleenex and stubs of pencils. She was frowning.

"It was boring this morning," she said. "The lady with the pink car didn't come."

"That's Mrs. Heydreich," Fanny said. "You can't go calling her 'the lady with the pink car.' It's rude."

"Mrs. Heydreich. Usually she comes by in the morning in the car and goes up to the club house. I love the pink car. I want a pink car like that when I grow up."

"I'm sure that will be very nice," Fanny said. She could have said, "You'll change your mind." She was sure that was true. Children hated being told they wouldn't want the things they wanted once they were all grown up.

Josh had started excavating his pockets, too. Fanny went over to him and took the bits and pieces of garbage out of his hand and threw them in the wastebasket.

"Come on," she said, trying to sound stern and serious this time. "We *really* have to go."

They went, this time, stumbling through the kitchen to the door to the garage, and then through the garage to the street. Fanny grabbed Josh's hand and tried to ignore the fact that Mindy no longer wanted hers held. It hardly seemed possible that Mindy was eight.

There were no sidewalks on the streets at Waldorf Pines. There were no school busses, either. The school bus stop was just off the grounds through the back gate, as if school bus drivers were like old-time tradesmen and not allowed at the front door.

Fanny swung them through the curve that passed in front of the houses of at least four couples without any children at all, and then down the cement path to the back gate. Waldorf Pines looked differently from this side than it did from the golf course. Fanny had never really understood the point of the golf course anyway. For the first three years they lived here, she'd woken up in the middle of the night, dreaming about golf balls sailing through the windows.

The back gate was, as always, very carefully locked. Fanny got out her key and opened it up. She had to try twice to make it work. Surely there had to be some better way than this to get children to the bus stop in the morning. Fanny always felt like a character in a fairy tale, having to unlock the enchanted mansion to release the prince and princess from their dreams.

Fanny always felt like a character in a fairy tale. That was the thing. That was the problem. She ran around and did things. She fed and bathed the children and helped with their homework. She slept with Charlie and washed his socks and ironed his shirts. She went out to dinner. She took the children to McDonald's. She bought books at Barnes & Noble. She watched television.

And none of it ever seemed as if it were real.

She shut the gate behind her after they went through. She heard the *click* that said it had relocked securely in place. She double-checked her pocket for her keys, even though she had just used them, because to forget her keys meant having to walk all the way around to be let in by the guard at the front.

There were other children waiting at the bus stop, and other mothers. The other mothers didn't talk to Fanny, because they were not from Waldorf Pines.

"She went out last night," Mindy said.

"What?" Fanny said.

"She went out last night," Mindy said again. "The lady with the pink car. Mrs. Heydreich. She went out. I saw her. But she wasn't in the car."

"Really," Fanny said.

"I thought it was funny," Mindy said, "because, you know, it was really late. It was after eleven o'clock."

"And what were you doing up after eleven o'clock?"

"I couldn't sleep," Mindy said. "I never can sleep when it gets too hot. You should let me have the air-conditioning on in my room."

"It was only forty degrees last night," Fanny said. "And you can't have the air-conditioning on just in your room. It would have to be on for the entire second floor. You'd be happy, but I'd be frozen into an icicle."

"I was just lying there trying not to be bored," Mindy said. "I mean, I'm not supposed to turn on the light or anything, so it's not like I can read. And if I turn on the iPod you always hear me. I use the earphones, but you hear me anyway. So I was just lying there. And then I heard them coming along the golf course, you know, so I got up and went to the window and looked out."

"The bus is late again," Fanny said. "What is it about this bus that it's always late?"

"I just thought it was funny," Mindy said. "I couldn't figure out what they were doing there that late and everything. I thought maybe they were burying treasure, because you're supposed to bury treasure in the middle of the night. But they weren't doing anything. They were just walking on the golf course. And they were laughing."

"Mr. and Mrs. Heydreich were walking? Maybe they couldn't sleep."

"It wasn't Mr. and Mrs. Heydreich," Mindy said. "It was Mrs. Heydreich and that guy, you know, the one who hangs around all the time at the pool. Except he wasn't at the pool, this time, he was just at the golf course. Maybe they were going to play golf. They didn't have golf things or anything, though."

"What?" Fanny asked.

The school bus was pulling up to the curb. The other mothers were herding their children toward the doors. The other mothers acted as if Fanny and Mindy and Josh weren't there, and Mindy and Josh acted as if the other children weren't there. It felt as unreal as everything else did these days, and Fanny didn't have a word for it.

"Sherry Carlson says Mrs. Heydreich and the guy from the pool are doing something nasty with each other," Mindy said, "but I think that's just because her mother has all of *Dallas* on DVD."

Fanny looked up, startled. Mindy was disappearing into the bus. Josh was right behind her. Fanny watched as the two of them sat down together in a seat and then turned to the windows to wave good-bye.

A second later, the bus and everybody in it was gone.

Fanny was left standing on the side of the road, thinking that this was just one more day, one more hour when she had no idea what was going on in her life. It all just came and went, and none of it made sense.

8

When it was time to leave, it was time to leave. Arthur Heydreich held fast to that thought, because it was the only thought he had that made any sense. He was a man of routine in the strictest possible sense. Only routine made sense to him. He could hear Cortina wandering through the rooms of the house, letting loose a soft stream of Spanish. He suddenly wished he lived in a time and place where he could forbid his maid from having a cell phone. She would be talking to all the other maids in all the other houses that ringed the golf course. She would be talking about the bright pink car in the garage. She would be talking about the pocketbook on the coffee table in the family room, the cell phone still in it. She would be talking and talking, and in an hour or two the maids together would have solved any mystery that might have arisen in the Heydreich house before eight o'clock in the morning. Except that they wouldn't have solved it. They would just have made it up.

Arthur went back upstairs to his bedroom and closed the door behind him. He was surprised. If he had been Cortina, he would have come up here first. He would have wanted to check out the story that the bed had been slept in. Maybe she was waiting for him to leave the house.

He went over to look at the bed himself. There was nothing to see that he hadn't already seen when he first woke up, nothing that had changed when he came out of the shower. The sheets and pillows and quilts were rumpled and twisted the way they always were when Martha had slept in them. He could remember her pulling them back across the bed and getting in under them the night before. He could remember her lying stretched out, talking about committees. He hadn't listened. He'd fallen asleep and slept like a stone for hours. Then suddenly he was awake, and she was not there beside him.

He went over to the windows and looked out on the golf course again. The houses that ringed it looked awake now. There were people on decks and patios. There were children making their way to the bus stop outside the back gate. It was an ordinary fall morning, and he was an idiot to think there was anything strange about it.

He left the room and went out into the hall. He went down the staircase and into the foyer. He went back through the kitchen to the breakfast nook. He could still hear Cortina somewhere in the house. Her Spanish sounded like music.

He went back into the foyer again and called out. "Cortina? I'm leaving for work."

There was something that might have been a muffled reply, or might not have been. He didn't want to spend the time finding out. He got his briefcase off the kitchen counter. He went out into the huge three-car heated garage. He got into his car and closed the door tight. He was having that odd feeling again. The air around him felt patterned.

Martha was Martha. She had committees. She had yoga and facials and all the other things that made him feel as if, talking to her, he was trying to make sense of an alien. It was not impossible that she had had something on her mind and simply forgotten her bag. It was not impossible that she had had something on her mind and preferred to walk instead of take the car. He liked to walk when he wanted to think.

And she had had something on her mind lately. He was sure of that.

He pushed the little button on his visor and the garage door slid open. The area in front of the garage was wide enough for cars to turn around in. It narrowed to a single lane that led out onto the thin access road that went around the houses to the front gate. This was his routine every morning. He did not have trouble following it.

His house was at the far end of the course, as far as you could get from the front gate. That was supposed to be an advantage. Real luxury was supposed to be to live away from people. He passed the back gate just as that Fanny woman—Bullstrode? Bullhorn?—was coming back through it. That would have been her children he saw on their way to the bus stop. Arthur had never been able to understand why anybody wanted to have children.

Fanny What's-her-name cut across the road and then through somebody's side yard. She went a little out of her way to do it. Arthur saw Walter Dunbar come out of the house she had avoided, and smiled a little. He'd go out of his way to avoid Walter Dunbar, too. Everybody did.

Stupid ass, Arthur thought, watching Walter pick up his paper from his driveway. Walter paid no attention to him, or pretended to—but that was what Walter did. He actually paid attention to everything. Then he complained.

The clubhouse itself was up at the front gate, far away from him still. He looked through the wide grassy areas between the houses at the green. Nobody was out there playing yet. They could have been. The club was ready and willing for most of the day and the night.

Going around the curve that would let him make the loop, Arthur caught a glimpse of the pool house and its ugly yellow caution tape. It struck the wrong note. It struck just the kind of wrong note Martha's handbag had. It was out of place. It felt wrong.

The curve continued relentlessly and he went around it very slowly, looking through the yards each time, looking at the way the grass was still green even this late in the fall, looking at the windows gleaming in the sun. The gates to the right of him were lined with evergreen trees. Nobody could see through them from the outside unless they came right up close, and then there would be sensors and other things, things to keep out the dark, to keep out the unsafe.

Arthur Heydreich was not like a lot of the people who lived at Waldorf Pines. He hadn't grown up rich. He hadn't even grown up lower middle class, in one of those neighborhoods where everybody knew everybody else and everybody's mother watched out for everybody else's children. He knew the world was not a safe place, and never would be.

The trick to the thing was people. That was it. There were a lot of different kinds of people, and most people were truly awful—but most people were not dangerous in any way that mattered, and that was what you had to watch out for. Arthur Heydreich watched, and he knew what he was looking for.

He was almost all the way up the other side of the curve when he saw it, the thing he would describe later, to the police, as "a flicker."

"Flicker" was the best word he had for it, and he was willing to admit that on another day, on a day when he was not already worried and a little upset, he might not have noticed it. It came up and bent a little in the wind. It shuddered in and out of sight. It was like looking at the flame on a candle on a birthday cake when somebody without much breath was trying to blow it out. And it was—*inside* the building.

He slowed his car to look and tried to see. For a moment or two there was nothing. Then the flicker came back. It rose and fell and rose again. It shuddered and died. It rose again. It shuddered and seemed to twist.

Fire, Arthur thought.

He brought his car almost all the way around and stopped at the small parking lot next to the pool house. He looked around. Most people traveled by golf cart inside Waldorf Pines. There were no golf carts parked in the parking lot. He looked at the pool house. It looked the same as it always did. He looked at the roof of it. There was nothing going on there that had not been going on there the last time he saw it.

He turned off his engine and waited. This was the back of the pool house he was looking at. The front faced the golf course, because people liked to swim and watch the play at the same time. He watched the back windows. He looked at the caution tape. He wondered where Michael Platte was, but not for long, because Michael Platte was never where he was supposed to be.

Arthur got out of the car. He put his keys in his pockets. He left his briefcase on the front passenger seat where he had put it when he left home. He closed the car door behind him and stood, listening.

The sound was definitely there. It sounded like paper crackling.

He walked across the gravel to the pool house door and stopped. The crackling sound was louder and louder. The closer he got to the doors, the louder it was. If he stepped back, it was very faint, almost as if he were making it up.

He went to the doors and tried them. He was sure he would find them locked. They were supposed to be locked. Instead, the door swung open easily.

He stepped into the foyer. There was a big glass case for trophies on the far wall. There were no trophies in it. The case looked forlorn and a little lame.

Arthur tried to listen again, but now he could hear nothing. He might really have been making it all up. He was upset with himself. He didn't like looking like an idiot. He didn't like looking like one of those old fussbudget perennial bachelors from the movies of the Fifties, either. He knew the kinds of things people said about him.

The door *snick*ed closed behind him, ending in a heavy *thump*. The lights were not on. He didn't know how to get them on. He tried to hear the noise again. He got nothing.

The pool was to his left. The changing rooms and showers were to his right. He went first to the changing rooms. He pulled the door of the men's room wide open and looked inside. There was nothing to see. He backed up and pulled at the door of the women's room, but he felt a little wrong doing it, as if women might still be inside. He stepped through and the door closed behind him. He was in pitch darkness now, but in a way that was reassuring. If there was pitch darkness, there couldn't be a fire, or not much of one, not yet.

He went back into the lobby and looked around again. Then he went toward the pool. There had been something about the pool at the last residents meeting. Something about the water being left in it until it could be properly drained by the people coming in to do the repairs. Something. He didn't remember what.

The doors to the pool were big and heavy. He thought he could hear water sloshing on the other side of them, but he was sure he was making that up. The water wouldn't be sloshing. There wouldn't be anybody in it.

He stared into the darkness. The darkness was very, very dark. There were no windows here. He let the door shut behind him. The darkness became even darker. He began to feel along the wall, slowly and slowly, inching his way in case there were things left lying on the floor that could trip him.

He found the first set of switches when he thought he'd gone a mile and a half, even though he knew he couldn't have, because he hadn't turned a corner.

He flicked the switches on one after the other.

A couple of dim lights came on and then the sound of air being pumped through a grate or a pipe—maybe he had turned on the air conditioner? He didn't know what he was doing. He'd never tried turning the lights on in the pool.

One of the dim lights was coming from under the water itself. That was all right. The pool had heat and light so that people could swim in the winter and at night.

Arthur turned and looked into the water, and for just a moment he did not know what he was seeing. There was somebody in the water, yes, but that wasn't the problem. The problem was the water itself. It was the wrong color, the wrong shade, something. There was something in there, something dark against the palish clearish blue, but—

But it didn't matter, because that was when the building went up in flames.

PART I

ONE

1

It was six o'clock on the morning of Monday, the fifth of November, and it was cold. It was so cold that Gregor Demarkian found himself staring down at the jacket his wife had laid out for him across the back of the living room couch and wondering if she'd gone insane. Insanity was never to be completely ruled out when it came to Bennis Hannaford Demarkian, but the forms that insanity took were not usually thin cotton jackets presented for wearing in the freeze that heralded the run-up to winter. Bennis was much more likely to do things that would not be considered illegal only because she was a very good friend of the mayor.

Gregor picked the jacket up and put it down again. It was the jacket Bennis had bought him a couple of years ago, when she had gone on one of her periodic campaigns to "update" him.

"Somehow or the other, you just don't seem to get the spirit of the times," she'd said.

He'd been at a loss to know what she was talking about. Maybe he was too stodgy for the business casual atmosphere of the twenty-first century? Maybe he was too rational for all the television shows about mediums and psychic children?

It had turned out that he didn't own any kind of outerwear that was not utterly formal, as if human beings would not be able to survive in the world of the Obama administration if they didn't own something called a "barn jacket."

The shower was on down the hall in the bathroom. Bennis was singing something that required her to hit the C above high C, which she couldn't do. This would be something by Joni Mitchell, who was the singer Bennis loved most in the world. All of that meant something, Gregor was sure. He just didn't know what.

He went down to the end of the hall where the bathroom was and knocked on the door. The apartment felt small and cramped these days, because it was filled with too much "stuff." The worst of the stuff had disappeared over the past few weeks. He didn't have to go on tripping over stacks of bathroom tile samples and books of dining room wallpaper samples. Bennis had made enough of the decisions about what would happen to this house they had bought to renovate that it wasn't necessary to live any longer with her indecision. Still, there suddenly seemed to be too much of everything in the apartment, as if she never put anything away anymore, on the assumption that they'd have to take it out and move it later anyway.

He knocked on the door again. The sound of the water got fainter. Bennis must have turned it down.

"What is it?" she called out.

"I'm going to go get Tibor," Gregor said. "I'm feeling too restless to stand around here. Do you mind?"

"Of course I don't mind. You ought to take another case."

"Yes, I know, I ought to take another case."

"I left the paperwork from the last case out on the kitchen table. You've got to give it to Martin as soon as you can. It's getting to be the end of the year. You can't just leave your paperwork in a mess. The IRS gets cranky."

"I'll get to the paperwork this afternoon," Gregor said.

He meant it, too. At least, he thought he did. He didn't remember that he'd always had such a hard time taking the paperwork seriously. There it was, though. If you got paid money for doing anything at all, you had paperwork to do, and the state of Pennsylvania and the government of the United States to answer to.

He went down the hall and into the living room. He went through the living room and into the kitchen. Bennis had not just left the paperwork from the Mattatuck case out on the table. She had spaced it out in neat stacks that, Gregor was sure, would turn out to be organized. Bennis had been "self-employed" for a lot longer than he had. She understood these things.

Of course, he'd been self-employed himself now for over a decade. He ought to understand these things.

He left all the paperwork where it was and went out into the hallway. The apartment door snicked shut behind him. He tried to hear the lock click into place, but it was difficult. Grace was upstairs with her door open again, practicing on a harpsichord. Either that, or she was practicing on something called "mother and child virginals." A lot of keyboard instruments were lifted up through the windows of Grace's apartment.

"Grace?" Gregor said.

The playing stopped. There was a slight pounding of feet and a head appeared at the stair rail above him.

"Hello, Gregor," Grace said. "Are you all right? Where's Bennis? Did I wake you up with my playing?"

"I've been up for an hour, and you never wake me up."

"I've got a concert tonight at the museum," Grace said. "It's too bad, don't you think? They call it early music and nobody comes, so we have to play in museums. A lot of people would like harpsichord music if they could hear it, don't you think?"

"I'm sure they would," Gregor said. "I like it when I hear you play it. Bennis wanted to know if we should make some special arrangements when you move downstairs. For the instruments, I think she

53

means. I know it won't be for months now. She seems to think she needs to know everything at once."

"Oh, that's all right," Grace said, "she just wants to be prepared. I understand that. I don't think there's going to be a problem. They pack up, you know, and it's not like we're trying to get them through the front door. Do you have any idea why they made that front door so narrow? I mean, I know most people aren't trying to get instruments in here, but still. It's like squeezing through a toothpaste tube."

"I think it was to discourage break-ins," Gregor said.

"On Cavanaugh Street?" Grace snorted. "The only person who's going to break into a house on Cavanaugh Street is Donna, and all she's going to want is to get at your windows so she can decorate. You'd think they'd know better than that, wouldn't you? I mean, they're supposed to be running the entire city."

Gregor had no idea if Grace was talking about the mayor's office, or the police, or who. He didn't think he'd learn much by asking.

"I'm going to go get some breakfast," he said. "You should talk to Bennis so she doesn't get too crazy."

"I will. Have a good morning, Gregor. And try not to be so depressed."

Grace's head disappeared from the stair rail, and a moment later Gregor heard playing again. It was the harpsichord he was listening to, he realized. That was Bach's Concerto in D Minor. It was one of maybe four harpsichord pieces he could recognize just by listening to it.

He turned down the stairwell and went carefully and slowly, as if he were afraid to trip. The apartments in this building were all "floor-throughs." There was one apartment on each floor, taking up the entire floor. The floor below Gregor's own, the second, actually belonged to Bennis, and was now part of the apartment above it. Bennis's first idea for making a home had been to knock out some walls and some ceiling and meld the two apartments together. Gregor had thought this was a very good idea, but for some reason it had never quite come off. The two apartments were melded together, but he and Bennis always stayed upstairs on the third floor, as if the second did not exist. Bennis did her writing on the second floor, but that was all. She hadn't even stored her renovating samples down there.

Gregor stood on the landing and stared at the door there for a while. He listened to Grace playing above his head. He thought he ought to go to Grace's concert tonight. It had been years since he had heard her play in person. He thought he and Bennis ought to do something unusual, like take a vacation. He would even be willing to take a vacation where there was sand. He thought he had spent too much of his life being narrowminded about vacations where there was sand.

He looked around and told himself he was spending this time of his life acting like a four-year-old who thinks he can make the bogeyman go away if he just pretends he doesn't really exist.

But the bogeyman did exist, of course. He existed and lived and breathed and was never far away from anybody's front door. It was just that, as a grown-up, he called the bogeyman "death."

Gregor made himself go down the last flight of stairs and into the foyer below. He looked out through the door with the glass panel that led to the vestibule with the mailboxes in the wall. Then he turned away and made himself look at the door to old George Tekemanian's apartment.

It was funny the way that worked, he thought. He could tell that the apartment was empty—not just empty because nobody was home, but empty because nobody lived there. He would have been able to tell that even if he'd never entered this building before, and if he'd never known old George Tekemanian.

Gregor went back to the door and turned the knob. It opened easily. He pushed it in. Most of old George's things were already gone. What was left was laid around in very neat stacks, most of them with white slips of paper taped to them. This stack was going to the homeless shelter. This stack was going to the yard sale. This stack was . . .

Gregor saw old George's sock baller, a machine Martin had given him once for a Christmas or a birthday. Old George and Father Tibor used to hang around old George's apartment sometimes and ball socks and let the machine fling them around the room. For some reason, the machine was never satisfied with just balling socks. It liked to play the catapult.

Gregor stepped back into the hallway and pulled the door shut behind him.

He didn't want to see the rest of the apartment. He didn't want to tell anybody about what he had just done. He had the odd feeling that everybody knew, anyway.

2

"Death is a part of life," Tibor said, when Gregor picked him up at the apartment in back of the church.

Tibor was muffled up as if it were the middle of February. He had on a long black winter coat and a scarf and the kind of hat that made Gregor wonder if Tibor ever looked at himself in a mirror. He had gloves on his hands and his hands in his pockets. Gregor could never get over just how short he was.

"The man was a hundred years old," Tibor said, as they rounded the corner into the alley and headed for Cavanaugh Street. "A hundred years old. The Bible says the days of a man are three score and ten. He was in overtime. And, sincerely Krekor, he knew it."

"He wasn't sick," Gregor said. "He wasn't ailing and in pain all that time. Not until the very end. The last week, maybe. He didn't have dementia. His mind was as good as mine ever was. It doesn't make sense to me."

"It doesn't make sense to you that people die of old age?"

"No," Gregor said. "I guess it doesn't. I mean, I understand that people's bodies break down, and they get sick, and that sort of thing. I understand that some people have minds that break down. But it just doesn't make any sense to me that somebody who is perfectly well, perfectly in charge of his faculties, should just die because— because of what, really? Because he'd been living too long?"

"That's the idea," Tibor said.

"Then I think there's something wrong with the idea. It's like cavities."

"Excuse me, Krekor, but you're getting away from me."

"It's like cavities," Gregor said. "Think about it. Your teeth exist for what? To make it possible for you to eat. Right?"

"Right," Tibor said. "Also, sometimes in some circumstances, if you know the wrong kinds of people, to help out in a fight."

"Okay," Gregor said. "I may even know those kinds of people, but that's beside the point here. Your teeth exist so that you can eat. But when you eat, just by eating, just by using your teeth for what they were made for—well, by doing that, you wreck your teeth with cavities, and they hurt and crumble and then fall out."

"There is the toothbrush—"

"Yes," Gregor said, "but why should you need a toothbrush? You're not misusing your teeth when you eat. You're using them for what they're supposed to be for. You're using them in just the way you're supposed to use them. So why are there cavities at all? If teeth were something a company made, and they did that—they broke because you used them properly—well, there'd be lawsuits, wouldn't there? There'd be congressional investigations. We'd do something about it."

"You want the United States government to do something about death?"

"I don't know," Gregor said. "I don't know what I want."

They were out on the street itself now. People were coming out of the tall brownstone buildings and wending their way toward the lighted plate glass storefront of the Ararat. Gregor saw Lida Arkmanian in her three-quarter-length chinchilla coat, hurrying to catch up with Hannah Krekorian and Sheila Kashinian. Sheila had on a coat that was some kind of fur and was supposed to look expensive, but didn't quite. Hannah was getting along with her usual wool, and if you'd asked her about it, she would have given you a long lesson on the stupidity of conspicuous consumption.

Except that she wouldn't have called it that.

Gregor slowed down a little. Lida might be in a hurry to catch up with those two, but on most mornings, he was not.

"Look at them," he said, pointing ahead to the women, now walking together. "We all grew up together on this street. I remember Lida in church when she was no more than four or five years old. I'd have to have been the same. She had a new dress for Easter, and her mother had bought her a hat to match. It was like a miracle had occurred right in the middle of the block. A matching hat. Who had the money for a matching hat?"

"Yes, well. While you were all growing up here, I was in Yekevan, and it would have been enough to have money for hats. Is that really what you're worried about now, Krekor, people's hats?"

"No," Gregor said. "No. It's hard to explain. We all did grow up here. It's odd to think about it sometimes. And we didn't have any money."

"Most people don't have money," Tibor said.

"We all have money now," Gregor said. "Even Hannah has more than she'd ever dreamed of all those years ago. She has a matching hat."

"I don't know why," Tibor said, "but I don't trust where this is going."

"Old George Tekemanian lived on this street when we were growing up," Gregor said. "You can't say he grew up here, because he was born in Armenia. He was from my parents' generation, not from mine. Can you imagine that? He was from my parents' generation. He remembered immigrating. He remembered what it was like when this was all tenements and some of them didn't have windows. He remembered doing all his business in Armenian and reading the Armenian language newspaper instead of *The Philadelphia Inquirer*. He remembered World War I. Can you imagine that?"

"I don't have to imagine it," Tibor said carefully. "There's nothing to imagine. It's just the reality of the real world. Of course he would remember all that. He had a good mind and it functioned well and he was a hundred years old."

"And now he's gone," Gregor said, "and all that is gone with him, and it makes no sense at all. It's wasteful, and arbitrary, and it makes no sense at all. You have to see that."

"What I see," Tibor said, "is that perhaps this time Bennis has a point. Perhaps you are depressed."

They were right in front of the Ararat now. The lights gleamed out into the dark of the November morning. Behind the glass, Linda Melajian was running back and forth with a Pyrex pot of black coffee.

"I'm not depressed," Gregor said. "I'm annoyed. I'm annoyed and offended, if you want to know the truth. It's a waste of time and resources and everything else I can think of that somebody like old George Tekemanian would die of nothing but old age. And it is not the way a well-ordered universe would be constructed to run."

Gregor grabbed the plate glass door, pulled it open, and went inside. The door sucked back toward Tibor, who stood unmoving on the sidewalk.

Gregor thought he should feel guilty about that, but he couldn't do it.

He was, he thought, right in everything he was saying, and he'd been thinking about it for weeks.

Cavanaugh Street was not the same without old George down there on the first floor, and it never would be.

3

Twenty minutes later, Gregor was sitting with Tibor and Bennis in the big benched booth near the windows, and Linda Melajian was delivering a platter with his favorite breakfast. He had two scrambled eggs, two pieces of buttered toast, two round breakfast sausages, three rashers of bacon, and a huge pile of hash brown potatoes. Tibor was having almost exactly the same. Bennis was having black coffee and a half of grapefruit, and glaring.

"Look at it this way," Gregor told her as he picked up his fork, "if

I die on you in the middle of the night, it won't be because of old age."

"Oh, for God's sake," Bennis said.

Linda Melajian swung around to see if anybody wanted more coffee, then took one look at Bennis's face and decided that they did not. She swung away again, back through the crowded dining room with its little knots of people bending over coffee cups and talking without bothering to take breaths.

There were times when Gregor sat looking at Bennis and marveling that he had ever married her. It was unusual to get lucky twice with wives. It was even more unusual to have reached the age he was now and never have been divorced. Bennis made him feel lucky most mornings, but this was not one of them.

He could look around the Ararat right now and see old George sitting there, at one of the interior tables, having breakfast with Lida and Hannah and Sheila or with Donna Moradanyan Donahue and both of her children, or with, well, anybody. Everybody had breakfast with old George once in a while.

He could see both Linda Melajian and her mother bending over old George's chair, scolding him about forgetting his gloves or his hat or eating the real butter instead of the nonsaturated-fat margarine.

These were the ordinary markers of an ordinary life. They were not vices, or risks, or natural disasters. They were not diseases or injuries. They were nothing but what everybody did everywhere with perfect safety, and there was something gravely wrong with the idea that someone would be punished for them after all.

I am being childish, Gregor thought. This is not the way grown-up people respond to death and dying. There are supposed to be stages of grief, and then at the end you are supposed to be all calm and accepting and ready to go on with your life. He had figured out in no time that what he was thinking and feeling did not fit into them.

"Do not go gentle into that good night," he said.

"What?" Father Tibor said.

"It's a poem by a man named Dylan Thomas," Gregor said. "Bennis probably had to read it at Vassar. He wrote it to his father when his father was dying. Do not go gentle into that good night. Death is the enemy."

"He's been like this for days," Bennis said. "Sometimes I get it, but sometimes I just want to kill him."

"Then there's the other thing," Gregor said. "The wages of sin are death."

Tibor shook his head. "If you're going to read the Bible, you should read the whole thing, not just bits and pieces of it that suit your mood. It doesn't do anybody any good taken apart like that. We've started wars doing that. We've killed people."

"I'm not going to kill anyone," Gregor said. "I'm arguing against killing anyone, that's the point. But the wages of sin are death goes to prove it."

"To prove what, Krekor?"

"That death is meant as a punishment," Gregor said. "It was in that book you gave me, too, that St. Augustine. The wages of sin are death. Death is a punishment. And George hadn't done one damned thing to be punished for that I know of. And if he'd ever done anything, it was so far in the past it couldn't possibly have mattered any more."

"You have read the St. Augustine, Krekor? You have read all of it?"

"He sits on the couch and pages back and forth through it," Bennis said. "Then he stops and reads some of it and mutters under his breath. I don't know what you were thinking, Tibor. That thing is a thousand pages long."

"With little tiny type," Gregor said. "But I'm not mistaking his meaning, Tibor, and you know it. The whole thing, the whole way you explained it all at the funeral, makes no sense. We couldn't run a criminal justice system this way. We couldn't write a code of law—doesn't it start with what's supposed to be a code of law? Could you imagine a code of law that gave the same penalty to somebody who cussed out his grandmother and, I don't know, pick somebody. Hitler.

That wouldn't be a code of law. It would be a travesty. And this is a travesty. And you know it."

"He's back on religion again," Bennis said.

"Yes," Tibor said. "I am sorry for this. I did not mean to cause this kind of a problem. I only meant to give George a proper funeral."

"And you did give George a proper funeral," Bennis said. "There was nothing wrong with anything you said. He's just grabbing hold of it and taking it to the zoo."

"I could have given the homily in Armenian," Tibor said.

"Then Martin and Angela wouldn't have understood it," Bennis said.

"I understood it perfectly," Gregor said, "and I'm not being an idiot here. That explanation made no sense. And if a God actually exists for whom that explanation does make sense, then He doesn't make sense, and there's no point in listening to Him. We don't have to figure out if God exists or not, we only have to figure out if He's sane, and apparently He's not. And that really ought to be all we need to know about it."

"Don't you think there's something really odd about the fact that this is the first time you've ever had trouble thinking that God makes sense?" Bennis asked. "I mean, Gregor, you were with the FBI for decades. You investigated serial murders. You've been investigating murders ever since. You see broken and ravaged bodies all over the landscape and you vaguely think you probably might not believe in God but it doesn't bother you—and then old George dies peacefully and without pain at a hundred years old and you get like this? You don't think there's anything odd about that?"

Gregor looked at his plate. There was too much food on it. He hadn't eaten like this in years. His back hurt.

"No," he said finally. "I don't think there's anything strange about this. I understand why people die at the hands of serial killers. I understand why they kill each other. And it does make sense."

He was about to go on with the thought—and it was a thought; he'd been working it out obsessively ever since old George's funeral—

when the front door to the Ararat opened and a man walked in Gregor was sure he had never seen. There would have been nothing strange about that at lunch or dinner, but breakfast at the Ararat tended to be the neighborhood and nobody else.

A dozen heads throughout the room swiveled around to stare. If it had been Gregor himself in that position, he would have backed right up and gotten out of there.

The strange man came inside instead and looked around. He was very small and very round and very bald, and he was about as nervous as he could be without giving himself a heart attack. Gregor found it hard to look at him. He was that twitchy.

The man looked around the room once, then twice, then again, and finally he turned his head enough to see the window booth. The twitchiness disappeared at once. The round bald head glowed. The oddly fishlike lips spread up and out in a grin. Then the little man hurried over, and stuck his hand out over the food at Gregor Demarkian.

"Mr. Demarkian," he said. "Mr. Demarkian! I've been looking for you!"

TWO

1

Gregor Demarkian had been a special agent of the Federal Bureau of Investigation for over twenty years, and he would have been one still if his first wife hadn't gotten cancer and died. It had been a long time since he'd stood at the edge of the bed in St. Vincent's Hospital and watched Elizabeth go, but he still thought about that day more often than he liked to admit, and he still thought about what his life would have been if that had never happened.

It wasn't that he didn't like his life as it now existed. He liked it wonderfully well, and he found himself surprised more often than not at how much more there was to life than he had ever expected.

As for Elizabeth, well, Gregor Demarkian had known Elizabeth Seroulian since they were both very small children. They had grown up together on Cavanaugh Street when to grow up on Cavanaugh Street was to be poor. They had gone to the same elementary schools and the same high school. They had "walked out" together when he was at the University of Pennsylvania, one of the sad little army of commuting students in an Ivy League school that had very little use for them.

In a way, Elizabeth had been, to Gregor, what old George Teke-manian had been: a repository of memories; a living, walking, breath-ing history. Gregor was getting to the point in his life when he needed people like that. When he looked around Cavanaugh Street, when he thought back to the days living in Maryland and Virginia and hauling out to Quantico every morning, he couldn't believe how much he had forgotten.

The little man with the bald head didn't look as if he had ever forgotten anything, but that was because he looked as if he had never known anything. Everything about him shone. Everything about him oozed.

Gregor looked to the side and saw that Bennis was staring at him with fascination. There was another thing he forgot, even though he was confronted by it every day. Bennis was endlessly fascinated with things he himself found perfectly ordinary.

It was what made Gregor realize that saying that two people came "from different worlds" was not just a cliché. He and Bennis Hannaford Demarkian had grown up less than ten miles from each other, and they might as well have been on different planets.

There was a cliché, he thought.

The little man with the bald head was standing next to their table, bouncing up and down on the balls of his feet. He had a hat, a plain little watch cap thing, the kind of hat Tibor wore to keep out the cold. The little man was twisting it in his hands.

Gregor took a deep breath and said, "Yes? You are?"

The little bald man bounced around on the balls of his feet some more. "I thought of you right away," he said. "Right at the begin-ning, right when it happened. But I didn't know how to go about it, you see, and then, at that point, there was nothing in it that looked really odd. But of course, I did know there was going to be trouble. There's always trouble when you have a case like this, and a place like Waldorf Pines. But I didn't think it was going to be big trouble. I didn't think we were really going to have something to worry about until today."

Gregor picked up his cup of coffee and took a very long drink of it. "Don't you think you ought to tell me who you are?" he said.

"Oh," the little man said, "oh, of course, you wouldn't know me to look at. But I didn't know how it worked, you see. I mean, I know you're a consultant, and I know there are police departments who hire you, and I knew right from the beginning that you'd be the perfect one, but I didn't know how to get in touch with you, did I? You're not in the yellow pages, are you? How is anybody supposed to know how to get in touch with you if you're not in the yellow pages?"

"You're in touch with him now," Bennis pointed out from her place over by the window.

The little bald man sighed. "Yes, Mrs. Demarkian, I am in touch with him now, but this is hardly the way to do it, is it? And it's the very last minute, which doesn't make me feel very good at all. And then, you know, what did I do? I saw that story about you in the style section last Sunday, and it said you always ate breakfast here at six o'clock in the morning, and so I came on out to find you. And if this isn't the way it's done—well, I'm sure it isn't the way it's done—if I've done absolutely everything wrong and you won't work for us, I think I'm just going to go jump off a roof. Because we're in a lot of trouble. And sometime today, it's going to get worse."

"Why is it going to get worse sometime today?"

"Because the lab results came back last night," the little bald man said. "And I know that lab results are supposed to be confidential, but we don't have our own lab. We have to send our stuff away. And it's all been such a big thing, so much publicity, that when it becomes obvious that we got it all backwards—well, I don't care how confidential it's all supposed to be. Somebody will leak it. They will. And if we don't have you to back us up, well, we're going to look like complete idiots, or something worse. And we won't hear the end of it, either. Not when it's about Waldorf Pines."

"Ah," Tibor said.

Gregor turned to him. "You know what this is about?"

"Yes, Krekor, of course I know. It was very big news last month, I think. A double homicide. A husband and a wife and a lover. The wife had a lover. The husband killed the wife and the lover. I'm surprised you didn't hear about it."

Gregor thought, but didn't say, that it was the kind of case he wouldn't pay much attention to, because it wouldn't present much of a challenge. The fact was, that wasn't entirely true. He paid attention to a lot of crimes that wouldn't present much of a challenge, because he was always interested in the way people thought and felt and acted. He'd always told himself that if he worked at it long enough, he'd finally understand why people committed murders. He had a feeling that this was not actually possible, but it was a nice goal to aim for.

The little bald man was now bouncing around so much and so fast, he looked like one of those lottery balls whipping around in the bubble before a drawing.

"That's the thing," he said, sounding anguished. "We thought the same thing. It all looked so cut and dried. The woman was almost certainly having an affair with this boy. Well, he wasn't a boy. He was nineteen. I suppose that's almost a boy. He was the son of one of the other people at Waldorf Pines and he'd had some trouble, lots of trouble, so he'd been expelled from school or something and then he'd got a job watching the pool house while it was closed for renovations. You know the kind of thing. Sit there in a chair all night and make sure nobody sneaks in. Or all day. I can't remember what his schedule was. I don't even know if it matters. But everybody we talked to said the same thing. They hung around together, this boy and this woman—"

"Did they have names?" Gregor asked.

"Oh," the little bald man said. "Yes, of course. His name was Michael Platte. Her name was Martha Heydreich. And there was the husband, of course, Martha Heydreich's husband. He's called Arthur. He says it like that, just like that: Arthur. He doesn't use a nickname. He's stiff, too. If she was a woman with anything to her, I wouldn't blame her for having an affair. But then he's just the type, you know. He's just the type to kill a wife who's having an affair. The ones who get all high on their dignity and can't stand the idea of their name being tarnished or something or the other. I don't think we were being negligent in assuming what we assumed. We're a small township. We don't have the resources you have here in Philadelphia. We don't have the expertise. But we're not bumpkins. And I think anybody would have made the same inferences we did, under the circumstances. It just made sense. It is usually the spouse that did it, isn't it? And in this case, as far as we could see, the spouse certainly had enough motive. But now there's this. There's this, and it's going to get out sooner rather than later. And then do you know what? We'll make the Philadelphia papers for sure, and everybody who lives in that godforsaken 'community' is going to come down on our heads with lawyers, and then I don't know what's going to happen to us. I hate communities. Anything that calls itself a community is nothing but trouble. And Waldorf Pines only exists to cause trouble."

"All right," Gregor said. "Do you have a name?"

"Oh," the little bald man said. "I'm sorry. I'm Larry Farmer. I'm chief of police in Pineville Station."

"And Pineville Station is—?"

"It's a small township in Lancaster County," Bennis said. "Way over at the far edge of it. It's not really all that far from here. It's just sort of rural."

"And Lancaster County is, what?" Gregor said. "The Amish."

"Oh, this isn't about the Amish," Larry Farmer said. "I wish it was. The Amish are easy enough to handle if you understand them. They mostly just want to be left alone, although of course there are all the traffic problems because of the horses and buggies. They had to build a special lane for them on the interstate just to keep people from plowing into them at eighty miles an hour. But that's just, you know. That's just a thing. Accommodation, they call it. I don't mind the Amish. But this is Waldorf Pines."

"What is Waldorf Pines?" Gregor asked.

"It's a 'gated community,'" Larry Farmer said. "God, I hate those, don't you? Fancy-ass ways of keeping people out, like we were all still in high school again and the dweebs don't get to sit at the cool kids' lunch table. It's got its own golf club, that everybody who lives there has to belong to, and it's got gates and guards and sensors and all that sort of thing, although they didn't work in this case, and if you ask me, they never work. Private security guards are a waste of time."

Gregor could think of cases when private security guards were not a waste of time, but that didn't seem to be the right thing to say here. He moved over a little on the bench and motioned to Larry Farmer.

"Sit down," he said. "And try to take this from the beginning."

2

Maybe the problem was that Larry Farmer didn't know how to take anything from the beginning. Maybe the problem was just that he was so deeply immersed in his "mess" that he didn't realize that everybody else in the world wasn't just exactly as immersed, so that all the details he needed to explain sounded to him like things everybody knew.

Whatever it was, Larry Farmer was a lot more organized about his breakfast than he was about the case he was nearly in a panic about. When Gregor gave him the opportunity to order breakfast, he ordered it, in quantity. His platter ended up being larger, and more complicated, than Gregor's own.

Gregor waited for a while, watching Larry Farmer shoveling it in. Considering the way the man ate, he should have been at least a hundred pounds overweight. As it was, Gregor didn't think he was overweight at all, just sort of naturally spherical.

Gregor waited until Larry Farmer showed some signs of slowing down. Then he said, "Let's try the beginning again. There was a double murder."

Larry Farmer sat back a little and stared at his plate. "It was about a month ago," he said. "Exactly a month ago, I guess. October fifth."

"That was when the murders happened? Or when you discovered them?"

"Oh, there was no lag in discovery," Larry Farmer said. "We discovered them right away. That's because the pool house caught on fire. And according to Arthur Heydreich, he noticed it. So he went in, you know, and found the bodies. One of the bodies. The body of Michael Platte was in the swimming pool and there was blood in the water. That was because he was hit on the back of the head with a blunt instrument. We're pretty sure about that."

"All right," Gregor tried again. "So it's, what—evening, morning, what?"

"A little after eight o'clock in the morning."

"Very good. And this Arthur Heydreich—"

"Well, that's the thing, you know," Larry Farmer said. "We just all assumed he was lying, but then maybe he wasn't. I mean, the way things worked out—"

"We'll get to the way things worked out in a minute," Gregor said. "It's the morning of October fifth. What happened?"

"According to Arthur Heydreich," Larry said, "he got up, and his wife wasn't on her side of the bed, but he wasn't really worried about it. Martha Heydreich is one of those women who are always on a lot of committees. You know the kind of thing. He said he woke up and saw her side of the bed empty but all crumpled up the way it was when she'd slept in it, and he didn't think anything of it. He got dressed for work and came downstairs."

"What does he work at?" Gregor asked.

"Some financial firm in Philly," Larry Farmer said. "And yes, it's quite a drive, but a lot of the people who live in Waldorf Pines work in Philly. And I've heard of people who live Philly and commute to New York, so maybe I don't know about commutes. I don't understand people, Mr. Demarkian. I really don't."

"Well, don't worry about it for the moment," Gregor said. "Arthur Heydreich woke up in the morning and found that his wife was not in bed but that her side of the bed had been slept in. He took a shower and got dressed for work. Then what?"

"He went downstairs. The maid was already there. A woman named Cortina Sanchez. That's when he found out that his wife wasn't down for breakfast, either. This Cortina Sanchez thought she was still upstairs asleep. Then it turned out that her car was still in the garage, but he wasn't worried about that, either, because the committees she volunteers for are usually with the golf club. They're right there in Waldorf Pines. He thought she'd just decided to walk for once. It was a nice day, that kind of thing. You know."

"And was she in the habit of doing that? Walking on the grounds of the club rather than taking her car?"

"Not on your life," Larry Farmer said. "She had this car, it was one of those two-seater sports things, painted bright, glaring pink. Neon-electric-bust-your-eyeballs pink. According to everybody we talked to, she drove that car everywhere. She drove it just to go next door. She even had vanity plates on it. 'GRLPWR,' or something like that."

"All right," Gregor said, "so the car was in the garage. Do you know if it was warm? Had it been driven anywhere recently."

"Not a clue," Larry Farmer said. His face fell. "I didn't even think to ask him about it. If he'd touched it, you know, and if it was warm. Because by the time we got there, of course—"

"It would have been stone cold," Gregor said. "Yes, I see that. What did Arthur Heydreich do after he found the car?"

"He says," Larry Farmer said, "that he came back into the house and got his cell phone and tried to call his wife. She was supposed to always have the cell phone with her, too. You should have seen the phone. It was bright pink, too."

"And did she have it with her?"

"No," Larry Farmer said. "According to Arthur Heydreich, he called her on his cell phone, and then he heard her cell phone ringing in the family room. When he went in there, he found her purse sitting on the coffee table. More pink. Everything was pink. And the cell phone had a ring tone that played 'I Enjoy Being a Girl.' Do you know that song?"

Bennis cleared her throat. Gregor ignored her.

"So," he said. "Now he's found his wife's purse. Was everything in it? Her keys? Her credit cards?"

"Everything we know of," Larry Farmer said. "We've got that, you know, under lock and key. Her keys are in it. Her wallet is in it. There's four hundred dollars in the wallet. Her credit cards are in it. And we did check all of that. He said he thought everything was there, but we double-checked just in case. The wallet had all her credit cards in it, all the ones we could find any mention of her having had out in her name, ever, anywhere."

Gregor nodded, thinking. "So," he said, "I have to suppose that once he found the purse, Arthur Heydreich called the police."

"No," Larry Farmer said.

"No?"

"He said he didn't want to jump to conclusions and act like an idiot and cause a fuss. This is Waldorf Pines. There's supposed to be lots of security. He figured she had to be safe because there couldn't be anybody coming in from outside to mug and rob her or anything, and besides she'd slept in her own bed so she probably wasn't out before the sun came up anyway."

"He didn't see her go to bed? They didn't go to bed at the same time the night before?"

"Oh," Larry Farmer said. "No, he saw her go to bed, or he says he did. He say he takes something to sleep and he never wakes up at night. And you should see this bed. A California king, they call it. You could hold a party in it."

"Did they?" Gregor asked. "Hold parties, I mean, the husband and wife?"

"Not that I know of," Larry Farmer said. "You've got to meet Arthur Heydreich, you really do. He's not the kind of person you'd

73

think would do something like that. Although you never know, I guess. Most straitlaced girl in my high school graduating class turned out to be a nudist when she got old enough. People get crazier than you'd believe."

"I'm sure they do," Gregor said, "but back to Arthur Heydreich. If he didn't call the police when he found his wife's purse, what did he do?"

"He says he did what he always did. He got his things together, got in his car and headed out for work. He figured he'd call in every once in a while during the day, and then if he still hadn't heard from her by dinner, he'd sound the alarm."

"That would have been a nice long stretch of time, don't you think?" Gregor said.

"That's exactly what we thought," Larry Farmer said. "That was one of the reasons we were sure he had to be the killer. I mean, who behaves like that? Your wife is nowhere to be seen. Her car is in the garage. Her purse with her keys and her credit cards and a whole wad of cash is lying on the family room coffee table. None of her clothes are gone from the closets, as far as you can see—did I tell you that? We checked the clothes."

"No, you didn't tell me," Gregor said, "but that makes sense."

"He said it made sense that she wasn't lying dead and mugged somewhere. I don't know. It didn't make any sense to me. And he could be wrong. She had a lot of clothes. There could be clothes missing he didn't know about or something. And, you know, there has to have been something missing, because she sure as hell wasn't wandering around the Waldorf Pines golf course in the middle of the night stark naked. Somebody would have seen her. These people spy on each other like those two guys in *Mad* magazine."

"What did Arthur Heydreich do?" Gregor asked. "Did he go straight to his office?"

"He was headed to go straight to his office," Larry Farmer said, "but he saw something that made him nervous. You've got to look at a map of Waldorf Pines sometime. The houses all back onto the golf course, and they front onto the one road in the place. It's one road, one great big loop, and it's one way. Arthur Heydreich lives in a house about halfway down the course from the clubhouse, but on the wrong side of the loop, so he has to go all the way around to get out the front gate. He says he got into his car, left his garage, and started around the loop. He says he was looking for his wife the entire time. Then, when he got almost all the way to the gate, he thought he saw something flicker in the pool house."

"Flicker?"

"Like a flame," Larry Farmer said. "He thought he saw the pool house on fire, except not really all the way on fire yet. He thought he saw a flame. And the place was all closed up, for the repairs, you know, and the kid who was supposed to be watching it wasn't too responsible about it—"

"This was the same kid that was supposed to be having an affair with his wife?"

"Same one," Larry Farmer said. "Anyway, he wasn't too responsible, so Arthur Heydreich said he parked his car in the little lot next to the pool house's back doors and went in to look around. There was still water in the pool—I don't know why, you'll have to ask the manager about that. He gave me an explanation, but it didn't make any sense to me. Anyway, Arthur Heydreich says when he came in everything was dark, and he looked around in the lobby and then he looked in at the locker rooms. He just looked in and he says he didn't see or hear anything. He thought he might have smelled something in the women's locker room so he went in and stood there, but it was absolutely black and he didn't see anything. Then he went back to the lobby and he heard the water sloshing and he went towards that because it was dark and he was having trouble finding his way around and he knew that way better than the way into the lockers. So he figured he'd check the pool first. And he went in there, and he found a switch that turned on a couple of low lights, and when those went on he saw a body in the water and dark stuff in the water with it. And then the next thing he knew, the building went up in flames."

"Interesting," Gregor said. "The body in the water?"

"That was Michael Platte. And the dark stuff was blood. He'd been hit hard on the back of the head, dumped in the pool, and left to drown."

"You're sure of that?"

"Absolutely. Michael Platte drowned."

"But you said there was another body," Gregor said.

"There was," Larry Farmer said. "In the women's locker room somewhere. I can only say somewhere because the place didn't just go up, it absolutely incinerated. It burned fast, it burned hot, and when we finally got firefighters out there to deal with it it was already all over and it still took another half an hour to subdue it completely. It was the most amazing thing I'd ever seen. The body was in there."

"And?"

Larry Farmer shrugged. "We assumed it was the body of Martha Heydreich. It was unrecognizable, you understand, but it made sense. Her lover's body is dead in the pool. She's dead in the locker room. Arthur Heydreich is right on the scene and he's got stuff all over him, he smells of the damned propellant—and yes, I know, the whole building smelled of it and he was in the building, so that wasn't conclusive. But still, you see, you've got to see, what it looked like to us. There's the fire, for one thing. Something had to start the fire. Arthur Heydreich was right there. The easiest way to start that fire is to have him be there and just start it. We didn't find any device for setting it off, or anything that could be that kind of device. We didn't find anybody who saw anybody else go into the pool house. So there we were. Easy as pie. Cut and dried. We almost arrested him on the spot. We did arrest him two days later. And this morning we let him go."

"Why?" Gregor asked.

"We sent samples from the body away for DNA testing," Larry Farmer said. "We thought we might be able to find some of Martha Heydreich's DNA on something. As it turned out, we couldn't—there's something that was gone, her toothbrush—but it didn't matter anyway. The results came back from the lab yesterday evening, and what we definitely do not have is the body of Martha Heydreich."

"How do you know?" Gregor asked. "Could you identify the body as somebody else?"

"No," Larry Farmer said. "The DNA did not match anybody in any database the lab could find. Apparently that's not all that odd. Most people don't have their DNA on file anywhere."

"But if you don't know whose DNA it is," Gregor asked, "and you don't have a sample of Martha Heydreich's DNA for comparison, how can you be sure it doesn't belong to Martha Heydreich?"

Larry Farmer put his head in his hands.

"Because," he said, "whoever the other murder victim is, undocumented or not, he's definitely and conclusively a man."

THREE

1

Arthur Heydreich knew that something was going on from the first moment the lights went on in the corridor outside his cell. For one thing, the lights actually did go on, rather than flickering and wavering for half an hour until somebody came along to set them to their daytime levels. Arthur had spent a lot of his time in jail thinking about those lights, and all the other lights, up and down the small building that was the Pineville Station Muncipal Jail. There were the lights in the cells themselves, that shut off abruptly every night at ten. There were those lights in the corridor, that seemed to have many different settings, but a schedule that varied for no reason available to him. Then there were the lights far down at the end of the corridor where the guard station was. Everything was arranged as if the Pineville Station Muncipal Jail had a regular clientele of rapists, murderers, and terrorists, liable to go bezerk at any moment and take the building by sheer force of physical power, or maybe lunatic rage. Instead, all there really were were a couple of petty thieves, three teenagers who'd been caught with marijuana, and Arthur himself. Only Arthur himself had been here more than forty-eight hours.

First the lights went on in the corridor abruptly. Then there was the low murmuring hum of people talking way up by the guard station, talking quietly, so that nobody in the cells could hear. Arthur lay in bed and tried to listen to it for a while, but it was useless. Whatever people were finding it so important to say to each other was obviously not meant for him.

He listened because it was practically the only thing he had to do. He had a few books they'd allowed him to take from home, but other than that there was nothing. Jail was nothing at all like he'd expected it to be. He'd seen a million movies where jail cells had one wall made entirely of bars and prisoners talked to each other through them. The corridors were open and the cells were open and there was a lot of conversation back and forth.

Here, each cell held exactly one prisoner, and instead of bars there were solid metal doors with just a tiny peephole in the center toward the top. Farther down there were flat slats that could be opened from the corridor side to slide in food trays for breakfast, lunch, and dinner. There was no prison cafeteria where hundreds of men would march together in a cafeteria line.

Of course, there were no hundreds of men, either. Maybe this arrangement was for small jails, and prisons were like what they were like in the movies. Arthur didn't know, and he didn't know why he was thinking about it. He only knew he was so mind-numbingly bored he could barely stay awake.

The murmurs were still coming from the other end of the corridor. He wondered what time it was. It had to be after six, but before seven, because at seven they brought the food trays around. The hum went on and on, spiking every once in a while and then falling back. Arthur stared at the ceiling of his cell and let himself drift.

He remembered the day they had come to arrest him, only two days after the fire in the pool house. He had been expecting them to come, but when he saw the cars pulling up outside his front door, he'd felt his stomach clench and his mind go numb. The only thing he'd been able to think of was the early warning system. At Waldorf Pines, no visitor was allowed onto the grounds unless the front gate had your permission first, and then, when the visitor did show up, he wasn't allowed in until you'd been found and notified. Obviously, the police were not the kind of visitors that had been meant in the brochure, but they were visitors nonetheless. Maybe he would have a cause of action because he hadn't been notified.

The murmurs went up again, and down again, and up again. There was the sound of shuffling feet in the corridor. There was another sound, farther off, that Arthur was sure was the breakfast cart bringing the trays in for the morning.

Arthur wanted to take a shower. He wanted to take a shower in his own shower in his own home, but right now he would have settled for the shower in the shower block next door. The idea that two showers a week were as many as anybody needed made him feel a little indignant. It was practically the only thing he felt at all.

The shuffling feet in the corridor stopped directly outside his door. Arthur knew the tread. It was the small Hispanic woman. He'd asked himself a dozen times why anybody thought it made sense to let this tiny little thing be a guard in a prison, even if it was really only a jail. Arthur was not physically fit, but he could have taken that woman down in a minute and a half or less, and if she hadn't had backup, he could have been off and on his way before anybody else knew he was gone.

The little Hispanic woman dropped the flap and said, "Come on. You're going downstairs."

"At seven o'clock in the morning?" Arthur asked.

"Your lawyer's here," the little Hispanic woman said.

Arthur got off the bed and turned his back to the door. He put his wrists together behind his back and pushed them through the slot. He felt the cuffs snap over his wrists.

He stepped away from the door and turned to look at it. The little Hispanic woman unlocked it and stepped back. He stepped out into the corridor and let her take his arm.

"You don't think it's a little odd for my lawyer to be here at seven o'clock in the morning?"

"Your lawyer's here," she said again.

"He's a public definder," Arthur said. "He doesn't go anywhere at seven o'clock in the morning."

The little Hispanic woman didn't say anything, and Arthur let it go. It was a break in the routine. He thought he should be grateful for it. He looked behind him at the cart bringing the breakfast trays. He had no idea what happened if he missed the breakfast tray. He probably just missed breakfast. He didn't like the idea. He never ate much of anything at home, but he was hungry all the time in here.

They went to the end of the corridor and around a corner. The little Hispanic woman opened another set of doors. They were in yet another corridor with doors, but these doors didn't seem to lead to cells. She stopped and unlocked one of them and then opened it wide.

"Go ahead," she said. "You've got to get dressed for court."

Arthur looked into the room and saw his clothes there, his jacket, his tie, his shirt, his trousers, the entire suit he was wearing when he'd been brought to this place. The suit was folded instead of hung up. It looked a little tired. He'd already worn it four or five times. They kept making him change into it when he had a court hearing.

"Am I supposed to go to court, really?" he said. "Now? At this hour of the morning? I didn't even think courts were open at this hour of the morning. What's going on here?"

"Get dressed," the little Hispanic woman said as she removed Arthur's handcuffs.

Then she locked the door behind him.

Arthur went over to the shelf where the suit was and looked at it. He remembered putting it on the morning he was arrested. He'd been very careful about picking it out. They were already looking at him oddly in the office. They were already talking about him behind his back. Then there were the secretaries, who hadn't liked coming anywhere near his desk. He kept expecting to be fired, or, if not fired— that might look bad, firing somebody who hadn't been convicted of anything, or even arrested—then put on some kind of leave of absence "until all this was over." People were supposed to be innocent until proven guilty, but it didn't work that way in everyday life. It was especially not the case once you'd been arrested.

He shucked off his orange jumpsuit and started putting on the parts of the suit, putting them on one after the other. His belt was not here, probably as a precaution against suicide, but that was par for the course with the way things were done around here. If he'd wanted to commit suicide, he could have used the tie, and they had given him that. Besides, why would anyone want to commit suicide in just these circumstances? He hadn't been convicted of anything. He wasn't on his way to the death house. The only thing that made him feel like he wanted to die was the endless boredom, and now the boredom had been relieved by all this.

He went to the door, knocked so that she'd know he was done, and turned his back so that she could put the handcuffs on. Instead, she swung the door open all the way and stepped back.

"He's in the conference room," she said.

Then she turned her back to him and started walking. Arthur was nonplussed. If this had been one of those movies he liked so much, this would have been a setup. She would have tricked him into following her down a corridor unbound, and then somebody would have raised the alarm that he was about to escape. Then there would have been a hail of bullets. Then he would have been dead.

She got to the elevator and pressed the button. The doors opened immediately. It had been waiting on this floor. She stepped back and waited until Arthur got inside. Then she pressed the button for the first floor and stared at the ceiling.

Arthur looked down at the thick curve of her neck. He thought again that he could take her any time he wanted to. He could leave her disabled and bloody on the floor. He could walk right over her and out and never be heard from again, except that there were all those other people around, and some of them had guns.

The elevator door bounced open. She stepped out into yet another corridor. Arthur stepped out after her. This corridor was full of desks and people, not prisoners but officers. They looked at him with interest as he came walking out, and as soon as he passed Arthur could hear the low murmuring of whispered conversations.

The little Hispanic woman went to the third door on the left and said, "He's in there."

Then she waited until he opened the door and went inside.

The room he walked into was largish. There was a big conference table in the middle of it, with chairs all around. His legal aid attorney was sitting in one of them, holding tightly to a stack of folders he had pulled out of a briefcase. Arthur tried to remember the kid's name, but he couldn't. He looked like he might be twenty-two.

"Well," he said, when Arthur walked in. "Sit down. Sit down. This is a development."

Arthur sat down and folded his hands in front of him "What's a development?"

"This is," the lawyer said. "Didn't they tell you? They're dropping the charges against you for killing your wife."

"What?"

"They're dropping the charges against you for killing your wife," the lawyer repeated. "And that changes everything, of course. It even changes the bail situation. They'll never be able to hold you on remand now. They might have, of course, if they weren't dropping one set of charges, but now with this—"

"Why?" Arthur asked carefully. "Why are they dropping the charges against me for killing my wife?"

The lawyer laid his hands flat on the conference table and sighed. "I don't actually know," he said, "but I've heard rumors. I've heard lots of them. We'll know for sure when we go into court, and that's in less than half an hour, so I want you to be ready. But the rumors are that the DNA evidence came back and the other body they found wasn't your wife's at all."

Arthur considered this. "They had DNA from my wife?"

"I don't know," the lawyer said. "I suppose they must have. Mr.

Heydreich, really, it doesn't matter right now. We can get to all that later when we've got a little time. What matters now is that we go into that hearing and if they insist on charging you for the murder of Michael Platte, then we get bail for you on that. I'm pretty sure that's more than perfectly doable. The judge is old Nancy Kildare, and she's got no patience with prosecutors as it is. So just get yourself into some kind of a good mental zone and let's go in there and get you out of here for good. Then you can get home and get back to some kind of real life."

Arthur thought of saying that he would not be able to get back to any kind of real life until somebody else was caught and charged and convicted of the murder of Michael Platte, at least, but he did not say that. He only wondered where the police thought his wife was now.

2

LizaAnne Marsh had gone into a state of nearly apoplectic mourning on the day she'd heard that Michael Platte had died, but it had been a month now, and it was getting harder to keep her focus. She was still really angry about what had happened to Michael, of course, and beyond furious at all those ridiculous stories about how he was having an affair with Martha Heydreich. It was ludicrous to think that somebody like Michael would have had an affair with somebody as old and ugly and extreme as that woman, when he could have had any girl he wanted in Waldorf Pines. He could have had LizaAnne herself. She knew he was interested. If he'd lived, it would have been just a matter of time before they had something going, and it would have been something a lot more attractive than anything he could have had with that stupid shrieking cunt. People just said things like that because they liked to sound as if they knew things.

LizaAnne was in her bedroom. Stretched out across her bedspread she had two hundred and twenty little thumbnail photographs, one for each of the members of the senior class of Pineville Station Senior High School. She loved having these pictures, because they made everything so much easier. Before this year, she'd had to get along with nothing but pens and pencils and notebooks. Even the computer hadn't been much help. Now she could actually see what she was looking at. That made all the difference.

Heather was in the bathroom, running the water in the sink far too long. Heather always ran the water in the sink far too long, and she took too long looking at herself in the vanity mirror, too. Heather didn't have a bathroom for her own bedroom at home. Heather's parents thought that would be "spoiling" her. As far as LizaAnne was concerned, Heather's parents were too retarded for words.

The water turned off in the sink. The swoosh of the air dryer went on. LizaAnne actually hated the air dryer, but so many of the people who came over were impressed with it, she didn't want to ask her father to take it out.

Heather came out into the room and brushed her hair off her face. "I don't think you're taking this seriously," she said. "My mother says it's all around the club today. It's everywhere. They're going to let Mr. Heydreich out of jail because they don't think he killed his wife."

"I don't care if he killed her," LizaAnne said. "I don't care who killed her. I'm only glad she's gone. Of course, it would have been better if Michael had still been alive to enjoy being able to live a normal life without having her skulking around him all the time, but that's the way things are. Do they still think he killed Michael?"

"I don't know," Heather said. "I was trying to overhear when my mother was on the phone, but you know what that's like. She doesn't like me listening."

"I've been thinking about Kathi Colson," LizaAnne said. "I mean, I know she was at my sweet sixteen party, but I don't think that should be the standard. I mean, I wanted lots of people at the party, so I let in people who don't really belong to the A group. I mean, I didn't let in dweebs or anybody like that. I didn't let in anybody retarded. But I think Kathi Colson belongs in the B group. Don't you?"

Heather looked down at the tiny picture in LizaAnne's hand, and

LizaAnne found herself thinking that she had been right all along. These pictures were really wonderful. She could see the faces of everybody in the class, and once she'd seen the faces she would know who belonged where. She was so glad she'd made friends with that retarded dork on the yearbook committee. She'd never have gotten them otherwise. It didn't matter that she'd have to invite him to a party this year. He'd figure out soon enough he wasn't wanted, and her own popularity was unassailable. She could never be touched when it came to that.

She put the tiny picture of Kathi Colson in the pile with the B group and searched around until she found the one of Didi Webb. Didi Webb was a special case. Didi had belonged to the A group, but then things had started to happen. First Didi's father had lost his job. Then the whole family had had to move out of Waldorf Pines, and there had even been rumors that the bank was about to foreclose on the house. Of course, nobody's house was ever foreclosed on in Waldorf Pines. The club had some kind of fund that stopped that from happening, but it didn't keep a family in the house they couldn't pay for. It just bought the house from under them and sold it to somebody else. Didi's family had actually packed up and moved in the middle of the night, so that nobody would see them.

At about that time, LizaAnne had moved Didi from the A group to the B group, which meant being very careful to make sure that there were no empty places at the lunch table when Didi wanted to sit down. There were musical chairs for a while, until Didi got the hint, and stopped trying. There were awkward moments in the girls' room, too, but LizaAnne could always cover up for those by concentrating really hard on her makeup. If things had stopped there, of course, Didi would just have descended to the B group, and that would have been that.

LizaAnne put the little picture down in front of Heather and waited. Heather looked away.

"It's not like it's her fault," Heather said finally. "She didn't make her father lose his job. It was just bad luck."

"I don't believe in luck," LizaAnne said. "And I don't think anybody ever loses a job unless he's done something wrong. I mean, think of all the things we don't know about. Mr. Webb might be an alcoholic. Or he might gamble. And, you know, even if he did those things, not everybody who does them loses his job. And people who lose their jobs get new ones. He's been out of a job for a year now. There has to be something wrong with him."

"That doesn't mean there's something wrong with her," Heather said.

LizaAnne brushed this away. "Of course there does," she said. "Families count. It's just like dogs, you know. There's a breed, and which breed it is determines a lot of things. The Webbs are—well, there must be something wrong with them. My father says that you can fool people for a while, but in the long run it all comes out. That's what must have happened here. Mr. Webb fooled people for a while, but now everybody knows what he is. He's no better than a bum, really."

"Oh, I don't think that's true."

"Of course it's true," LizaAnne said. "And if he's a bum, she's a bum. But even if she wasn't, we'd still be where we are, and that's that she doesn't have a car anymore. She comes to school on the bus. We've seen her."

"Lots of people come to school on the bus," Heather said.

"Of course they do," LizaAnne said. "But they're all in the C group or lower, and you know it. And I'm not the only one who feels that way about it, either. Didi's been hanging around with Norma Antonelli for weeks now, and I heard Norma talking about it to Sally Carr in the girls' room. I mean, I'm not asking for her to have some fancy car the way she used to, but practically everybody has something to drive. Even dweebs have something to drive. It's impossible."

"If her father is out of a job, maybe he doesn't have enough money to get her something to drive," Heather said. "Maybe she'd have to get a job to have something to drive."

"Well," LizaAnne said, "if she got a job, that would be very good.

And if she got the right kind of job, she could even get back into the B group. But I think she belongs in the C group and I'm going to talk to Norma and Sally about it. If things keep going the way they're going, she's going to drop all the way down to D, and then nobody will talk to her. Don't be retarded. Tell me what I'm supposed to do about Lisa Breen. She's started dating Peter Halliday, and usually that would mean a step up, but you know Lisa. I can't stand brainy girls, can you? I mean, who do they think they are?"

Heather went over to the window and looked out. LizaAnne stared at her back for a moment and then turned away. Heather was always a problem. She was only in the A group because she was LizaAnne's ugly friend, and she knew it, and LizaAnne knew it, and everybody else knew it. LizaAnne had considered the possibility that it might one day be necessary to ditch her for a substitute, but she didn't like the idea. Substitutes were actually very hard to find. You wouldn't think so, but they were. A lot of ugly girls seemed to think it was better to be outcasts in the F group than to be some pretty girl's ugly friend.

LizaAnne picked up Lisa Breen's picture and frowned. Lisa wasn't bad looking, and she had wonderful clothes, but there was the brains thing. Lisa was in all the honors classes, and in AP everything, and people said she was applying to Harvard. Nobody with any sense applied to someplace like Harvard.

Heather came back from the window and sat on the bed. "It's true," she said. "I just saw him."

"Saw who?"

"I just saw Mr. Heydreich. He's back. He just came out onto his deck. He was wearing a suit. You know, a regular suit. Not an orange suit for jail."

LizaAnne put down the picture of Lisa Breen. "Well," she said. "I guess that's interesting. Although I don't like it, and my dad doesn't, either. It's not nice to live in a place with a murderer."

"But maybe he isn't a murderer," Heather said. "They let him go."

"They arrested him in the first place, didn't they? They must have had a reason. The police don't just go running around arresting people for no reason. He must have done something."

"Do you think so?"

"Of course I think so," LizaAnne said. "Everybody thinks so. Besides, somebody has to have killed Michael. Everybody goes on and on about Martha Heydreich, but it was Michael's body they found in the pool all bloody. Who do you think did that?"

"I don't know," Heather said.

"I do," LizaAnne said. "There were two murders, not one. People don't just go around murdering people like that. Especially not people in a place like Waldorf Pines. There can't be two murderers running around. Whoever killed the one had to kill the other."

"Maybe."

"Absolutely. And you know what?" LizaAnne said. "I'll bet that if I had to, I could prove it. Forget about it, won't you? He probably has some fancy lawyer that found a technicality to get him out of jail. It happens all the time. That's what my dad says. Just wait. He'll be back in jail in no time. What do you think I should do about Lisa Breen?"

"What?" Heather said.

LizaAnne rolled her eyes. Heather was so retarded. Really. LizaAnne took the picture of Lisa Breen and dropped it into the C group.

"I don't care who she's going out with," LizaAnne said, "she's just retarded."

FOUR

1

When Gregor Demarkian had first started to do the work he did now, he had not given much thought to the people he would do it for. Even the word "client" had been foreign to him. He had worked for twenty years as a special agent of the Federal Bureau of Investigation. Special agents of the Federal Bureau of Investigation did not have clients, and did not think well of most of the people who did. Lawyers had clients, and lawyers were always trying to get the perpetrators off, or to pretend that the perpetrators were crazy, or just filing motions because otherwise they'd get bored. Even federal prosecutors were lawyers. Their job seemed to be to tell everybody else that the case was hopeless, and that there would need to be at least another hundred man hours of scut work before they could even think of getting anything done.

Of course, when Gregor had joined the Bureau, all special agents had been required to be either lawyers or accountants, so many of the agents Gregor had known had been lawyers, too, but that somehow hadn't seemed to count. Gregor himself had been trained as an accountant and had become a CPA before first arriving at Quantico.

Once he was in training and part of the organization, nobody had ever mentioned that again.

Part of the reason Gregor had never thought about clients was the timing. He had come back to Cavanaugh Street after Elizabeth died, just after. He'd bought his apartment in a kind of daze, not really knowing where or who he wanted to be. As long as Elizabeth had still been alive and there had still been something to do he had been "all right" in the sense of "pretty nearly functional." It wasn't until it had been all over for months that he'd realized that "pretty nearly functional" had been a euphemism for "just like a zombie." Still, as long as he had doctors to talk to and a hospital to visit and medical bills to negotiate, he'd been able to get along day by day, doing the things people did, lying down in a bed he could never remember sleeping in, putting away food he could never remember eating.

At the end, he hadn't even been living in the apartment he had shared with Elizabeth all those years. He'd put that up for sale and moved into something efficient and modern closer to the hospital, and he'd gone on leave so that he didn't show up at the office every morning just to spend all day listening for the phone. It had been a long, bad stretch that last year. When it was over, he had not really had any idea of what he wanted to do next. He hadn't even had any idea that there was a "next," and coming home to Cavanaugh Street—*coming home*—had just seemed like something natural that might one day make sense.

Working as a consultant to police departments with difficult-to-solve murder cases had not seemed like something natural or something that might make sense, but that was because he had not thought of it at all. His very first case had been an accident and not one he'd gotten paid for. His next had been set up by friends who thought he needed something to do with his time. Then the cases had come on down the line and people had started sending him money, and it was only when old George Tekemanian's grandson Martin had gone out on his own as an accountant that Gregor had been forced to think about making the whole situation regular. Now he had a "billing department" of sorts, and a standard hourly fee that seemed to have been concocted out of thin air. He had somebody to send people to when they asked him what he charged. He still had no handle at all on clients, or where they came from, or what they really wanted out of him. It was easy to say that what they wanted was their cases solved, but it was never that simple. If all you wanted was your case solved, you could hire somebody a lot cheaper who wouldn't suck up all the publicity as soon as he arrived in town.

"What they want is cover," Bennis told him, over and over again. "They want you to suck up all the publicity. It's usually bad publicity. They want to be able to sit back and say, look, we went out and got the hottest guy out there, it's not our fault this is the way it turned out."

"I don't usually leave a case until it's been solved," Gregor pointed out. "I don't usually leave them with an open murder file."

"It's not just a matter of solving the case," Bennis said. "It's also how it gets solved and who it gets solved in the face of. That didn't make any sense, I know. But I think a lot of these times, a lot of these cases, what they're worried about is not necessarily solving it, but solving it by arresting the wrong person."

"They bring me in as a kind of Innocence Project?"

"No," Bennis said, "not that kind of wrong person. I mean they don't want to think that the person who is really guilty is the richest guy in town, maybe, or the mayor, or somebody else they would rather not arrest. I don't think they're going to call you in if they think the perpetrator is the local high school drug dealer. They bring you in when the murderer is going to be somebody—normal."

"I don't think murderers are normal," Gregor said. "I never did buy that thing about how any one of us could be a murderer under the right circumstances. Most of us could be killers, yes, but that isn't the same thing."

"You're not really going to give me one of those lectures about the fundamentally altered mind of the murderer," Bennis said. "I mean, the first time I heard you give one of those was the week after we met, and that was—"

Gregor sat in Larry Farmer's car and thought that his theory was fine as far as it went, but that he'd never developed it to the point of determining how you could recognize such a person when you first met him.

Larry Farmer had pulled up right outside the Pineville Station Police Department's front door. It wasn't much of a police department as far as Gregor could see, but the departments that hired him almost never were. Larry Farmer looked around a bit and then sighed with relief.

"That's all right, then," he said. "I was sure we'd already be inundated. It's just the kind of thing, you know. There'll be trucks down here before the day is out. It's been enormous news locally for weeks. This is going to make it worse."

Gregor sat where he was, without moving. Larry Farmer didn't seem to be moving, either.

"We're going to want to call a press conference," Larry Farmer said. "I hope you don't mind, but it's absolutely vital. We can't be seen as just sitting on our rear ends or not doing something to repair the situation. Especially now that we seem to have made such a mess of it. There's going to be a lot of local publicity and there's going to be a lot of, well, people."

"People?"

Larry Farmer shrugged.

Gregor leaned back a little. "My wife says that people hire me when they know who committed the murder, but it's somebody they don't want to take the responsibility of arresting. That they call me in to take the heat when the murderer turns out to be the mayor."

"Oh, the murderer isn't the mayor," Larry Farmer said.

"I wasn't suggesting he was," Gregor said. "I was trying to find out if that was why you had hired me. To take the heat of the publicity which you know is going to be bad."

Larry Farmer squirmed. "Is that unacceptable? Would you be unwilling to work for us if that was what we wanted? Because, I have to admit, Mr. Demarkian, the publicity is an issue. The publicity and the pressure. There's going to be a lot of pressure, because it's Waldorf Pines. And we haven't talked money yet, but I've heard about what you charge. You're not cheap. I don't think I could justify your fee if it wasn't for the problem with the publicity. And, you know, the pressure."

"I've got nothing against taking the heat with the publicity," Gregor said, "but I do think that if you've got a good idea who did this and why, or even just who, that it might save us both a lot of time if you just told me now. Making me stumble around until I stumble on the obvious just wastes time. And even if you're wrong, knowing who you suspect and why is useful information."

Larry Farmer fluttered his hands in the air. Everything about the man fluttered.

"But that's the thing," he said. "That's the thing. You know who I suspect? Arthur Heydreich. Or at least, I would have suspected him if that body in the pool house had been his wife. What would you think? Here's a man found right at the scene with two dead bodies. One is definitely the body of the kid who was screwing his wife, or at least who everybody said was screwing his wife. The second was unrecognizable but, you know, arguably—"

"It made sense to expect it belonged to the wife," Gregor said. "We've been over this before."

"Now I don't know what happened, or why," Larry Farmer said, "The kid who's dead? The body we can identify? Well, he belongs to a Waldorf Pines family. He was a first-class screwup. His parents bought him out of some legal trouble on and off, and he got expelled from college for something drug related. But dead in the pool with his head bashed in from behind? Who would do that? He wasn't a major dealer. He didn't know anybody who was, that we can tell. His parents moved to Waldorf Pines after he left for college. And I refuse to believe all that nonsense about the Marsh girl. It's ridiculous."

"Who's the Marsh girl, and what's the nonsense about her?"

Larry Farmer sighed again. "LizaAnne Marsh lives in Waldorf Pines. She goes to high school. She's a senior, I think. She's one of those people. She's a sociopath in training, if she isn't full blown there yet. She had one of those parties, those sweet sixteen parties, that they show on television."

"What?"

"It's a reality television show," Larry Farmer said. "*My Super Sweet 16*. Girls have sweet sixteen parties and they film them, the preparations, the party itself, everything. I don't know how to explain them to you if you haven't seen them. The families spend a ton of money on them, hundreds of thousands of dollars."

"Seriously?" Gregor said. "Then this Waldorf Pines place is, what, an enclave for multimillionaires?"

"No," Larry Farmer said, "not at all. If there's one thing I've learned in the course of my life, Mr. Demarkian, it's that people with real money would never let some television show come and film some big party they gave for their daughter, and they really wouldn't let some television show make a big fuss about what everything costs. The people who live at Waldorf Pines are well off, more or less, but it's nothing like that. LizaAnne Marsh's father owns a bunch of car dealerships. High-end cars, multiple dealerships, he's definitely making money. It's just not that kind of money."

"And yet he gave his daughter a party that costs a hundred thousand dollars?"

"Three hundred and fifty thousand dollars by the time they added up the final tab," Larry Farmer said. "But you know what people like that are like, Mr. Demarkian. They like to throw it around. Old Herb Marsh likes to throw it around, and as much of it in public as he can. He's probably in debt up to his eyeballs."

"You haven't checked?"

"I haven't got probable cause to check," Larry Farmer said. "I'd love to see the guy's financial statements, though. I'd be willing to bet just about anything we'll be seeing him back here on fraud charges in a couple of years. Either that or the feds will get him for playing games with his taxes. Or, hell, you know, the state of Pennsylvania. But I don't have anything that sounds like he's involved in this."

"But you think his daughter is?"

"No," Larry Farmer said. "It's the people in my department. They've come up with this ridiculous theory that it's LizaAnne who killed Michael Platte, because LizaAnne had the hots for him, and he wasn't buying. He was chasing around after Martha Heydreich instead."

"And the other body?"

"This was back before we knew the other body wasn't Martha Heydreich's," Larry Farmer said. "We thought it was, and they thought LizaAnne could have killed her, too, for the same reason. Out of jealousy, I guess, or spite, or just the attitude that what LizaAnne wants, LizaAnne gets. And it's like I said, the girl is a sociopath. It's just that I can't see anybody murdering anybody for a reason like that. Can you?"

Gregor shook his head. "People commit murder for a lot of completely silly reasons," he said. "They commit murder for reasons that would sound trivial to you and me. I don't think the apparent triviality of the reason is the problem with that theory."

"What is?"

"You're back to the second body," Gregor said. "You have two bodies, both of them men. You'd have to have a reason for this girl to kill another man."

"Maybe she was snubbed by this one, too," Larry Farmer said. "I told you it was all just crazy. She can't go around killing every guy who doesn't want to date her. There's got to be a ton of them."

"Unpleasant personality?"

"Heavyset and not very attractive physically," Larry Farmer said. "Back when I was growing up in this town, a girl who looked like that wouldn't have been on the map socially. But that's what you get when you're stuck with a place like Waldorf Pines. It changes the entire equation. Popular used to be about being pretty and talented and socially adept. Now it's about how much money your father has and whether he's willing to spend more than most people would spend for a house giving you a party where you ride in on an elephant."

"What?" Gregor said again.

"That's how LizaAnne Marsh made her entrance at her party," Larry Farmer said. "She rode in on an elephant. You would not believe the amount of trouble it caused. Handlers. Permits. The state animal control people. A circus license. I don't remember all the details. But we were stuck doing days of work just so that they could make it happen, and then the party needed extra security because of all the drunken teenagers who hadn't been invited and who wanted to get in. I just about killed somebody myself in the middle of all that."

Larry looked out and around at the Pineville Station Police Department building.

"It's the Waldorf Pines people," he said. "I don't know. Maybe it's just the way things are in places like Philadelphia. You've got the Main Line and all of that. It just never was the way things were out here, and I don't like it. I just wish they'd all pack up and go away somewhere and leave the rest of us alone."

2

The Pineville Station Police Department was like a thousand others across the United States, small, neat, and built to be "modern" in 1958. There was a long, blond wood counter where members of the public were supposed to present themselves to do their business. There were a few desks behind that counter, most of them unoccupied at this time of day. There were two small offices to the back, one of which Gregor assumed must belong to Larry Farmer. A young woman sat at a desk just behind the counter and did things on the computer. A tall man stood aimlessly next to her, talking without raising his voice and looking as if he had nowhere to go. The tall man was the most formally dressed person in the place.

"Oh, good," Larry said. "Just who we need. That's Buck Monaghan. Buck! Buck! I brought back Gregor Demarkian. I told you I would."

The tall man straightened up and held out his hand to Gregor. "I hope he didn't kidnap you," he said. "The situation is pretty dire, but

I don't think we're at the point where we have to start committing felonies just yet."

"We're not the ones committing felonies," Larry Farmer said. "I wish you'd stop saying things like that. I know you think it's funny, but it just gets everybody all confused, and then they're mad at me again. Of course I didn't kidnap him. I explained the situation, and then he agreed to come. I don't know what it's going to cost, but it's better to have him here than not. You said that yourself just this morning when I asked you about it."

Buck Monaghan seemed to sigh and stare up at the ceiling, but the movements were so slight, Gregor wasn't sure he hadn't imagined them. When Gregor took another look, the impression was gone.

Buck Monaghan leaned over the counter and picked up a manila folder. "It's very definitely a very good thing that we have Mr. Demarkian here, and I never meant to suggest otherwise. I'll admit I was a little surprised at how fast you got it done. Has he filled you in on anything at all, Mr. Demarkian? Or has he just been panicking?"

"I think I'm more or less filled in," Gregor said. "Two bodies, one too damaged to identify immediately. DNA came back without providing positive identification of any person but ruling out the person who had been supposed to be the victim—"

"Well," Buck said, "yes, but not because we've got Martha Heydreich's DNA, either. I sometimes find it more than a little disappointing that the world does not work the way it does on television. If this had been *CSI*, Martha's DNA would have been in half a dozen databases and the only reason it wouldn't have been would be because otherwise the show wouldn't last long enough. I used to think it would be interesting to get a case like this, a case that wasn't completely cut and dried. I spent a lot of my time doing plea deals with idiots who think it's just common sense to rob convenience stores being tended by some kid you've known since high school and then expecting he won't recognize you in a ski mask. The ordinary run of criminal leaves a lot to be desired."

"It's not the criminal I'm worried about," Larry Farmer said.

The young woman at the computer looked up. She gave Gregor Demarkian a long stare and said, "It's Waldorf Pines. It's always Waldorf Pines. When anything goes really wrong in this town, you can bet your wallet it's going to have something to do with Waldorf Pines."

Gregor shook his head. "Just a few minutes ago, Mr. Farmer here was telling me that the people who live in Waldorf Pines weren't all that wealthy or all that influential. Car dealerships, I think he said. But if they're not all that wealthy and they're not all that influential, how can they cause you all this trouble?"

Buck Monaghan and Larry Farmer and the young woman all looked at each other.

It was Buck Monaghan who finally spoke. "It's not the people who live in Waldorf Pines who are the problem," he said.

The young woman snorted. "They're a problem, all right. If I get my hands on that little bitch, I'll—"

"That wasn't the kind of problem I was talking about," Buck Monaghan said.

"Well, it's not just LizaAnne, queen of the universe, who's trouble," the young woman said. "There's the alleged victim, the one who isn't a victim and is probably in Monte Carlo by now under an assumed name. She was a prize and a half on Sundays, let me tell you."

Buck Monaghan cleared his throat. "Miss Connolly's sister wasn't invited to the Marsh party," he explained, "and as for Martha Heydreich—well, whatever. Let's just say that she isn't a very polite person."

"She drove that car around like she wanted to kill somebody," Miss Connolly said, "and the somebody she wanted to kill was definitely one of us peasants. Honestly, Larry, stop shushing me. Who do these people think they are? It's not Bill Gates living out there and it isn't the president of the United States, either. Since when does being able to borrow enough money to ride around in a pink sports car make you queen of the May?"

"Do you even know what that means, being queen of the May?" Buck Monaghan said.

Miss Connolly shook that off. "It's something my mother used to say. And Sister Agnes Haloran at school. Why should I care what it means? The whole lot of them up there act like somebody just appointed them God, and they don't care what kind of damage they do in the process. It's not just that Jen didn't get invited to the Marsh party, it's that she tried to kill herself over it. Because that's Waldorf Pines and they can't just not invite you. They have to go around telling everybody at school that they shouldn't ever talk to you again because you're such a freak, and probably a lesbian, and then—"

Gregor straightened up. "I see," he said. "That's why some people had the other theory. This is about that girl again."

"LizaAnne Marsh," Larry Farmer said.

"She's not a girl," Miss Connolly said. "She's a hatchet-faced snake and a tub of lard. And it wouldn't surprise me if she'd killed off half the state of Pennsylvania."

"It sounds more like half the state of Pennsylvania has a reason to kill her," Buck Monaghan said, "and she's very much alive, and at her usual business. And that may be very unfortunate on a number of levels, but it is not our problem at the moment. Our problem is Waldorf Pines."

Miss Connolly had turned back to her computer. "They're not worried about the people who live there," she said, "they're worried about the people who run the place. Not that anybody really knows who runs the place. It's a private corporation."

"People have a right to form private corporations," Buck Monaghan said. Miss Connolly shuddered, and he frowned at her back. "But as it turns out, it's not the owners of the corporation we're concerned with immediately, it's the man they hired to manage the place. Waldorf Pines is a private, gated community where anyone who buys a house must be a member of the golf club. You're from Philadelphia, so you're probably thinking of how those traditionally work, places where there's been a club in place for generations and then the members decide to build residential housing on the grounds. This isn't like that. Waldorf Pines was invented pretty much out of whole cloth not more than fifteen years ago. They built the club, they built the golf course, they built the houses, they worked up the club rules, they did the whole thing like they were making a set for a movie. The rumor, and it's a reliable rumor, is that they sunk a ton of money into doing it, and they've got a continuing interest. I've been trying to get some information about exactly how the financial arrangements go for the people who are living there, but so far all I've heard is that the arrangements don't have anything to do with this murder and I don't have an excuse for getting what is supposed to be privileged communication. But there's something, some way in which the company is continuing to be financially involved, because they've got a full time manager out there and he seems to be charged with protecting their interests."

"Horace Wingard," Larry Farmer said.

"Horace Wingard," Buck repeated. "He was right in our faces the moment we made the arrest, and he's been in them ever since. Until today, we were able to fend him off, because we had Arthur Heydreich in jail and the situation looked fairly straightforward. Now nothing looks straightforward, and my guess is that we have maybe an hour or two before he's back down here ready to clean our clocks. At the very least, he'll sue the town, and whoever's hired him will make sure he has the resources to do it. And it won't really matter if he wins or loses, either. He doesn't have to win. He just has to bankrupt us."

"Waldorf Pines," Miss Connolly said, without turning around again.

"You're here," Buck Monaghan said, "so that we can be sure that they'll either back off, or that we'll have good grounds to recouping our expenses in a countersuit. If you could manage to make the murderer Horace Wingard himself, none of us would mind. But we're not expecting to be that lucky."

FIVE

1

Horace Wingard heard the news on the television in his office at the club, and as soon as he heard it he jumped out of his chair and started pacing. Pacing was not good for much of anything, and he knew it, but it was the only thing he could think of. He'd never been under the illusion that he'd be able to get what he really wanted out of all this. That was because the best-case scenario was that no body should ever have been found on the grounds of Waldorf Pines at all. Still, he'd thought the very least he could expect was that the police would be competent at their jobs, the "mystery" would amount to anything but, and the perpetrator would be taken off the grounds and stuffed away in jail as quickly and as quietly as possible. That would be less quickly and less quietly than it might be under other circumstances, but that came with being associated with a place like Waldorf Pines. People were always much more interested in richer people committing crimes than in poorer ones. That was because, with poorer people, crime seemed almost inevitable.

It took him a few minutes after hearing the news to figure out what was going to happen and why. In the end, there were always two all-important factors: the publicity and the money. The money was always more important than the publicity, but the publicity could cause money, and it could cause it to go away. There were also different kinds of publicity. The publicity about a resident of Waldorf Pines having murdered his wife and her teenaged lover was bad, but it was by no means as bad as it could possibly get.

He was standing at the window of his office when Arthur Heydreich came into the complex. His window looked out on the golf course, but he had television sets following security cameras along one wall, and he could see the whole scene at the gate. Arthur was not driving his own car. He was being driven by somebody in a battered Ford sedan. Nobody at Waldorf Pines had a car like that sedan. Even the residents who had Fords had big, new, and shiny ones. This thing looked like it belonged to a social worker who lived with the very clients she served in South Philadelphia. Either that, or to a high school teacher who couldn't quite get a job in a decent neighborhood.

The car passed through the gate. Horace switched to another monitor and saw the sedan begin the long curving drive around the outside of the complex. He wondered how many people would be out there, standing at their windows, waiting to see what would happen next. It was a small mercy that it was already after the rush hour, and most of the men, at least, would be at work.

The Ford sedan went out of sight behind a small cluster of trees. Even this late in the fall, some of the trees were still full of leaves, bushy and obstructing. Horace went back to his desk and buzzed Miss Vaile.

"Could you come in here?" he said. "We have things to discuss."

Miss Vaile was an excellent secretary. She was in his office and by the side of his desk in an instant. She carried the notepad she never used. She looked as if hell could overrun Disney World and she wouldn't have batted an eye.

"Mr. Wingard?" she said.

Horace looked across the room at the monitors. He couldn't

really see them from the desk. It might not have mattered if he could, since there was no security camera directly on Arthur Heydreich's front door. He wondered what it was like over there: Arthur getting out of that awful sedan in the drive; Arthur walking up the steps to his own front door; Arthur going inside. He wondered if women were looking out their windows now. There would be if Arthur went out to the back deck. Somebody would almost certainly be taking pictures.

Miss Vaile was waiting. Horace had a terrible urge to ask her if her first name was Vicki. Then he couldn't remember if that was the right way to spell "Vaile."

He sat down behind his desk and put the palms of his hands down on either side of the green felt blotter. Miss Vaile continued to wait.

"Well," he said. "Have you heard the news this morning?"

"Yes, Mr. Wingard. I keep the window to the WKVT Web site open at all times when I'm at work."

"WKVT is a local station?"

"That's right, Mr. Wingard. It's the local Fox affiliate."

Horace Wingard made a face. He had no politics to speak of, but in his mind, Fox was definitely downmarket. Fox was the kind of thing plumbers listened to. Horace would have been happier if Miss Vaile were monitoring NPR.

He put those considerations aside.

"Well," he said. "Let's see if I have this straight. The police are now saying that the second body in the pool house was not the body of Martha Heydreich."

"That's right," Miss Vaile said. "The DNA tests came back, and it's the body of a man, not a woman. So—"

"Yes, I see. Do the police know who this man was?"

"Apparently not, Mr. Wingard."

"Do we know? Is there a resident missing somewhere? Do we know if any of our families have filed a missing persons report?"

"If anybody here had filed a missing persons report, we would have heard about it," Miss Vaile said. "We've got that kind of thing very well organized. I can check just to make sure, of course, if you'd like me to. It's not impossible that with all the fuss there's been about the murders, some things are falling through the cracks."

"Do that," Horace said. "I take it you don't think it's likely."

"No," Miss Vaile said. "I do not."

Horace contemplated the situation for a little longer. "The first concern," he said finally, "will simply be the novelty of it. If the police had just announced that they'd found the bodies of two men in the pool house to begin with, it wouldn't matter much now one way or the other. News gets old. It's the switch that will supply the point of interest, because the switch is an anomaly. After we get past that, though, the issues are trickier. The best thing would be to require Mr. Heydreich to move out of the complex. I've looked at the residential agreement, and I'm fairly sure that we do have a right, under that agreement, to ask him to go. But I also think it isn't going to be that simple. There's always the possibility that he could sue."

"I doubt if he could win such a lawsuit," Miss Vaile said. "This is a private association. We're entitled to have our own bylaws. And to run by our own rules."

"Oh, I know that, Miss Vaile. I know that. And I'm sure that if we asked our lawyers, they'd say the same. But it's really not that straightforward when you get down to the day-to-day tactics lawyers will use. I presume Mr. Heydreich has a lawyer?"

"It said in the paper that he had one assigned by the court." Miss Vaile sniffed. "I don't know if you could call that a proper lawyer."

"I don't know if you could, either. And I'd be a lot easier in my mind if I thought that the only lawyer Arthur Heydreich was going to have was a public defender. But my instincts say it isn't going to be that way. Arthur Heydreich can afford a private attorney. We do know that?"

"Yes, of course," Miss Vaile said. "I ran a check on his financials as soon as he was arrested."

"And was there anything we could use? Is he in a lot of debt? Does he gamble? Did he have a life insurance policy on his wife?"

"Mr. and Mrs. Heydreich both had life insurance policies, and each of those policies named the other as beneficiary," Miss Vaile said. "Mr. Heydreich's policy is for three million dollars. Mrs. Heydreich's policy is for one million dollars."

"That's standard enough, I suppose, for people around here. And it's not quite relevant, is it, under the circumstances? Anything else? A fall in the credit score, something?"

"Not a thing," Miss Vaile said. "I'll admit it did surprise me a little. I would have thought that getting arrested for murder would have some impact on your credit score, but apparently the credit reporting agencies don't follow that kind of news."

"Yes, well," Horace said. "That causes us something of a problem, doesn't it? We've got the legal right to put him out just because he's been arrested. It doesn't matter what for, and it doesn't matter if he's guilty. We can do that under the clause forbidding activity that would damage the reputation of Waldorf Pines. But having the right isn't the same thing as having the ability, and having the ability isn't the same thing as being able to act with impunity. The simple fact is that he hasn't been convicted of anything."

"That's true."

"And from what I heard this morning, it's possible he won't even be charged with anything."

"I think that was what the news said, yes," Miss Vaile said.

"There are several different possibilities here," Horace said, "and they all make us look bad in the short run. And in the long run, too, depending on how they work out. We can make him leave, and he can refuse to budge. Then we'd have to—what? Send the sheriff and some vans out to take possession of his house? How would we do that? It would make an enormous fuss, which is just what we're trying to avoid. And whether we got him out or not, there would be stories in the press about how we're taking the law into our own hands and presuming him guilty before he was proven innocent, or however that goes. If he sued on grounds like that, the process could take years. We'd be all over the Internet."

"I'm afraid so, yes."

"And there would be the legal issue," Horace said. "It's possible that there is some kind of protection under the Fifth Amendment. It's possible we're not allowed to ask him to leave when he's not been proven guilty."

"I don't think that's the case," Miss Vaile said. "The residential agreements are perfectly plain. We may ask anybody to leave if he engages in any behavior detrimental to the reputation of Waldorf Pines."

"Yes," Horace said. "But the letter of the law is one thing, and the real world is another. Do you know what I'd like to know? Do you know the one thing nobody seems to be asking?"

"What's that, Mr. Wingard?"

"If the other body doesn't belong to Martha Heydreich, where is Martha Heydreich?"

"I think the speculation is that she's run off," Miss Vaile said. "At least, that was what was on the Internet this morning. She committed both the murders, and she's run off to live under an assumed name. I'm not sure it made much sense, but it's still early days. We'll have new theories by tomorrow."

"I'm sure we will. But there's always the most obvious possibility. There's always the possibility that Arthur Heydreich killed all three of them, and Martha Heydreich's body is buried in his basement. Can you imagine that? Police vans and forensics teams and all the rest of it, just like before, but going through Arthur Heydreich's basement."

"I think the police already went through Arthur Heydreich's basement, Mr. Wingard. I don't think there's anything to be found there."

"Maybe not," Horace said, but he was thinking, and all his thoughts were nasty. He didn't care what the police were saying this morning. He didn't care who the other body in the pool house had been.

He thought Arthur Heydreich had murdered Michael Platte, at least, and that if he was left at large, he'd murder half of Waldorf Pines.

2

Fanny Bullman didn't think she had ever been as shocked in her life as she was by the way people at Waldorf Pines were behaving toward Arthur Heydreich. She wondered what Charlie would think of it, if he were here. Fanny had always thought of Charlie as the single most upright person she had ever met. It was true, some of the ways things were shaping up looked bad. There were the bodies in the pool house and everything that had gone with them. Fanny could remember standing on her deck and trying to see something of the police going in and out on the morning of the discovery of the bodies.

Women from all over the complex had come out onto their decks to look. Women Fanny had never seen had gathered in little clutches and cliques to talk about it. And it had looked bad. Of course it had looked bad. There were the two bodies, one of them burned so badly it was unrecognizable. In fact, it was burned so badly, it wasn't even really a body. Maybe they shouldn't have jumped to conclusions that way, thinking that it had to be Martha Heydreich who was dead, but then it had made so much sense. If Charlie were here, Fanny was sure he would agree with her, because he always agreed with her, except when he didn't.

And lately, of course, he didn't. He didn't because he wasn't here. Fanny could walk around the house and feel him, but he was really somewhere else. Sometimes she wished he'd come back. Sometimes she thought that if he did come back, she would pick up a knife and carve her initials on his face. Those were not times she liked. She wasn't used to having strong emotions. She didn't think she wanted them.

And there were all the other things, too—the fact that Arthur had been right there on the scene, the one who had discovered the bodies and the only one, as far as anyone knew, who had entered the pool house in days. Well, the only person who had done that and was still alive. And then there had been the smell of him. People who went over there after the alarm was sounded, back when it looked like all that was happening was a fire—well, those people said that Arthur Heydreich absolutely reeked of the smell of nail polish, and the accelerant that was used to make the fire burn so quickly was something to do with nail polish.

Fanny still didn't think it was right, the way people just assumed that Arthur Heydreich must be guilty of murder. That was not the way it was supposed to be in the United States of America.

Fanny heard the news on the radio just after she'd dropped the children off at the bus stop. She came into her own kitchen and heard the announcer's voice doing that breathless "breaking news" thing that sounded as if he were having an asthma attack. She tried to make sense of it and found herself wishing the man would be replaced by a robot, or by anybody, someone who could talk and not sound as if he were having an orgasm.

When the radio finished, Fanny went to her computer and began to look around the Web sites. The only one that had anything up was WKVT, and it was very sparse. DNA testing had revealed that the unidentified body in the Waldorf Pines case belonged to a man. The police had dropped the charges against Arthur Heydreich in the murder of his wife. There was no news on whether or not they would drop the charges against Arthur Heydreich in the murder of Michael Platte. Fanny had to go back and read the story twice. She thought her head was going to explode.

There, she thought, sitting at her kitchen table and rubbing her hands together. There. What had she tried to tell everybody? It was wrong to jump to conclusions, no matter how obvious those conclusions seemed to be. You never really knew what was happening until all the evidence was in. People were going to be embarrassed when they realized they had made this mistake. They were going to be ashamed of themselves.

And what about Arthur Heydreich? He'd been left sitting there in jail for weeks, with nobody to visit him. Fanny had wanted to visit him, but she hadn't had the courage. She had always lacked courage, all her life. She had always been very sensitive to injustice, but she had never been able to do anything about it. It had made her cry, that was all. The people at Waldorf Pines who had been talking about Arthur Heydreich made her cry, too, but there were so many of them, and she wasn't sure what she was supposed to do about them anyway. People were just people. They did what they did, and nothing much ever changed them.

She saw the strange, ugly car come around the curve when she went out to check her mailbox. It was much too early to check her mailbox, but she was feeling restless and at loose ends. She was at loose ends most mornings, but it usually didn't bother her. Today, she was finding it hard to stand still.

She saw the ugly little car stop at Arthur Heydreich's house and then, a moment later, Arthur Heydreich getting out. He was wearing what Fanny thought of as his "always suit." She was sure he had more than one of them, but they all looked alike. She couldn't tell them apart.

Arthur walked up the driveway and to his front door. He leaned over and picked something up from the edge of the step that Fanny couldn't see. Then he opened the door and disappeared inside.

Fanny found herself suddenly, oddly breathless, as if something had sucked all the air out of her world. She went back into her own house and tried sitting down. She tried sitting down at the kitchen table. She tried sitting down on the love seat in the living room. She really could not sit still today, and she couldn't breathe.

She got up and went to the front door again. She went out to her driveway and looked up the road. The front of Arthur Heydreich's house looked blank, as if nobody had ever lived there, and nobody ever would.

If Charlie had known what she was going to do next, he would have had a fit and a half. This was not the kind of thing Charlie approved of people doing.

But then, Fanny thought, Charlie had no right to complain if he wasn't around for her to ask for his advice.

Fanny stepped out onto the road. It was impossible for anybody to go anywhere in Waldorf Pines without being watched by somebody, but Fanny found she really didn't care. What was it that these people were supposed to do to her if they didn't like the way she behaved? There were a lot of complicated things about the residential agreement, but she had never understood those.

She walked up Arthur Heydreich's driveway to his front door and stared for a moment at the button for the bell. She had not thought out what she was going to say, and she didn't know if she was going to say anything he wanted to hear, anyway. She looked around her at the leaves and the grass and the houses, everything just a little gray and dark, because it was autumn. She turned back to the door and pushed the button for the bell.

For a moment, there was no sound at all from inside the house, and Fanny felt stupid. Of course Arthur Heydreich wouldn't answer his door. He wouldn't want to see people. He probably felt persecuted. He had a right to.

Fanny considered going back home. She considered her shoes, which were canvas and looked drowned by the wet on the morning lawns. She looked up again and pressed the button again. This time, there were footsteps behind the door.

Fanny thought he'd call out from behind there and demand to know who it was. Instead, the door swung back and he was just there, his tie undone, his jacket off. If Fanny had expected to see prison pallor or the start of a nervous breakdown, she was disappointed. Arthur Heydreich looked the way Arthur Heydreich always looked. He looked sensible. He looked sane. He looked calm.

"Yes?" he said.

"Oh," Fanny said. She really did not know what she was doing here. She did not know what to say.

Arthur Heydreich was standing in the doorway. He was waiting. He was polite. He did not seem to be restless or in a hurry.

"Oh," Fanny said. "I'm sorry. I'm—I'm Fanny Bullman. I live up the street. I live, in the, well, they're all mock Tudors around here, aren't they? I live up the street. And I just wanted to say. I wanted to say—"

"Yes?" Arthur Heydreich said again.

Fanny looked away again. There really was no sensible way to do this. There was no sensible way to do anything at all.

"I just wanted to say," she said, "that I think it was horrible. I think it was horrible the way the police treated you, and the press, when they didn't really know what they were talking about and you hadn't done anything at all. They didn't even stop and think about what they were doing, about what kind of damage they could cause. They just jumped to conclusions and went ahead and did it. And I didn't want you to think that everybody felt the same way. That we all thought you were guilty without thinking about it. I didn't want you to think that everybody at Waldorf Pines—"

"You have the children," Arthur Heydreich said. "The small ones. You take them out the back gate to the bus stop every morning."

Fanny looked up. She felt more than a little flattered that he'd noticed. "That's right," she said. "A boy and a girl. They're both in elementary school."

"I see you walking them in the mornings," Arthur said. "That must be hard to do. I think it's why Martha and I never had any children. There are so many things you have to do for them. Maybe it wasn't that. I don't know. It's hard to remember things now."

"It would be hard for me to be in one of these big houses by myself," Fanny said. "I think that's why I came over. I didn't like the idea of you being in there all by yourself. These places are so big, they echo."

"They do echo," Arthur said.

Fanny felt exposed where she was. There was a slight breeze. It was making her feel cold. She shoved her hands in her pockets and said,

"Well. I'm sorry. I mean, I didn't mean to bother you. You must be busy. I just thought I'd say it was terrible the way you were treated."

"It was very nice of you to say."

"I think people should be more careful about the things they say and do," Fanny said. "Too many people just want a story because it's exciting. It doesn't have to be true. I don't understand people sometimes. But I did always think you were—"

"What?"

"Very nice," Fanny said firmly. Then she rushed. "I always thought you were a very nice person. I didn't see any reason to change my mind just because somebody had accused you of something. And it didn't make any sense to me that you would, you know, that you would kill—you were always so good to her, to Martha, I mean. I met her at meetings sometimes. I just didn't see how you could be like that with her, day after day, and then—well, you know. I'm sorry. I really am intruding. I didn't mean to do this. I just wanted you to know that, well, you know. Well—"

Fanny thought she ought to get out of there as quickly as she could. She ought to run all the way back to her own house.

She was just about to do it when Arthur Heydreich stepped back and pulled the door more widely open.

"Would you like to come in?" he said. "I'm trying to make some coffee."

"Trying?"

"It used to be the maid who did it. She came in and did it every morning. She's not here, now, of course. I don't know what's happened to her. I suppose she just disappeared when I went to jail."

"A lot of them disappear when the police come around," Fanny said. "That's because they're not, you know, legal."

Arthur stood all the way back. Fanny could see the entire foyer.

"Come in," he said again. "I really can make coffee if I think about it."

Fanny did not know why they were talking about coffee, but she did know that she wanted to go into Arthur Heydreich's house.

SIX

1

The mayor was a man named Kenneth Bairn, and Gregor knew from the moment he saw him that Ken would insist on being called "Ken," and glory in the idea that he was a "hands-on boss." Gregor had had a number of hands-on bosses in the course of his life. He'd even liked some of them. He'd found all of them irritating. From the look of him, Gregor thought he was going to find Ken both irritating and insufferable. It always surprised the hell out of him, the way so many insufferable people, women as well as men, managed to get elected to things. The basic requirements of democracy should have worked against it.

Ken's office was in the only other substantial building in the middle of town, and the only other one made of brick. Unlike the Pineville Station Police Department building, it was not in any way new. Gregor thought it had probably gone up just after the Civil War. It had that odd architectural confusion that was part of the second Greek Revival. The generation of the founders had known the Greeks and Romans the way they knew the small and struggling states from which they had come. Many of them were "learned" only to the extent that they'd been able to piece out such learning on their own. Most of the others had had the kind of old-fashioned formal education that ignored the practicalities of everyday life for drilling in Greek and Latin. The generation that came up out of the Civil War was different. They acquired their learning self-consciously, as the badge of a kind of person they wanted the world to think them to be. They were unsure of what it meant. They wore it like a suit of clothes that didn't fit. That was how you got buildings like this one, stolid red brick with immense three-story white marble columned façades that imitated the façade of the Parthenon but looked like . . . Gregor wasn't sure what.

The building with the mayor's office in it also held what few municipal offices there were—the local tax collector; the probate judge; the land records office. Gregor walked across the street to it with both Buck Monaghan and Larry Farmer in attendance. They went up the wide front steps—more white marble, faring badly in the Pennsylvania weather—and through the tall doors into a foyer that was actually cramped and small and that led to a corridor that was even more cramped and smaller. Gregor could see the tax collector's office, which was closest to him in the corridor. It had a window and a well where you could slide your payments through. The window had bulletproof glass.

"Interesting," Gregor said, looking at that.

Then he saw a young woman dragging some kind of equipment down toward them. It looked like a lectern taller than she was.

"That's for you," Buck Monaghan said. "We're going to hold a press conference after we meet with the mayor. It's set for ten thirty, I think. I hope you don't mind speaking at it."

"You're not opposed to press conferences," Larry Farmer asked. "Are you?"

Gregor promised that he was not opposed to press conferences, and left off any mention of just how much he disliked them. He understood their usefulness for the towns he worked for, even if he thought they were counterproductive to the investigations themselves. There was a small, narrow staircase to the side of the foyer. They went up that.

"Sorry about the lack of an elevator," Buck Monaghan said. "It's an old building."

"I don't mind the stairs," Gregor said. "I was just thinking, though, that Pineville Station is in reality what the town who called me in last only pretended to be."

"And that's what, exactly?" Buck Monaghan said.

"Small," Gregor said.

Larry Farmer was huffing and puffing and wheezing behind them. "I read all about that case," he said. "You've got to wonder at some people, don't you think? They think they can get away with anything."

Gregor didn't respond to that one, mostly because he had no idea how to do that. It seemed to be just one of those things Larry Farmer said without really intending it to mean anything. Or maybe he intended it to mean everything. It was hard to judge.

The corridor at the top of the stairs was filthy, as if nobody had bothered to wash down the floors in a decade and a half. The walls were painted two-toned yellow and green, but it was a dull mustard yellow and a washed-out olive green, so that the whole space looked as if somebody had poured a thin film of mud over it and then let the mud dry. It was an unpleasant space to walk through. Gregor couldn't imagine people working here.

They went to the end of that corridor to a tall wooden door, and then through that door into the outer office of the mayor. It wasn't much of an outer office, but at least it was clean, and very brightly lit. The middle-aged woman at the desk was clean and neat, too, and just plain enough to remind Gregor of the secretaries in Forties movies where the businessman was having his staff chosen by his wife.

The middle-aged woman had a little laminated nameplate on her desk. It said DELORES MARTIN. She looked up as the three of them walked in and then looked over her shoulder to a door at the back.

That door had a nameplate screwed into it that said OFFICE OF THE MAYOR.

"I'm sure there isn't going to be any problem with your going right in," Delores Martin said. "I'll buzz just to make sure. But it isn't as if he doesn't have anything on his mind this morning. Horace Wingard called."

"Did he," Buck Monaghan said.

"Oh, it was the usual kind of thing," Delores Martin said. "Yelling and screaming and threatening to sue everybody. Sue Connolly's right, you know. You do have to wonder just who these people think they are. And what's Ken worried about, really? That he'll lose votes if Waldorf Pines is unhappy? There aren't that many of them, and most of the residents of this town would be happy to see them unhappy. How's Sue, Buck? Is she holding up in the middle of all this?"

"She's fine," Buck said. "It's been a while, you know."

"I know it's been a while," Delores said, "but it can't be something you get over quick. Your own sister trying to commit suicide and you find her yourself, and it's all over what? Some party being given by a girl none of us would have wanted to be seen dead with in our day. It's terrible what's happening to the world. It really is. And it's only going to get worse."

Gregor had no idea how this woman knew that things were only going to get worse, but he had an odd feeling that she did. He watched as she stared down at the little intercom box on her desk and frowned. Then she got up and went to the wooden door at the back and knocked. A voice came from inside. Delores Martin poked her head in.

"They're here," she said. "Buck and Larry and somebody I presume to be Mr. Demarkian. Don't you think you'd better see them before your ulcer explodes?"

There was more from the voice behind the door. Delores turned to look at them.

"Go right in," she said, flinging the door wide. "I told you he wouldn't have anything more important on his plate. Forgive me if

I've been rude, Mr. Demarkian, I've had a lot on my mind this morning. And I can't say I've liked having it on my mind. I knew when they wanted to build that place that it was going to be a bad idea."

A tall, reedy man suddenly rushed through the wooden door and out into the anteroom where they were all standing. He was loud in every way. Even his tie was loud. He was trying hard to look younger than he was. Gregor was sure his hair was dyed, although he couldn't imagine anybody wanting hair that was that particular shade of jet black.

"Delores, for God's sake," he said. "You can't just keep going on and on about it. And we couldn't have done anything to stop them in the long run anyway. They'd have gone to court and gotten any ruling overturned. What was the planning and zoning commission supposed to say? It wasn't wetlands. It wasn't historic."

"All he could see was the tax revenue," Delores said, shaking her head. "Bunch of big houses, bunch of big real estate tax assessments, money, money, money. They don't understand what kind of damage those places cause. Jen Connolly trying to commit suicide. At seventeen, imagine that."

"Jen Connolly didn't try to commit suicide just because Waldorf Pines got built in Pineville Station," Ken said. "And it went up when she was something like two years old. You can't blame everything on Waldorf Pines just because you don't like them."

"Oh, for God's sake," Delores said. "Go have your meeting. Go do something. I'm tired of talking myself hoarse."

Ken held open his door and said, "Come right on in, Mr. Demarkian. I'm Ken Bairn."

2

Ken Bairn's office was, Gregor had to admit, not bad. It had high ceilings and a tall window that looked down on Main Street. Gregor could see the car he'd been driven up in sitting in the Pineville Station Police Department's parking lot. He could also see across the empty space that was most of the town to what looked like a small complex of school buildings. He thought that they would have to be new, too, or close to it. Even as late as his parents' generation, school buildings were built in the centers of small towns, where most of the students could walk to them.

Buck Monaghan noticed what he was looking at and nodded. "Those are the Pineville Station public schools," he said. "One elementary school, one middle school, and one high school. Except they didn't start out that way. They were built in the late Sixties, and nobody had ever heard of a middle school. Or at least, nobody around here had. We ended up having to do some renovations to make the new system work back around nineteen eighty."

"It's not that big a complex," Gregor said. "Or is that an illusion created by the distance?"

"It's no illusion," Buck Monaghan said. "Last year's high school graduating class was under a hundred and fifty. A lot of towns with schools that size go in on consolidated regionals. It makes sense, on a lot of levels. There's more money to go around. You can buy more equipment, not strain so much with teacher salaries no matter what the state unions come up with, participate in elaborate class trips and field programs—"

"Pineville Station has what every parent wants in an education for their child," Ken Bairn said. "It has a school system where every teacher knows every student. It has small classes where every student gets individual attention."

"Ken can talk such a good game, you'd even think we'd planned it all this way," Buck said. "But it was inertia, really. We'd always had public schools right in town. We went on having public schools right in town. Even when the town started shrinking. And we have been shrinking. There's not much to do here if you're ambitious."

"Pineville Station has the perfect mix of friendly small-town values and access to upscale shopping and entertainment," Ken said.

"He means it's not that far from here on the interstate to the King of Prussia Mall," Ken said. "It's also the reason why people like Delores and Sue Connolly are opposed to Waldorf Pines and all it stands for. If it can be said to stand for anything. Well, maybe I just mean all it brings with it. If your high school class numbers only a hundred and forty-five students, and one of them gives a party and invites everybody but maybe fifteen of you, then it's suddenly a big deal in a way it would not have been if your school was bigger."

"Crap," Ken Bairn said. "You are not going to get me to believe that little Jen Connolly tried to kill herself because she didn't get invited to a party. I've known that girl all her life. She's not that much of an idiot."

"It would have been different if what was coming into town was really rich people," Buck said. "Really rich people send their children to private schools. They live their lives as far out of the limelight as they can get them. They settle in. They keep to themselves. They try to avoid their taxes. They don't get in anybody's way as long as nobody gets in theirs. With these people, though—let's just say they make a point of getting in everybody's way as much as possible, and their children have absolutely taken over the school."

"Oh, for God's sake," Ken Bairn said.

Over in the back, Larry Farmer coughed. "Not to make too much of a big deal about it," he said, "but we do have a limited time frame here. We've called a press conference. We have to know what we're saying in the press conference."

"That's right," Ken Bairn said. "And this has nothing to do with that. That party was a year ago. It's already been on television."

"They had some wonderful shots of LizaAnne Marsh shopping for dresses in Philadelphia," Buck said. "She bought two, so that she could change halfway through the party. One of them cost three thousand dollars."

"It doesn't have anything to do with this," Ken Bairn said firmly. "Larry's right. We're going to have to concentrate. We're going to have to have something to say when we get to that press conference. And it's not going to be as easy as you think. How we could have made a mistake of this kind is beyond me."

"The body was burned to ashes," Larry Farmer said. "I saw it myself. There was nothing to use to identify it with. And as for dental records—well, forget it. We didn't find half the teeth. What were we supposed to do?"

"Not jumping the gun might have been a good thing," Ken said. "You could have said the body was unidentifiable."

"Wait," Gregor said.

They all turned to look at him.

"Are you saying you had nothing to identify the body with?" he asked. "Nothing at all? Nothing left over in the ashes?"

"No, of course we didn't," Larry Farmer said. "If we'd had something like that, we wouldn't have gone off and identified it as Martha Heydreich's."

"Yes," Gregor said, "I know. But you're actually talking about nothing at all here. Absolutely nothing."

"Yes," Larry Farmer said. "I mean, what can you possibly—"

"Jewelry," Gregor said. "Mrs. Heydreich was a married woman. Didn't she have a wedding ring that she wore regularly? Would she have taken that off when she was having sex with her lover?"

"Oh, wonderful," Larry Farmer said. "He gets here and the first thing he does is make us all look like idiots. Of course she had a wedding ring. And no, we didn't find it. Not that we were specifically looking for it, mind you, but we sifted through everything. If it was there, we would have found it."

"It's worse than you think," Buck Monaghan said. "We should have found a lot of jewelry, not just a wedding ring. From everything we've been told about Martha Heydreich, she was usually decked out like a Christmas tree. Necklaces. Bracelets. Rings. She wouldn't have taken them all off just to hop into bed with somebody."

"Was there any indication that she had hopped into bed?" Gregor asked. "Or, I should say, that the corpses had?"

"Well, one of them was charred beyond recognition," Larry said.

Buck Monaghan was shaking his head. "They did check—I have the case files back at my office, you can look at them sometime—

there wasn't anything on Michael Platte to say that he'd had sex that night with anybody. I think I can see where you're going with this. The misidentification of the body affects more than the misidentification of the body."

Gregor nodded. "You've got two bodies. I take it they weren't in the same room."

"They weren't even close," Buck Monaghan said. "Michael Platte's body was in the pool room, and in the pool. Directly in it. In the water. And he'd gone into the water alive, because he bled into that pool for hours. The water was full of blood. The other body was in the locker room—"

"The men's locker room or the women's locker room?" Gregor asked. "Or is there only one of them?"

"Oh, there are two," Larry Farmer said. "And now that you mention it, that's odd. The other body was in the women's locker room. But it was the body of a man. So what was it doing in the women's locker room?"

"Let's worry about that later," Gregor said. "What I want to know now is how close that locker room was to the pool."

"It was close enough," Buck Monaghan said. "It's across a big foyer with a trophy display case in it, but the display case didn't have much in the way of trophies. Or maybe any. I've got some pictures of it. It got partially destroyed in the fire. You had to cross that foyer to get from the pool to the locker rooms and back again. It wasn't too far but it wasn't right there, if you know what I mean. I remember thinking it was a silly way to design a pool facility."

"It sounds like it," Gregor said, "but what bothers me is this. What evidence do you have that these two people died at the same time?"

"What?" Ken Bairn said.

"Well, as far as I can see," Gregor said, "there's no reason to assume that these two people ever met each other, never mind that they were killed together for the same reason. It's different if you assume that what you've got is the wife and her lover, because then it makes sense that they'd be there together. And it makes sense that somebody, certainly the husband, might come along, find them engaged in sex, and have at them. After that, the circumstances are rather elaborate but they're not out of the question. The guy finds himself with two corpses and tries to cover his tracks. He hauls one body across the foyer, lets the other one drown where it is and then sets the fire. There would be a few problems, but you could solve practically all of them by assuming that the murder was planned."

"I thought you just said that the murder was not planned," Buck Monaghan said. "I thought you said he came in and found them in a tryst—"

"Yes," Gregor said, "but he wouldn't have had to go there and find them unexpectedly. He could have known the tryst was about to take place and gone there deliberately. With a plan, as I said. That way, he would have brought an accelerant with him. I'm making a sloppy job of this, but you must see what I mean. If you assume that what you've got are the bodies of Michael Platte and Martha Heydreich, then you can make everything else fit. But once you assume that the bodies you've got are not Michael Platte and Martha Heydreich everything starts to come apart, and not just the case against Arthur Heydreich."

"We had noticed that," Ken Bairn said sardonically. "That's why you're here."

"I know," Gregor said. "It's just begun to occur to me, however, just how much of a tangle this all is. You have two bodies, one of which you can't identify. They're not in the same room, and you have no way to tell if they've both been killed in the same way. Or have you?"

"No," Larry Farmer said.

"Which means you also have no way to tell if they were both killed at the same time," Gregor said. "One of them was left perfectly recognizable and, at the time, not even dead in a swimming pool, which sounds like the work of panic. The other was found so completely disfigured and so completely stripped of identifying articles that there was no clue as to identity, which sounds like the work of not only careful planning, but emotionless planning. You've got a possible motive for the murder of one of them, but no idea what the motive might be for the murder of the other. You have, in fact, no evidence at all that these two murders are in any way connected to each other."

"Oh, my God," Ken Bairn said.

Larry Farmer looked a little wild. "But that doesn't happen, does it?" he demanded. "You don't get two completely unrelated murders like that in practically the same place at practically the same time. Maybe you get them in Philadelphia, where there's crime all over the place, but there's practically no crime at all in Pineville Station. And there really isn't any murder."

"You know that isn't true," Buck Monaghan said patiently.

"We're not talking about domestic violence cases," Ken Bairn said. "We're not talking about some idiot getting liquored up or those fools in the trailer park trying to make crystal meth. We're talking about two completely separate people committing murder on the same day, or at least in the same twenty-four hours, and in Waldorf Pines of all places. Why Waldorf Pines?"

"Sue Connolly would say those are just the people who'd commit them," Buck Monaghan said. "Ask Delores out there. She'd say the same thing."

"Don't be a complete idiot," Ken Bairn said.

"There's one more thing," Gregor said. He hated to interrupt them. As it was, they all turned in his direction at once, and stared. He cleared his throat. "Are you sure the murders were committed by somebody or more than one somebody from Waldorf Pines?"

"What do you mean?" Buck asked.

"Well," Gregor said. "You keep telling me this Waldorf Pines is a gated community. Gated communities are gated. They have guards. They have fences. They almost always have video surveillance cameras. In fact, I'm pretty sure one of you mentioned those. Lots of video surveillance cameras in lots of places. I've got to assume somebody on the police force looked at the footage from those cameras for the times in question. And yet none of you has mentioned a single thing about those cameras, or a single thing about the video footage. So—"

"Oh, God," Larry Farmer said.

"We did look at the footage from the morning the bodies were found," Buck Monaghan said. "There was nothing on it that we didn't already know. There was Arthur Heydreich driving around and entering the pool house. There was Arthur Heydreich in the foyer."

"Was there footage of Michael Platte's body in the pool?" Gregor asked.

"There are no direct video surveillance cameras in the pool room itself," Buck Monaghan said. "You should ask Horace Wingard to make sure I'm remembering this right, but I think the deal was that there had been cameras in there, but the wet kept ruining them. Cheap equipment, I suppose."

"What about the women's locker room?" Gregor asked.

"No, there isn't one in there, either," Buck Monaghan said. "There are cameras in the men's locker room, but the women complained, and Wingard apparently thought they had a point."

"But there are cameras in the foyer," Gregor said. "So there should be footage of Arthur Heydreich going into the locker rooms if he went."

"Well, there's footage of him stumbling around in that direction in the foyer," Larry Farmer said. "But there weren't any lights on in that building anywhere. So—"

"This is awful," Ken Bairn said. "They're going to crucify us. Didn't we do any of the investigating we should have been doing? Didn't we use any common sense at all?"

"Don't talk to me about using common sense," Larry Farmer said, suddenly incensed. "You're the one who wanted the case closed in fifteen minutes so that Waldorf Pines would see we were doing our jobs. I wasn't the one who was in that kind of hurry. I'd have—"

"You'd have dithered around for a week and gotten nowhere,"

Ken Bairn said. "You wouldn't even have thought of getting Gregor Demarkian here if I hadn't suggested it. What you think you're doing in that job is beyond me. Hell, you don't even want a job. You want—"

"Excuse me," Gregor said. "There is one more thing."

"Thank God," Buck Monaghan said.

"The rest of the security tape," Gregor said. "You looked at the rest of that? Was there anything on it? Anything at all."

"You mean aside from the time between ten forty-five and twelve thirty the night before when the system went on the fritz?" Buck said. "Nope. Not a thing."

"The system went on the fritz?" Gregor asked.

"It was shut off," Buck Monaghan said. "Or somebody shut it off. Just turned it off. Then turned it back on again. We think. From ten forty-five to twelve thirty on the night the murders were committed."

"Interesting," Gregor Demarkian said.

Ken Bairn looked like he was going to lunge for Buck Monaghan's neck. He was stopped by the sudden, flustered entrance of Delores Martin.

"Will the lot of you get out there and hold a press conference?" she demanded. "They've been there for ten minutes and they're out for blood."

PART II

ONE

1

It was the doorbell that got Gregor Demarkian out of bed the next morning, and he had to admit that the doorbell was not his favorite thing to hear even when he was fully awake and dressed. He got up to answer it because he couldn't be sure it didn't represent an emergency. There were cell phones these days, of course, and there was the land line, with the phone on the night table right next to his head, but he couldn't trust the people of Cavanaugh Street to think like that. He couldn't even trust them to call 911. There was something visceral about responding to an emergency by rushing across a cold night street in your pajamas and your robe.

He looked across the bed, at Bennis sleeping as if she'd never had anything to worry about in her life. He'd never understood how Bennis could sleep like that, considering all that she *had* had to worry about, but then, he'd never understood Bennis. She was, in her way, the anti-Elizabeth. She came from a world so remote from any he had ever known that she might as well have been a Martian.

He gave a little thought to Bennis as a Martian, and then sat up. He grabbed his robe from the chair. He stood up and put it on.

Whoever was ringing the bell certainly acted as if it was an emergency. The bell rang and rang and rang in a staccato of small bursts. Then it went silent for a second. Then the ringing started again.

Gregor went out into the hall and down the hall to the foyer. He was surprised Grace from upstairs hadn't come out to find out what was going on. He'd have come out to find out what was going on, even if only to have the chance of killing whoever was causing it.

He got to his front door and tried looking through the peephole. Peepholes were never of any use. All you saw was distortions. He pulled the door open and looked at Lida Arkmanian, fully dressed in three-inch heels and that chinchilla coat, holding a stack of three large baking pans. The three large baking pans were each covered with aluminum foil, and they each had something in them.

"You brought food," Gregor said. "It's, what—before five o'clock in the morning?"

"It's four thirty," Lida said, brushing past him with her baking pans. "I've been up all night. We're all worried about you, Gregor."

"I wish you'd worry about me dying of lack of sleep," Gregor said.

He closed the door behind her and didn't bother to lock up. It was too early in the morning and it wouldn't serve much of a purpose anyway. Lida was already marching through the living room on the way to the kitchen. Gregor followed her.

In the kitchen, Lida had put the baking pans down on the kitchen table next to Gregor's stacks of folders about the Waldorf Pines case. She opened the refrigerator and looked inside. Then she shook her head.

"It's impossible," she said, shaking her head. "I love Bennis very much, Gregor, you know that, and we were all very happy when you two found each other and very relieved when you actually got married, but how is it possible that a woman of her age doesn't know how to cook? Anything? What is this supposed to be?"

Gregor peered at it. "It's yogurt," he said. "It's Dannon fruit-on-the-bottom cherry yogurt. It's her favorite kind. She eats those for lunch."

"These and what else?"

"I don't think there's an anything else. I think she just eats one of those. I don't keep track, Lida. I'm not walking around writing down everything Bennis eats every day."

"Maybe she is? Maybe she has one of those eating disorders? I've read about those, Gregor. These people, they have little notebooks, and every time they eat anything they write it down in the notebook with the calories, and then they make themselves throw it up."

"If Bennis had bulimia, I think I'd notice," Gregor said. "She doesn't throw anything up. What are we doing here at four thirty in the morning talking about Bennis's eating habits? You know she doesn't have an eating disorder. You see her eat at the Ararat all the time."

Lida put the yogurt back in the refrigerator. Yogurt was practically all there was in the refrigerator. There was also a small carton of cream, which Gregor liked in his coffee, and the leftover takeout from some Indian restaurant they'd gone to in Wayne.

Lida started putting baking pans in among the yogurt.

"I couldn't sleep," she said. "I kept worrying about your refrigerator. I knew it would look like this. It always looked like this. But before you weren't married. Now we all think you have a wife to make sure you eat, and she doesn't even eat herself. I've got some manti in here. I made a hundred and six of them. More of them wouldn't fit in the pan. Oh." Lida got her shoulder bag and looked into it. A second later, she brought out a big plastic tub. "I've got some yaprak sarma, too. It's not as much as I'd wanted to bring, but this was the biggest container I could find."

"You got up in the middle of the night and cooked manti and yaprak sarma because you thought I wasn't getting enough to eat?"

"There's also imam biyaldi. I'm never happy with that. It doesn't do as well in the microwave as some of the other things. But you need real food, Gregor. You can't go running around on nothing but yogurt and green beans and expect to stay healthy."

"This is insane," Gregor said.

Lida looked at the things she had put in the refrigerator and checked that they wouldn't fall out as soon as somebody opened the door. Then she closed up and sat down at the kitchen table.

"We've been worried about you," she said. "I've been worried about you. Ever since old George died, you haven't been yourself."

Gregor sat down at the table, too. He pushed away some of the folders. "I've been entirely myself," he said. "If you mean I haven't been in a very good mood, that I could see."

"Even Tibor is worried, Gregor. And I'm—well, we've known each other all our lives. I know what I'm talking about when I say you're not yourself."

"I've maybe been a little depressed."

"No, Gregor. After Elizabeth died, you were depressed. You didn't sleep. You didn't eat. You didn't respond to people when they talked to you. I was like that after Frank died. I know what that is. And that sort of thing is inevitable, I think. It is to be expected. But this is not that. It's nothing like that."

"No, it's not the way I was feeling after Elizabeth died," Gregor said.

"It makes no sense for you to be arguing with Tibor about God," Lida said. "We know you're not a believer. And those of us who didn't know have guessed, I'm sure. But you seem to be arguing about—about the possibility—"

"About the logic of it," Gregor said. "That's all. I don't see the logic of it. But I wasn't trying to get Tibor to stop believing, or anything like that."

"You couldn't get Tibor to stop believing, or any of the rest of us. What you're saying is entirely senseless to anybody who does believe. But I do not think it is a good sign for you."

"I'm fine," Gregor said. "I really am. And I can't believe you stayed up all night to do this. Which doesn't mean I don't appreciate it."

"That is all right, Gregor. And part of me understands it, too. It's all going now. The old neighborhood. It's disappearing into dust."

"You might say the old neighborhood went a long time ago,"

Gregor said. "You remember what this street was like when we were growing up. There weren't any town houses. There weren't any floor-through apartments. The buildings were here, but they were run down, there wasn't much heat, the apartments were small and everybody was crowded. And nobody had a three-quarter-length chinchilla coat."

"The people were here," Lida said. "Now the people are going. And I'm not saying that they're going because they're dying, like old George. None of us has children living on Cavanaugh Street except the Ohanians, and they won't stay after they've finished college. Donna and Russ are thinking of moving out, did you hear that?"

"Bennis said something about it to me," Gregor said. "But it's not like they're going next week. They're mostly worried about what happens when Tommy gets ready for junior high school."

"And they have to worry," Lida said. "The schools are bad here, and the private schools are expensive. Were the schools as bad when we were in school, Gregor?"

"They were bad relative to the better neighborhoods of Philadelphia, yes," Gregor said. "But it was a different era, with different priorities."

"I don't think it's about death and dying, the things that are wrong. Going wrong. I don't know what I'm saying. But I'm not like you. I grew up here, and I never wanted to leave here. I still don't want to leave here. I suppose I'm being ridiculous."

"No," Gregor said. "I'll admit I did want to leave here. I got out as soon as I could. But I understand why you wouldn't."

"Are you and Bennis going to leave, Gregor? I was thinking maybe not, since it's unlikely that you'd be having children. Not that I'm saying anything about Bennis's age, of course, but—"

"Bennis and I are not going to leave here," Gregor said. "It's going to take at least another decade to get that house we bought into livable shape. And that's right down a couple of blocks and squarely on Cavanaugh Street."

"It's not going to take a decade to get the house finished," Bennis said, showing up suddenly in the kitchen doorway. "It may take till next Valentine's Day."

"She said Thanksgiving at first," Gregor said. "Then it was Christmas. Now it's Valentine's Day."

"Societies die if they don't have children," Lida said.

Bennis came in and sat down at the kitchen table. "What are the two of you doing here at this time of the morning?"

2

Three hours later, Bennis was helping Gregor pack the folders into the sleek Coach briefcase she had bought him a thousand Christmases ago, and Gregor was thinking yet again that the thing didn't look big enough to hold even a few sheets of paper.

"Briefcases used to be substantial," Gregor said. "They looked like pieces of furniture. You could carry an entire federal budget bill in them."

"Nobody should carry an entire federal budget bill in anything," Bennis said, "and this will hold these folders without a problem. Although I don't understand why you use these. You've got a perfectly good computer."

Gregor knew he had a perfectly good computer. It was packed into the briefcase with everything else.

"I like to move things around," he said. "It helps me think. I make little stacks of things here and little stacks of things there and it works better than just staring at a screen. There's something hypnotic about staring at a screen. I start to go to sleep."

"So did it help, spending last night moving around little stacks of paper?"

Gregor looked at the folders going into the briefcase. "It did," he said, "at least a little. The problem is that they didn't really start thinking about this case objectively until they came and got me, and even then they weren't doing it. They had their preconceived little scenario, they gathered the information they needed to confirm their preconceived little scenario, and then when the monkey wrench landed in the works, they had nowhere to go and nothing to go there with. There are a million things I need that aren't here because nobody thought to ask about them."

"Like what?"

"Well," Gregor said, "let's start with the murder victim whose identity we know, Michael Platte. Everything they have seems to say that Michael Platte was having an affair with Martha Heydreich. But I looked through there evidence on this, and all they've really got is local gossip. Somebody saw them together. Somebody else says they were spending too much time together. It's all that sort of thing. There's no indication that anybody ever caught them in an actually compromising position, no proof of their having rented a hotel room somewhere, nothing. When you actually look at what they've got here, it could mean anything at all. It could mean nothing. Martha Heydreich wasn't a very well liked woman. It could be spite. Michael Platte himself was something of a problem child. There's nothing substantial here. Do you see what I mean?"

"I think so," Bennis said.

"Then," Gregor said, "there's information that definitely should be here that isn't. For instance, we know that Michael Platte was murdered. Somebody should have checked up on his life. There's a note in the files about the incident that got him kicked out of college. He got caught selling cocaine in the dorms, apparently not for the first time. The parents were steady donors. The college didn't go to the police about it. All right, but then what? Was he still selling drugs? Was he selling them at Waldorf Pines? Was he selling it in town, or farther afield? What kind of money did he have on him? Where did it come from?"

"You mean you think this could be some kind of drug deal murder?" Bennis said.

"For what it's worth, I don't think this has to do with drugs," Gregor said. "Or at least not with your regular run of drug dealer and drug buyer. It's the wrong kind of murder. They both are. Your friendly neighborhood drug lord doesn't usually respond to problems by hitting somebody over the head and drowning him in a pool. A fire to make it impossible to identify a body is more like it, but in that case there should have been a bullet or a casing somewhere in the stuff they picked up at the scene, and there doesn't seem to have been either. Somebody went through a lot of trouble to erase not just all possible signs of identification of that body, but all signs of how it might have ended up dead. To pull the same thing on you that I did on them yesterday, mostly out of frustration—we couldn't actually prove it as a matter of fact that the unidentified body was the result of a murder at all. There's more than one reason why you might want to get rid of a body and erase all possible means of identification."

"I can't even think of one," Bennis said.

Gregor watched her as she closed up the briefcase. "I've got a list in there of things that have to be done before we can even think of solving this case," he said. "It's the longest list I can ever remember having. It's one thing to come in at the beginning of a case, before anything has been done. It's something else to come in in the middle of a case that's been horribly bungled. I find myself looking at this stuff and doing just what they were doing, because all the information I have has been skewed to make me think in that direction. I don't mean me personally, and I don't mean deliberately, but—"

"I know what you mean," Bennis said.

"So I made a list," Gregor said. "I didn't do any of the things Marty told me to do. I know I should. I know I should be more businesslike about all these things. I don't even have an agreed fee with Pineville Station, and you know what it's like when I don't get that settled up front. But, try as hard as I can, I just can't find the financial side of things anything but boring."

"Didn't you train as an accountant?"

"Absolutely," Gregor said, "but to tell you the truth, I found accounting boring, too. That's why I joined the FBI. It was a sheer fluke they didn't put me on tax cases with the rest of the accountants. I'd better get dressed. I ordered the driver for seven twenty."

"You ought to learn to drive so that you don't continually get into these situations where you need a driver," Bennis said. "Is Lida all right? Is there something going on that I should know about?"

"Lida's fine," Gregor said. "Or, at least, she's as fine as she's ever been. She's getting old. I'm getting old. Even Cavanaugh Street is getting old. But I do know how to drive. I've even got a driver's license. I just don't like to do it."

"You're changing the subject. If you don't want to tell me, don't tell me."

"No," Gregor said. "It's the absolute truth. Lida and I are having the kind of crisis people have when they realize they've gotten old without noticing it. Not old in the sense old George was, you understand. Just sort of out of time."

"Does this mean you're going to buy a private jet and start dating blondes who don't know when Pearl Harbor was?"

"No," Gregor said. "It means I've spent a lot of my life in recent years assuming that things will always stay the same even though I know that nothing ever does. Do I have something besides that awful tie with the red and green starbursts on it? I swear Howard gave me that because he knew it would make me look ridiculous."

"I've got your *Looney Tunes* tie," Bennis said, heading out of the kitchen.

Gregor was going to call out that that one would make him look even more ridiculous, but he felt a little guilty about it. It was Tommy Donahue who had given him the *Looney Tunes* tie, and Tommy Donahue had been seven years old at the time. Tommy had not thought the tie would make Gregor look ridiculous. He had thought it would make Gregor look cool.

Gregor got up and headed out of the kitchen himself.

3

Gregor was sitting in the car taking him to Pineville Station when he found the thing he'd missed all four of the times he'd gone through the paperwork. It was not the kind of thing he would usually miss, but it had been noted in the oddest and least helpful way imaginable. And it had only been noted once. He had only pulled the folder halfway out of the briefcase. He'd been half pulling out folders and checking through them for most of the ride. Now he pulled this one all the way out and laid it down on the seat beside him.

It was a beautiful day out, bright and crisp. He had hoped to miss the rush hour traffic by leaving early, but seemed to only have half made it. There were a lot of cars on the road, and long stretches when they barely seemed to be moving. That actually worked to his advantage. The papers didn't slosh around too much. He was able to keep track of what he was looking at. He did worry, just a little, that he would look from the outside like somebody who was "being driven."

He got the paper he needed from the folder next to him and held it up to the light. He reread it twice, just to make sure he wasn't imagining it. Then he got out his cell phone and accessed the address book.

One of the things Gregor insisted on when he agreed to take a case was that he have contact numbers for all the people responsible for it. And the contact numbers could not be limited. He had to have a way to call anybody anytime, twenty-four/seven, for any reason. Twenty years ago, he would have found that kind of thing excessive. Now he knew better.

He found the entry that said "Farmer, cell," and punched it. He listened to the ring and wondered what Larry Farmer was doing at this hour of the morning. It wasn't even eight o'clock. Larry Farmer could be in the shower. He could still be asleep. Gregor didn't care.

The phone rang long enough so that Gregor began to get worried that it would go to voice mail. If it did, he would simply call it again, and not worry for a moment that he was disturbing someone. Still, voice mail was a nuisance, and calling again was a pain.

The phone was finally picked up, and Larry Farmer sounded as bouncy and perky as he ever did. Gregor gave a brief thought to the idea that Larry Farmer was bouncy and perky when he slept.

"Mr. Demarkian!" Larry Farmer said. "Good to hear from you! Are you here already? I can get right out to the station—"

"I'm in a car on the way," Gregor said. "I just found something. It's in the scene of crime notes from the morning when the bodies were discovered, but it's not in the Buck Monaghan notes for the prep for the prosecution. I have no way of knowing if Buck Monaghan even has this information at all. And that makes me nervous."

"Really, Mr. Demarkian, we're very careful to give Buck all the information we have. And he insists on it. He says that if we don't give him all the information, we're just asking for the defense to be able to pull something on us at trial. And he's right, you know, he's really right. I don't know what defense lawyers do these days, but they think of everything. Even the public defenders do that. And the kind of lawyer that would be hired by somebody at Waldorf Pines, well—"

"Didn't Arthur Heydreich have a public defender?" Gregor asked.

"Well, yes, he did, but that was only temporary," Larry Farmer said. "He'd have gotten a better one eventually. We all knew it."

"Okay," Gregor said. "Listen very carefully. I have here a piece of paper with the notes from the scene of the crime on it. It includes a list of things found in Michael Platte's pocket when he was fished out of the water. You got that?"

"Yes, of course. I remember that. I was there when it was done."

"Fine," Gregor said. "The list includes keys, a wallet with fifty-two dollars in it, some loose change amounting to ninety-three cents, a condom still in its wrapper—"

"They all have condoms these days, did you ever notice that, Mr. Demarkian? We never had condoms, not even in college, nobody would give us any. Now they have condom dispensers in the men's rooms at these places. Anything for safe sex."

"Back to the list," Gregor said. "He had a pack of cigarettes and a lighter. The lighter was a standard Bic. Got all that? Okay. Now go back a little, to the keys. The officer very carefully described each of the keys. He's got two house keys, both identified later and noted as being to his parents' house at Waldorf Pines. He's got a trunk key and an ignition key to his own pickup truck, also identified later. Then there are a little collection of keys that are described and not identified. Most of them are irrelevant to anything. One of them sounds like the key to his dorm room at college. He was almost certainly supposed to return it before he left, but he wasn't the world's most responsible person, so we won't worry about it. It's got the college's name on it. There's another one labeled U.S. Post Office. That will be to a post office box. I don't suppose anybody has checked that out, what post office he had the box in, here or at college, what he used it for, anything like that?"

"Oh," Larry Farmer said. "No, no we didn't. We could, of course, I can see how it might seem significant now—"

"Yes, it's definitely significant now," Gregor said, "and it definitely ought to be checked out. But the one I can't believe is this one. 'Silver, two inches, bulbed hold, four prongs.'"

There was silence on the other end of the line. "I remember that," Larry Farmer said. "But there was nothing on it to say where it was from. And it didn't look very used. I remember that, too. What could that possibly have to do with anything?"

"Did you keep the keys?" Gregor asked.

"Oh, of course we did. We kept everything. We explained to Mrs. Platte that she couldn't have them until the case was finished because we might need them for evidence, although I do have to admit that I don't see how any of that could be important."

"Did anybody show that key to Buck Monaghan?"

"I don't know if we showed any of those keys to Buck," Larry said. "We gave him the lists, of course, but I'm not sure—"

"Did you give him this particular list with these particular descriptions on it?"

"I don't know," Larry Farmer said. "I suppose you could ask the officers who responded to the scene, or the evidence clerk, or whoever it was, but I still don't see why this is so important. Do you know where the key is from? Is it something to do with Waldorf Pines security or that kind of thing? I'd really like to know how all those security cameras were made to malfunction at once for two hours. I'd really like to know that."

"I'd like to know that, too," Gregor said, "but right now, I've got this key. Get it ready for me when I come in. Because from this description, I'd be willing to bet just about anything that what you've got there is the key to a safe-deposit box."

"What?" Larry Farmer said.

Gregor closed his eyes and wished that Larry wouldn't say "what" so much.

TWO

1

For most of her growing up, Eileen Platte had envied her older sister. Eileen Platte had been Eileen O'Brien then, and her older sister had been named Margaret Mary. Margaret Mary was a special name. It was the name of the nun who had seen the Virgin Mary on an altar in her convent and been given the design of the Miraculous Medal to reveal to the world. All the girls at St. Rose of Lima School loved the Miraculous Medal best, because it was the most beautiful of all the medals. There was a picture of the Blessed Virgin on the front of it with her arms outstretched. Rays of light come from her fingertips, and words came from the rays of light: O MARY, CONCEIVED WITHOUT SIN, PRAY FOR US WHO HAVE RECOURSE TO THEE. Neither Eileen nor her sister nor anybody else they knew understood what "recourse" meant, but it didn't really matter.

Now Eileen stood in the middle of her kitchen, looking down at the long granite counter, and wondering what she had been thinking. She knew what "recourse" meant now, but it seemed to her that it was a trick, and always had been. The Virgin Mother would pray for those of the human family who had a right to ask her to pray for them. If you didn't have a right to ask—well. You could ask away forever, and none of your prayers would be answered.

It was odd the way things had been, all these weeks since Michael had died. At first, Eileen had barely felt it. There was no body she could look at. There was no funeral. There wasn't even a death notice in the papers. The whole thing was drifting and unreal, as if she'd dreamed it. Dream was the wrong word, but she didn't know what else to call it. Sometimes she had nightmares that woke her up screaming. Sometimes she had the same nightmares, but all the emotion was gone. Michael was gone. A policewoman had come to the door and told her that. They had both sat down at the kitchen table. The policewoman had touched her hand, and Eileen had had to force herself not to recoil at the touch. There was something wrong with that policewoman's hand, she was sure of it. There was flecks of black and green across the knuckles, that looked like they'd been poisoned.

After about a week, Eileen had found herself thinking of it as actual. That wasn't quite the same thing as real, but it was close. The house was big and silent and empty. Michael was not in his bedroom snoring off a night doing God only knew what. Stephen was not storming around the house, delivering lectures about Michael's faults and all the awful things that would happen to him if he didn't straighten up. Stephen was not saying anything, really, and that was the strangest thing of all the things that had happened so far.

Actually, there was one thing Stephen did say, and it mattered. Eileen couldn't make herself forget it.

"You shouldn't be helping the police," he said. "They're professionals. They've got a job to do. You should let them do it."

"But what if I have information," Eileen had said. "Don't the police always want information? Don't you want to see the person who did this go to prison?"

"They got the person who did this," Stephen said. "They don't need any more help from us."

That conversation had happened at the kitchen table, too. It seemed to Eileen that all conversations happened at the kitchen table now.

Except that they weren't really conversations, because she didn't really take part in them. She said things. Other people said things. There was no connection. She knew what Stephen was thinking of when he gave her his orders. She'd been thinking about it herself ever since the policewoman had come to the door. She had no idea why she hadn't told the policewoman about it then and there. Maybe it was instinct. Maybe she had just known, without having to ask, that Stephen would hate the entire idea of her telling the policewoman about what she had found in Michael's bedroom.

For a while after that, Eileen had relied on the news. There were news reports every day about the "progress of the investigation," and lots of speculation about what Arthur Heydreich had done and why. There was one terrible picture of Martha, made-up like a circus clown, that they played over and over again. Eileen wondered if they used that one because it was so extremely bizarre, or just because it was the only one they could find. The few other shots that appeared anywhere had been taken in groups at club events, with Martha as usual in the background, tall and thin, but the wrong kind of thin. Eileen had stared at all the pictures and wondered what Michael had found so fascinating in the woman. It didn't matter if he was sleeping with her or not. It didn't matter if he was gay. There must have been something that had drawn him there.

Eileen thought she might have gone on feeling like that forever, if it hadn't been for yesterday. Yesterday there were other stories in the news, and suddenly nothing seemed to be settled at all. Arthur Heydreich was out of jail and not even charged with one of the murders anymore. The television stations said he would soon have the charges dropped on Michael's murder. Now it was Martha herself everybody was asking about. There was a poster showed on television, and a "nationwide campaign" to discover her "whereabouts." It sounded even less real than the rest of it had. It sounded like a movie.

When Stephen came home last night, Eileen had tried to put it to him again. There was something about this new circumstance, about Arthur Heydreich getting out of jail, that made it through the thick fog of defense around her and let her know that this was final. Michael would never be coming home. She could stay up night after night. She could get in the car and drive into Philadelphia and look through all his old neighborhoods until she was sure somebody was going to murder her for whatever she had in her purse. She could do all the things she had always done, but this time, at the end of them, there would be no Michael needing to be rushed to the emergency room and no Michael needing to be left to sleep it off and no Michael angry and mocking because she'd appeared out of nowhere to spoil his fun.

Eileen had sat down at the kitchen table one more time and tried to talk sense. She was aware that talking sense was not something Stephen thought her capable of doing. It was important, though. It was important to make things work out right.

"It will be different now," she'd said, rubbing her palms together over and over and over again. This was not something she was doing just because this was the subject she was trying to talk about. This was the way she always was when she talked to Stephen. "It will be different now," she said again. "There are going to be more questions. And they've hired this man, this Gregor Demarkian. I don't think they hire somebody like Gregor Demarkian unless they mean to do a serious investigation."

"I don't care about Gregor Demarkian," Stephen had said.

Eileen had tried again. It was, really, very difficult. The house felt like a huge prison rising up around her head. It was endless. It had too many rooms. All the rooms were full of people whispering.

"Don't you see," she said. "It might be important. It might be a clue. Or—or evidence. It might be something they need to convict whoever killed him. You have to know somebody killed him. It couldn't have been drugs that bashed his head in."

"She was a cunt, that woman," Stephen said. "I don't care what happens to her."

"You don't care if she goes free and is never punished for Michael's murder?"

"What difference does it make if anybody is punished for Michael's murder? For God's sake, Eileen. The kid was a wreck. He'd have died sooner rather than later anyway. What's a month or two ahead of time?"

"But it matters if it was a month or two ahead of time," Eileen said. "Something might have happened. He might have turned himself around. He might have gone to rehab again and had it stick—"

"Rehab doesn't stick," Stephen had said. He'd used that voice she'd come to think of as "patience in the face of wanting to kill somebody." "Rehab is a fraud. You know how many people get off drugs and stay off drugs when they go to rehab? Five percent of all the people who start. Five percent. You know how many people get off drugs and stay off drugs without rehab, just because they want to do it and do it on their own? Five percent. If Michael had ever wanted to get off drugs and to be off drugs, he'd have done it, with rehab or without. You just can't accept the fact that he never wanted to get off drugs."

"I don't think what's upstairs had to do with drugs," Eileen said. "I think it had to do with her. I think she gave it to him."

"Gave it to him," Stephen said. "And why would she do that?"

"I don't know," Eileen said.

Actually, she did know. At least, she had a suspicion. She had been working it out in her head ever since she heard that the other body in the pool house didn't belong to Martha Heydreich. It was very hard to make it come clear in her head. There were so many turns and wrinkles in it. Still, she had an idea.

"I think," she said.

Stephen got up from the table. "I think you just don't get it," he said. "You can't tell the police about something like this. You can't go off and get us into the papers this way. They can throw us out of Waldorf Pines for something like this. Did you know that?"

"They didn't throw out Arthur Heydreich," Eileen said.

"They were afraid they'd get sued," Stephen said. "Innocent until proven guilty and all that kind of thing. But they won't have any trouble sticking it to us. They've been wanting to get us out of here for a year. That Horace Wingard. He's been ready to give us the shove at the first excuse."

"Horace Wingard was always very good about Michael," Eileen said. "He gave him that job. And he kept him on that job, you know, even though Michael—"

"Even though Michael didn't show up half the time?"

"It was just a phase," Eileen said. "He was young, that was all. He thought he knew everything. He'd have grown up eventually . . ."

Her voice had trailed off. She couldn't remember the last time she'd believed that.

"The trouble with you," Stephen had said, "is that you just can't face reality."

Then he had gotten up from the table and walked away, out the swinging doors to the dining room. Across the foyer. Eileen had heard his feet on the stairs. Everything in this house echoed. There was a television in nearly every room, but she never put them on.

She heard a door open upstairs. That would be the door to Michael's room. It was a very clean room. She kept it clean. When Michael came home, he threw things on the floor and messed it up.

The footsteps were in the hall again. Then they were on the stairs. Eileen looked down at her hands and waited.

Stephen came back across the dining room and into the kitchen. He had a Bass Weejun shoe box in his right hand. It flopped and shuddered as he moved. Eileen thought that it was going to fall, and then everything would be all over the place, right there in the kitchen.

Stephen put the shoe box down in the middle of the table.

"I'm going to take this out of here," he said. "I'm going to move this somewhere, and you won't find it. And if you ever tell the police, or anybody else, that it was in Michael's room, or that I've got it, I'll say you're lying. And make no mistake about it, Eileen. They won't believe you. They'll believe me."

Eileen did not see how there was any way to deny this. This is what had always been true.

2

Caroline Stanford-Pyrie was not the kind of person who panicked, ever. If she had been, she would not have landed safely at Waldorf Pines, and she would not have been able to bring Susan Carstairs with her. She had long been of the opinion that any catastrophe could be survived if it was handled properly. The difficulty lay in knowing what "properly" was meant to be. There was also the rule that you had to be most careful when the police were involved. The police were always the enemy.

Of course, at the moment, her problem was not the police, who had no reason to be thinking about her. Her problem was Susan, who was doing her usual fluttery, addled thing when danger approached. It had started with the news, yesterday, that the charred body in the pool house was no longer thought to be Martha Heydreich, and that the charges against Arthur Heydreich for the murder of his wife had been dropped. Then Arthur Heydreich had been released, and Susan had had something like a nervous breakdown.

"You can't say it doesn't matter," Susan had wailed. "How can it not matter? It was different when he was dead and she was dead and everybody knew who did it. They don't ask questions when they know who did it. But now what, Alison? Now what?"

"Caroline," Caroline had said automatically.

Susan had blushed.

"I'm not worried about the police asking questions," Caroline said. "I'm worried about that. I'm worried about you—"

"I won't do it again," Susan said. "I'm sorry. I just get upset. I can't understand how you can blame me for being upset. After everything that's happened—"

"After everything that's happened, I should think you'd know better than to get upset at every little thing," Caroline said. "And it is a little thing, Susan. The situation hasn't really changed. There are still two dead bodies, and the police still think they know who the murderer is. It's just a different murderer."

"I don't know what you're talking about," Susan said. "How can they know who the murderer is? They let Arthur Heydreich go."

"Yes, they did," Caroline said. "They let him go, because now they're looking for Martha. There are two dead bodies and Martha's missing, so naturally they think it was Martha who killed them. It's what I'd think."

Caroline watched Susan try to process this. It was like watching an old woman trying to knead bread dough. It was painful. Susan thought about it. Susan thought about it again. Caroline wanted to tear the hair out of her head.

"Do you think that's possible?" Susan asked finally. "Do you really think Martha could have done something like that, killed two people?"

"I think Martha could have had sex with the devil if it would have gotten her where she wanted to go," Caroline said.

Susan shuddered. "I didn't like that movie. I never like movies with the devil in them. I just can't see it. They said Michael Platte was hit over the head and thrown into the pool. I know Martha was athletic, but could she have done something like that? And what about the other one? Whoever it was. Burned to a crisp is what they said on television. Burned down to nothing but ash. It just sounds crazy, that's all."

"It doesn't matter if it sounds crazy," Caroline said. "It's what happened."

"But how would she do that?" Susan insisted. "She must have been there at the same time Arthur was. To start the fire. Or almost at the same time, anyway. He must have seen her. Somebody must have. It was the middle of the morning commute. There are people everywhere. And you know what people are. They pry."

"Well, these people didn't pry," Caroline said. "Maybe they were talking on their cell phones. Maybe they were texting while driving. What does it matter? Let the police do their jobs. Sit tight. Don't talk too much. Let it pass. They'll find Martha. They'll put her in jail. Nobody will have paid the least attention to us."

"What if they don't find Martha?" Susan said. "What if she's dead, too?"

Caroline had wanted to scream. "Then," she'd said, "maybe it will turn out that Arthur Heydreich killed all three of them. It has nothing to do with us."

Maybe, Caroline thought now, it would have been easier to convince Susan if it had been true. Susan had been up all night with it, pacing around in her room, crying when she thought Caroline couldn't hear her. There had been times during the night when Caroline had wanted to burst into that bedroom and have a complete and unalloyed fit. Only the possibility that somebody might hear her and call security had stopped her.

It didn't help that, if somebody called security, Caroline knew who it would be. Everybody said they could make a list of the people willing to kill off Martha Heydreich, but Caroline was willing to bet that the list of people willing to kill off Walter Dunbar would be longer.

She got coffee going in the percolator and set out the cups and saucers on the kitchen table. She had always been careful to set the table for breakfast as she was used to having it set, just as she set the table for dinner as she was used to having it set. She sometimes thought of herself as one of those representatives of the British Empire in the deep jungles of Africa. It didn't matter if there was no toilet and lions were lurking in wait just outside the comforting ring of the fire. She would don her tuxedo and be served like a gentleman.

Except that lions didn't live in the jungle. They lived in the grasslands. She remembered that from *The Lion King,* which was the last movie she had seen in a theater. She had been with her youngest son that day. She had not been angry at him.

Susan was moving slowly this morning, as if she hated the idea of coming downstairs to start the day. Fortunately, there were no committee meetings to attend today. There had been very few committee meetings since the murders. People didn't like the idea of spending time with each other when one of them had two bodies on his conscience.

"It's going to get worse now," Caroline said, not meaning to say it out loud.

Susan appeared in the kitchen and blinked. "What's going to get much worse now?" she asked. "You said yesterday that it wouldn't matter. You said it had nothing to do with us. You said the police had already decided it was Martha who committed the murders and then ran away."

The coffee was finished. Caroline brought the percolator to the table. She sat down in front of her own place mat with her own set of silverware. It was her own silverware, too, brought from the house, carefully wrapped in that fuzzy warm blue cloth from Tiffany's. Caroline used to have a service for thirty-six in this pattern.

"I wasn't thinking about the police," she said. "I was thinking about the people. The people who live here. They've been skittish with each other since this started. Now it's going to be worse."

"Why would it be worse?" Susan asked. "They'll still know who killed them. You said that yourself. You said they used to think that it was Arthur Heydreich who killed them, and now they'll think it was Martha."

You had to go over and over things with Susan. You had to explain and explain and explain again, and then you had to start all over from the beginning.

Caroline had toast and jam and butter on the table. The toast was in a silver toast rack. The jam and butter were in small ceramic bowls. She did not allow jars and boxes from the supermarket on her breakfast table.

She tried it again. "The police will know that," she said, trying to say it slowly, and trying not to scream. "And the people at Waldorf Pines will hear it from the police. But it's much the way it was before. They'll only partly believe it. With some other part of their brains, they'll wonder if the police couldn't be wrong. And this time, of course, they'll wonder all the more, because the police were wrong the first time. Then they'll do the even more natural thing, and start to suspect each other."

"I don't see why that's the natural thing," Susan said.

"It is the natural thing, nonetheless," Caroline said. "It's the way people are. They'll suspect each other, and they'll gossip about each other, and then all sorts of things will come out that wouldn't have otherwise. That's why it's so important for us to just stay away from these people as much as we possibly can. And since that's what we were already trying to do, it ought to be easier for us than it will be for some people."

Susan was still standing there, shifting back and forth on her feet as if she were in the first form and being reprimanded by the head of the Lower School.

"Are you going to give up organizing the cotillion?" she asked. "That's where we see other people most of the time."

"I know," Caroline said. "Part of me doesn't understand why they'd want to have their wretched cotillion after all this. I mean, think of it really. They don't want a real cotillion, a private thing for private people. They want something they can splash all over the newspapers, and maybe even have television cameras for. You'd think they'd have had enough of publicity with all that's been going on with the murders. Have you been remembering to go in and out the back way?"

"I've hardly been out of the complex at all," Susan said. "And yes, I did remember, only the back way and then with a scarf and sunglasses, although what good the sunglasses are supposed to do, I never did understand. I didn't understand it with—with—you know. I never did see the good it was supposed to do. I was always recognized anyway."

"You were recognized because they were looking for you," Caroline said. "Nobody is looking for you now. Nobody expects to find either of us in Waldorf Pines, and the newspeople aren't chasing that story anyway. It really is just a matter of keeping our heads. Nobody is interested in us."

"They would be interested in us if they knew who we were," Susan said.

"But they don't know who we are. And there's no reason for them to find out."

"They'd be interested in us if they knew about us." Susan walked over to the percolator stand, as if there was something there to see. "It's not the same as if we had nothing to do with them at all. Martha and Michael, I mean. We did have to do with them. We couldn't help it."

Caroline took a piece of toast out of the toast rack. They'd been talking for so long, it was cold. She hated cold toast. She hated this house, if it came to that. Everything was too obviously expensive. Everything was too florid and overdone.

She took a butter knife and went at the butter, real butter, whipped to make it possible to spread. Caroline did not believe in margarine. She did not believe in anything contrived or fake.

"There is nothing," she said, very carefully, "to connect us to either Martha Heydreich or Michael Platte except what inevitably arises from the fact that we lived in the same housing estate. There is no reason why anyone, anywhere, should make any other connection between us. And there is no reason why anybody, anywhere, should connect either one of us with—with what happened before. I suppose there are people who would like to do it for spite, but they don't know we live here and they have no reason to connect us to this place. Not even my children know we live here."

"You should talk to them," Susan said. "It's not good, what you're doing to them."

"They should have thought of that before they did what they did to me," Caroline said. "Now sit down and have your breakfast and start behaving like a grown-up, or you're going to blow this whole thing into the stratosphere. And you know you don't want that. You've been there before."

THREE

1

The key was waiting for him when he got to the Pineville Station Police Department, lying on what looked like a mouse pad. Larry Farmer paced and struggled back and forth in front of Miss Connolly's counter. Buck Monaghan had left word to be called as soon as Gregor got in. Gregor himself had begun to feel a little foolish about the whole thing. There was always the chance that he could be wrong. There was always the chance that whoever had written the evidence descriptions couldn't describe a basketball without making it sound like a toaster.

As it turned out, the person who had written the evidence descriptions had not been bad at the job, and the key lying there on the counter was almost certainly a key to a safe-deposit box. Gregor looked at it for a moment without touching it. Then he said,

"Tell me this has already been through the wringer. It's been fingerprinted. It's been tested for blood. It's been—"

"Yes, yes," Larry Farmer said. "We did all that. We may not have the kind of forensics you see on television, but we do get things done here. And we've got a mobile evidence lab."

He leaned over the key as Miss Connolly picked up the phone to call Buck Monaghan. He turned the key over in his hand. It was like every other safe-deposit key he'd ever seen. It was small. It was blank. It was without identification. Gregor put it back down.

Buck Monaghan appeared from upstairs and looked over the scene. "Well?" he said.

"Mr. Demarkian thinks it's a safe-deposit key," Larry Farmer said. "I don't see why he thinks that. It looks like any other key to me. It looks like one of those keys you lock luggage with. Why he'd think it was a safe-deposit key, that's beyond me."

Gregor picked up the key and handed it to Buck.

"Ah," Buck said.

"I don't see what the 'ah' is about," Larry Farmer said. "It's like there's some secret code here and nobody's let me in on it."

"If it was a luggage key, it would have some identification on it," Buck said. "It would have the name of the luggage company. It would have something. The point of safe-deposit boxes is that they need to be both secure and discreet. So the keys don't have identification on them. They don't have the name of the bank. They really don't have the number of the box. The idea is that if you have a right to the key, you already know the bank and the box number."

"Well, that helps us out," Larry Farmer said. "We have a key. We have no idea what bank it came from and no idea what box it will open. And don't you need two keys to open a safe-deposit box?"

"You definitely do," Gregor said. "I don't think a bank would have a great deal of trouble accepting that they ought to come forward on something like this when the box holder has been murdered, and even if the bank doesn't want to do it, we could always get a warrant to open the box. But that assumes two things, neither of which I think is going to help us."

"What two things?" Larry Farmer looked definitely put out.

"The first is that the box belonged to Michael Platte," Gregor said. "Just because he had the key on him doesn't mean he owned it.

He could have stolen it. Which, given the things you've said to me about him so far, wouldn't be a shock. He could have been given it by somebody else. In either of those cases, you might find that a bank would not come forward to admit that the key was theirs, if they even knew it. And you'd have a hard time convincing a judge to give you a warrant to open the box even if you could find out who it belonged to and what bank it was at."

"If he stole the thing," Buck Monaghan said, "then he had no right to it, and it's not likely that whatever is in it is germane to his murder. Although it might be. But you must see how the banks will think. People keep all kinds of sensitive information in safe-deposit boxes. They wouldn't do that if they thought their confidence could be violated for any excuse at all."

"Two murders isn't an excuse," Larry Farmer said. "Even a judge should be able to figure that out."

"Why don't we worry about all that when we're farther along," Gregor said. "Right now, we've got Michael Platte dead, an unknown person dead, Martha Heydreich missing, and a safe-deposit key. Michael Platte has family at Waldorf Pines, doesn't he?"

"A mother and a father, at least," Buck Monaghan said. "There may be siblings. I'm not sure."

"A mother and a father will do," Gregor said. "Let's talk to them. There's always the possibility that this is something completely unimportant. Maybe the kid had a safe-deposit box because it was where he kept his savings bonds for college money. Maybe he inherited something from a grandparent. Maybe his parents got it for him at birth to keep things like birth certificates and passports in. Let's talk to the family and find out, and if all that comes up negative, we can start thinking about how to find the bank."

"Do you think it's going to be something like that?" Buck asked curiously.

Gregor shook his head. "I'm almost dead certain the key didn't belong to Michael Platte at all, but we've got to check out the obvious. It's imperative. Then we can get on to the esoteric."

"Well," Larry Farmer said, "obvious or whatever, we're not getting into Waldorf Pines to talk to the Plattes unless we talk to Horace Wingard first, and that's not going to be a piece of cake."

2

Gregor Demarkian had counted on having Buck Monaghan with him throughout the investigation. He'd counted on it without ever bringing it fully into consciousness. If he had, he'd have realized that that wasn't going to be possible. Buck Monaghan was the town prosecutor. He had other work to do. It was Larry Farmer's business to deal with the policing. And in spite of being called "chief of police," Larry was not exactly at the head of a huge cohort of law enforcement officers. In fact, as far as Gregor could tell, Pineville Station had no more than two officers for each of its three shifts. There was no homicide bureau, no detective squad, no drug detail.

Larry, unfortunately, was the kind of person who talked, and he talked nonstop all the way out to Waldorf Pines.

"It's the tax base," he said, more than once. "That's what Ken's so upset about. It's not the way it used to be, Mr. Demarkian. Everything is about money these days. Everything. And the people who live here, the ones who've always lived here, they don't have a lot of it. It's people like the people at Waldorf Pines we need to pay taxes. Ken looks around and all he sees is one disaster after another, and you can hardly blame him for wanting to bring in more people who will pay taxes. There's a rumor that the people who built Waldorf Pines might want to build another one of those things, an even more expensive one. And Ken really wants that."

"And you don't."

Larry Farmer looked away. "No," he said finally, "I don't. I keep thinking we got along without money for all this time, we should get along without it now. But here it is, Mr. Demarkian. Right up ahead of us. That's Waldorf Pines."

What was actually right up ahead of them was a stone and

wrought iron wall punctuated with a stone and wrought iron gate, the words WALDORF PINES sunk into the stone just to the left of the little guardhouse where everybody had to stop before entering. It was much less impressive than Gregor had expected it to be from everything he'd heard at the Pineville Station PD. There had to be thousands of housing developments across the country just like this, with their walls and their gates and their pretensions to exclusivity. Anybody who had ever seen the real thing—who had seen, for instance, Tuxedo Park—knew what was wrong with them.

There was an elaborate ritual to wade through before they could go inside. First they had to stop at the gate. Then Larry Farmer had to present his credentials to the guard. Then the guard had to wave them through and point at the big dark wood clubhouse just to the left. They had barely pulled up to the clubhouse's curb when a little man came rushing out from inside, waving his hands in the air and going bright red in the process.

"I've told you and told you," the little man said. He wasn't screaming. His voice wasn't raised. Even so, there was something about the way he was saying what he was saying that was like a scream. "I've told you and told you," he said again, "I don't want you on the grounds with a police car. Sometimes it can't be helped. We can't do anything about that. But this isn't one of those times. This isn't one of those times. I don't want that thing parked in front where every television news program in Pennsylvania can see it."

"There weren't any television cameras out there," Larry Farmer said as he climbed out of the car. "The whole front gate is clear now, Horace. You've got nothing to worry about."

"Somebody will call it in," Horace Wingard said. "They'll have seen you, and they'll call it in. You've got to get that car out of sight somewhere and you've got to do it now."

"This is as out of sight as it's going to get," Larry Farmer said. "We need to use a car. This is Mr. Demarkian, by the way. Last I heard, you thought it was a wonderful idea for us to hire him."

"I thought it was a wonderful idea for you to hire someone," Horace

161

Wingard said coldly. "You don't have the capacity to investigate a crime of this complexity. I did not say I thought it was a wonderful idea for you to hire *him*. The man is a publicity hound. He's on television more than Paris Hilton."

"He's the best there is," Larry Farmer said. "You told Ken you wanted the best there is."

"I'm going to call Mr. Bairn right now," Horace Wingard said. "You can't get away with this. You can't ruin the reputation of Waldorf Pines. This is a quality complex."

"Last I heard, your quality complex had two dead bodies in it, and a missing person who's either the murderer or dead herself under a tree somewhere."

Horace Wingard managed to go a little redder. Then he turned on his heel and marched back into the clubhouse. He was wearing shoes with heels on them. They were very discreet heels. They couldn't be mistaken for cowboy boots. Even so, they were heels.

"Asshole," Larry Farmer said.

Farmer started toward the clubhouse door, and Gregor followed him. The drive he was walking across was gravel. The front doors of the club were double doors, and wider than standard ones at that. The foyer just inside was heavy with wood and beams. It was as if someone had tried to replicate a golf club from the Twenties—or, more likely, the fantasy of a golf club from the Twenties from a movie made of *The Great Gatsby*.

Horace Wingard was in an office to the left of the front doors. The door to that office was open, as was the door to the anteroom office that opened onto the foyer. There was a tall, thin, youngish woman in the anteroom office, sitting at a desk at a computer and behaving as if she couldn't hear her boss in spite of the fact that he was now actually yelling, and at the top of his lungs.

Gregor bypassed Larry Farmer and went in. "How do you do," he said to the secretary at the desk. "My name is Gregor Demarkian."

"I have seen you on the news," the secretary said. "I'm Miss Vaile. I'm sure Mr. Wingard will be out in just a moment."

"If he doesn't give himself a heart attack with the way he's behaving," Gregor said.

Miss Vaile looked through the door to the other office and shrugged. "It's been a strain, all this happening at Waldorf Pines. It's been a strain on all of us. I'm sure you must realize this is not the kind of thing Mr. Wingard is used to."

"I take it there's not a lot of crime at Waldorf Pines," Gregor said.

Miss Vaile hesitated just a second too long. "I suppose it depends on what you mean by crime," she said, "but this kind of thing, violence and thuggery, no. That's what our people come to get away from. The world has become a violent and insecure place."

"I'm afraid I don't really see that," Gregor said.

There was the sound of a phone receiver being slammed into an old-fashioned cradle, and then Horace Wingard was with them once more. He was not so red, but he looked as if he was sweating. Gregor thought that this was probably going to turn out to be Horace Wingard's biggest dissatisfaction with himself: the fact that he sweat easily and heavily, and apparently could do nothing about it.

He marched past Miss Vaile's desk and planted himself in front of Larry Farmer, almost as if Gregor wasn't there.

"Come on in," he said. "And Miss Vaile, please bring your pad. I want a record of everything we say here, and I intend to use it."

3

Horace Wingard's office was just what Gregor had expected it to be. It was so much what it ought to have been, Gregor got the impression that it had been staged. Horace himself was so much what he ought to have been that Gregor felt that he was staging himself, and he filed the observation in the back of his mind for later.

Horace sat down behind his desk and looked at the both of them. He didn't ask them to sit. Gregor sat down anyway. Horace Wingard made a face.

"I presume," he said, "that you have come here because you have something to report. I expect you to have a great deal to report."

"We came because we need to talk to the Plattes," Larry Farmer said. "Mr. Demarkian here had found something we need to ask them about."

"And can I ask what this something is?" Horace Wingard said.

"No," Gregor said. "Mr. Wingard, this is a police investigation into a double homicide. I do understand that you have a special relationship with the municipal authorities, but no such relationship gives you the right or the power to interfere in such an investigation. The Plattes are within their rights to refuse to talk to the police if that is what they want, and they are within their rights to hire an attorney to tell us that that is what they want to do. Neither they nor you, however, have the right to use Waldorf Pines's status as a gated community to attempt to keep the police away. So I would appreciate it if you would stop pretending to be Truman Capote having a snit and behave like a grown-up."

"You are not," Horace Wingard said carefully, "a member of the Pineville Station Police Department."

"I'm a consultant who has been hired by the Pineville Station Police Department, and my status as an active investigator will be held up in court if you insist on taking it there. I know, because other people have insisted on taking it there. Did the Plattes request you to run interference for them in this matter?"

Horace Wingard licked his lips. "No," he said finally. "I have no idea how the Plattes feel about talking to the police. I know how I feel about having police on the premises of Waldorf Pines."

"Fine," Gregor said. "That's the way everybody feels about having the police on the premises. I would like to ask you a few questions. Then I would like to go out to talk to Michael Platte's parents."

"He isn't there," Horace Wingard said. "He's already left for work. She's there all the time. I'm not going to let you go there without warning her."

"That's fine," Gregor said. "Warn away. This isn't a stealth mission. I said I wanted to ask you a few questions."

"If you want to ask me about Michael Platte, I know less than you'd think," Horace Wingard said. "He was a problem. It's a terrible thing to say, I know, but there's nothing to do but admit it. It's everywhere these days, very nice families, good families, and one of the children just doesn't turn out right."

"I didn't think Michael Platte was a child."

"He was nineteen," Horace Wingard said. "We gave him the job at the pool house because we didn't want him doing something irrevocable. Breaking into people's houses, for instance, in an attempt to get money for drugs. We thought if we just provided him with a way to spend his time—well."

"And this job consisted of what?"

"He was supposed to stay at the pool house and make sure nobody went in or out except the repair people," Horace Wingard said. "It wasn't an entirely make-work job. For complicated reasons I do not completely understand, the repair company does not want us to empty the pool of water until their own people can come in and do it, and their own people cannot come in and do it for weeks. Still. We didn't want children to come in and drown in the water, or anything like that."

"Don't you have a staff for the pool?"

"Yes, we do," Horace Wingard looked uncomfortable. "And the pool is usually open all year round. It's heated. However, when we were informed we would not be able to keep the pool open this fall while repairs were being done, well, I—"

"You fired your staff," Gregor said.

"There was no reason—" Horace Wingard said.

"Who were probably all illegal immigrants anyway," Gregor said.

"I've never knowingly hired a single undocumented worker at Waldorf Pines, or any other property I've managed," Horace Wingard said. "You have no right at all to make such accusations."

Gregor didn't say that he couldn't see how it would be possible to run a place like Waldorf Pines without "undocumented workers," because he knew Horace Wingard couldn't see it, either.

He looked around at the hunting prints and golf memorabilia on the walls and said, "Let me ask you for a bit about Martha Heydreich. You knew her better than anybody I've talked to so far. Do you believe the things people say about her having had an affair with Michael Platte? Was she the kind of woman who might have had an affair with a much younger man?"

Horace Wingard made a face. "Oh, it's no use asking what kind of a woman Martha is," he said. "It didn't surprise me when I heard she was dead—thought to be dead, I suppose. It didn't surprise me that somebody would want to kill her. If I was her husband, I would have killed her years ago."

"She was an unpleasant woman?"

"She was loud," Horace said, "and exaggerated. Everything was too much. Too much makeup. Gestures that were too overly dramatic. A voice that could pierce tempered steel, and she was never quiet. Clothes that were extreme in ways that would be difficult to explain if you hadn't seen them. Violent colors. Evening gowns with constructions that were practically like architecture. Bathing suits that were barely this side of pornographic. A breast enhancement that made her look like Dolly Parton was having an affair with a bicycle pump. Oh, and hats."

"Hats?"

Horace Wingard nodded. "She always wore hats. Very retro hats, not quite high-fashion hats but aspiring to that kind of area. Things that she had to pin on to get them to stay. Feathers curling under her chin. Little veils. And everything pink. It was like watching a high-fashion runway show where all the models were truck drivers."

"Truck drivers?"

"She had no grace," Horace Wingard said. "She was awkward when she moved. She was big boned and tall and outsized in every way, and she moved like she'd been put together with parts. But, you know, that's the thing. She barged around. She barged in. It was what she did. She was a barger. But at the same time"—he shrugged—"tiny waist. Tiny hands. Even those were exaggerated. They were just smaller than life rather than bigger."

"I've seen two pictures of her, and neither of them were very clear," Gregor said. "Do you happen to have a better one?"

"I probably gave Mr. Farmer here the pictures he's got," Horace Wingard said, "unless Arthur did, of course, and I suppose Arthur might not have been cooperating at the time. She didn't take very clear pictures. It was surprising, really, because she was the sort of person who liked to call attention to herself. We've probably got a hundred pictures of her, and in every one of them she's either in the back of the crowd or so made-up she might as well have been wearing a mask."

"Well," Gregor said, "maybe she was."

"I don't think even Martha Heydreich went quite that far," Horace Wingard said.

"Possibly," Gregor said. "But what you've been describing to me is someone who will be almost impossible to recognize if she stops putting on all that makeup. We've got to at least consider the possibility that that was deliberate. It's possible that Martha Heydreich was intending to disappear all along."

"And kill two people when she went?" Larry Farmer interrupted. "What do you mean by 'all along'? Since she's been living at Waldorf Pines? Since before?"

"I don't know," Gregor said. "And I don't know about either. But I think we should at least consider the possibility that what went on here was not spur of the moment, not even relatively spur of the moment."

"Well, it couldn't have been that," Horace Wingard said. "There must have been some kind of device, or something, to set off the fire. Granted, the police haven't found that device, but there must have been—"

"It's not that we didn't look for it," Larry Farmer said. "We went through that place with a sieve. Whatever it was must have been destroyed in the fire."

"You weren't looking for it at all," Horace Wingard said. "You thought you knew exactly what you had, and you didn't look for anything that could disturb your precious little theories. I know how you operate. I have to deal with it every day."

Gregor got up and began to walk around the office. He didn't need to listen to the two of them fight. He checked out a bookcase with volumes in tooled black leather. The books actually looked as if they'd been opened. He checked out a marble bust of somebody he thought he was supposed to recognize, but didn't. He stopped at the window and looked out across the golf course.

That was when two things happened to him at once.

First, he had an idea he should have had before. It was such an obvious idea that he thought he might be going senile not to have thought of it.

Second, he saw a woman walking at the edge of the golf course, making her way to the clubhouse, and recognized her immediately.

He turned back to Larry Farmer and Horace Wingard and asked, "Who is that woman?"

"That?" Horace came to the window. "That's Caroline Stanford-Pyrie. She lives just down the right side of the course, there, with her companion, if you know what I mean. Not that we're prejudiced here, of course, but the way these old money women conduct affairs of that kind is truly bizarre, don't you think?"

"What I think is truly bizarre," Gregor said, "is that the murderer only went to the trouble of destroying one of the bodies."

FOUR

1

To Walter Dunbar, everything that had happened in the last month—and especially everything that had happened in the last few hours—was proof positive that the world was a pack of idiots. Sometimes what had to be done seemed so obvious to him, he just didn't believe that other people didn't see it. Sometimes he was convinced that the world was full of people who existed only to spite him. Horace Wingard, to name one, would be willing to see Waldorf Pines and everything it supposedly stood for sink into the sea and drown before he'd admit that Walter was right about anything.

And Walter was always right about everything.

Walter had no idea what had started him thinking, this morning, about his mother. He only knew he had woken up and walked out onto the deck as usual, and suddenly his head was full of the sound of her voice. She'd been dead now for nearly thirty years, but Walter could still remember the last time he'd talked to her. He'd gone to the little town house she'd lived in in the "retirement community" where he'd found her a place after his father died. The place had started out being called an "adult community" until he complained, because of course, by then, "adult" had come to mean "pornography."

"It's not a very nice thing, saying your mother lives in an adult community," he'd told the management not a week after he'd moved his mother in. "It makes it sound like she's going to put tassels on and buy fans."

The snot-nosed idiot at the management office hadn't the faintest idea what he was talking about. He'd probably never even heard of a fan dancer. There was something that had come and gone without a trace. Walter remembered fan dancers. They were the "respectable" strippers, and Perry Mason even had one as a client on the old television show.

He'd had to go up the chain of command, then, to talk to somebody old enough to have much sense—not that even older people had much sense. He'd made enough of a stink about it to force the change of name, and he'd put his foot down about calling the place a "senior" community. If there was one thing Walter hated it was all that crap about "senior citizens." It was as if the world was supposed to be one big high school, complete with class colors and junior–senior balls. Walter had hated high school, much as he'd hated elementary school, much as he'd hated college. Education was a pile of crap, anyway. You slogged your way through a lot of meaningless bullshit, and then they let you make a living.

The last day Walter had seen his mother, she had been watching the neighbors' grandchildren in the neighbors' yards. She had a pair of binoculars to do it with, and the longer she watched, the more agitated she got.

"You're not supposed to have children here," she told him, "not even for the afternoon. It's against the rules. It upsets the residents."

Walter could see how the children would upset his mother. They were on both sides of her, and they were very wild and noisy. People didn't know how to keep their children well behaved anymore. The children ran and screamed and shouted and broke things. These children were climbing on the cellar doors and pretending to slide down. Then they were crying that they had splinters. Some of them had

Frisbees. The Frisbees sailed right over the hedges into his mother's own yard and the children climbed over after them.

"I'll go do something about it," he'd said.

Then he'd walked right over to the management building to complain. It was Saturday. The crew that was on for the weekend was all young, and none of them really wanted to take responsibility for anything.

"But it's grandchildren," the little girl in the office had said, looking confused. "You don't want people not to be able to have their grandchildren visit?"

The little girl in the office made the statement as if it were a question, but Walter could see it in her eyes. She thought he was crazy. She thought nobody on earth would mind if people's grandchildren made a fuss and a bother and came running onto people's lawns, because they were grandchildren, and everybody had to love grandchildren.

"They're throwing those Frisbees right into my mother's yard," he'd said, "and then they're running into the yard to get them. They're going to break something. A window maybe. And I don't care whose grandchildren they are, I want them out of there. That's why there are rules."

Then he'd gone back to his mother's town house. He'd let himself in by the front door and called out to her. He'd listened to the silence as if it were music.

Then he'd walked all the way to the back and found his mother dead on the kitchen floor.

After that, he'd sued the "retirement community" for not keeping their own rules and allowing the fuss of the children that had given his mother her fatal heart attack. It had taken ten hours for his lawyer to talk him out of suing the neighbors on both sides for having the children there.

"You can't prove it was the children who caused the heart attack," his lawyer had said. "She was an old woman. It could have been anything."

That was the kind of thing people said these days. Whether they made any sense at all, people said them. That was why Walter was hearing his mother's voice in his head today.

"You should never think you know somebody unless you check," she'd said. "You should check and check again. People lie more than they tell the truth."

This was absolutely true. Walter knew it from experience.

He stopped looking through the kitchen window and backed up to get the papers he had put on the table. Jessica was sitting there, not really drinking a cup of coffee, the way she had been all morning.

"Don't tell me why I shouldn't go," Walter said. "We had all that out last night."

Jessica looked down. "I thought you were looking at something," she said, mostly mumbling. "I thought there was something out there you wanted to see."

"It's Horace Wingard and those asshole cops," Walter said. "The cops are back. They've fucked up everything and now they're going to muck around here again, making a scene. I told you they were going to fuck it up. I told you right from the beginning. Yes, I did. But nobody listens to me. I'm just a jerk. I'm just a bad-tempered old man. And here we are. That man is out there."

"What man?" Jessica looked confused.

"Gregor Demarkian. The detective the police have hired to cover their asses. Never mind it's just locking the barn door. We could all be dead by now."

"I don't see how we could all be dead," Jessica said. "He didn't kill anyone, Michael Platte. He was killed himself."

"She killed someone," Walter said. "Don't tell me you didn't know it as soon as you saw her. Why the two of them ever got let into this complex, I don't know. Waldorf Pines. An exclusive community for discriminating people. An advertising slogan meant to gull the idiots, and the world is full of idiots. Exclusive doesn't mean expensive. Exclusive means you keep the people you don't want out."

Jessica shook her head. She was staring so hard at her coffee, it was as if the thing was a crystal ball, a place where she could see visions. Walter wanted to hit her.

"Think what it must be like for his mother," she said. "She is his mother, no matter what he turned out to be. Mothers don't stop loving their children because the children don't turn out well. Think of what she must be going through."

"If it were me, I'd be damned glad I was rid of him," Walter said. "And all I want right now is to make sure this doesn't happen again. You can't stop me, Jessie. You shouldn't even try to stop me."

Walter headed out for the foyer and the front door, the door that led to the road and not the green. Jessica did not try to stop him, but he hadn't really thought she would. Back when they were first dating, she had tried to stop him sometimes, when she thought he was going off the handle too quickly. It had never worked out well.

It would be a better place if other people understood him as well as Jessica did. It would be a better place if everybody just stopped being idiots.

"Never have children," his mother had said to him, when he was twelve years old. "Never have children. They'll only be a disappointment to you."

She had been absolutely right.

Walter stepped onto the road and watched the scene just ahead of him. His house was the one right next to the pool house and clubhouse on the right when looking up the green, so he was right next to the action as it happened. He saw Horace Wingard come out, leading Larry Farmer and the big man Walter assumed was Gregor Demarkian. He saw the three of them stop at the pool house door and look at it. It was ridiculous. What did they expect to get by looking at it? It was the kind of things detectives did on television shows, to make themselves look intelligent.

Walter clutched his papers in his hand and walked faster. He could walk very fast, even at his age. He walked every day. You didn't have to become a cripple at sixty unless you wanted to. You didn't have to let yourself go to hell. Most people did, and then they called it arthritis.

Walter got all the way to the pool house and stopped. From his own house, it was difficult to see the burned part, because the burned part was around the other side. From where he was standing now, he could see the blackened edges of the roof and the walls where the fire had come through before the fire department had made it onto the scene. Then there had been a lot of trouble at the gate, because nobody had notified the gate guard that there was a fire. Idiot. The fire was right there, right in front of his nose. He was just waiting for orders.

Walter stopped in the little parking lot. Gregor Demarkian had gone into the pool house. Horace Wingard and Larry Farmer were still standing in the parking lot, looking useless.

Horace Wingard saw him coming and said, "Mr. Dunbar. I hope you're not thinking of going into the pool house. The pool house is off limits to residents until the damage is repaired. If you left personal items in a locker, we'll be more than happy to send a staff member in to collect them for you."

Horace Wingard always sounded as if he were saying tongue twisters. All the words came out very fast. Walter wasn't listening to him anyway.

"I'm going to the clubhouse," he said. "I'm going to file my petition again. And don't tell me I need the signatures of a third of the residents, because you know that's hogwash. I could sue you over it if I wanted to. An exclusive community for discriminating people. Hogwash. Bullshit, if you don't want to put too fine a point on it."

Horace Wingard sighed. "Mr. Dunbar, the residents of Waldorf Pines are already subject to a background check—"

"To a financial background check," Walter said. "There should be a criminal background check. Criminals have money. Criminals have parents with money. Criminals have husbands with money. We could have a serial killer here, and you wouldn't know it."

"Mr. Dunbar," Horace Wingard said.

"There's trouble here whether you like it or not," Walter Dunbar said. "There's that hose that was thrown right up on my porch the night of the murder. I told you about it. I told the police about it. Nobody pays attention to me."

"Mr. Dunbar," Horace Wingard said again.

Gregor Demarkian came out of the pool house. Walter saw Horace Wingard throw him a nervous glance.

"Great detective," Walter said.

Then he turned his back on all of them and marched on in the direction of the clubhouse.

2

LizaAnne Marsh didn't know when she had decided that she needed to Do Something about the things that were going on in Waldorf Pines, but she did know what it was that had to get done. People were being woefully stupid about all this, as if the only thing they could do when disaster struck was to dither around and sound like people on television, saying things that didn't mean anything.

LizaAnne was not worried about Martha Heydreich coming back in the night and murdering them all, which is what her father and mother kept talking about. She hadn't been worried about Arthur Heydreich murdering them all, either, which was what her parents had talked about in the beginning.

Death was not all that interesting to LizaAnne. She thought it was probably only really interesting to old people, because they were so close to having to die. People who were not so old did not think about death. They thought about sex.

LizaAnne had started thinking about sex the first time she'd seen Fanny Bullman go into Arthur Heydreich's house. Well, no, that wasn't exactly right. LizaAnne thought about sex a lot. She thought about what it would be like to have sex with Brad Pitt. She thought about how awful it must be for him, married to that woman with the lips that made her look like a fish. It was scary the way things happened sometimes. People did things to their lives. They married people. They ran away. They hit people with their cars. People just did things, and then everything was a mess.

LizaAnne had started thinking about sex and murder the first time she'd seen Fanny Bullman go into Arthur Heydreich's house, and the more she thought about it, the more interesting it got. The idea of older people having sex was a little confusing, except for movie stars, because movie stars always looked young. LizaAnne didn't know what people saw in each other at that age. She did know what people that age saw in people her age, which was why she was never really upset when one of the teachers came on to her.

Still, she knew that older people had sex, and had sex with each other, and had affairs. They even did the things younger people did to mess up their lives. If Fanny Bullman was having sex with Arthur Heydreich, she was probably going to mess up her life. Arthur Heydreich wouldn't mess up his, because his was already down the toilet.

She kept seeing Fanny Bullman going into Arthur Heydreich's house. Sometimes Fanny Bullman went by way of the green, walking across the grass as if she were doing nothing more important than taking her children to the bus stop. Sometimes Fanny Bullman went by way of the road. Then, if LizaAnne had caught the start of the walk, she had to go out to the stairwell and look through the window there. It was always the same walk, though, and always the same little ritual when Mrs. Bullman got to Mr. Heydreich's house. First she would stand still on the doorstep, as if she wasn't sure she wanted to go in. Then she would turn around and look up the green or up the road, to see if anybody was looking. Then she would knock on the sliding glass doors to the deck or ring the front door bell. It would take Arthur Heydreich a moment or two to open the door, but he always did.

What Arthur Heydreich did not do was come out into the open, or go to Fanny Bullman's house, ever. It was as if, coming home from jail, he had become a vampire, and couldn't stand the sunlight.

LizaAnne amended this. Arthur Heydreich was nothing like a

vampire. Vampires were truly awesome. She had seen every movie in the *Twilight* series, and she had the books. Someone like Arthur Heydreich would never be cool enough to be a vampire. He had probably never been cool at all.

LizaAnne had tried to get Heather to go with her, but she wasn't having any.

"I know he's not arrested anymore," Heather had said, "but you never know. He could have killed them and killed his wife, too, and her body could be under his house or something. It could be anywhere. I'm not going to make him think he'd be better off if I was dead."

"Oh, for God's sake," LizaAnne had said. "Don't be retarded."

"I'm not being retarded," Heather had said. "Think about all the murders you hear about. Who do murderers kill? People like us, that's who. Girls in high school and college. You can see it on television all the time."

"Television isn't real."

"I don't mean that kind of television," Heather had said. "I mean the kind of television where they tell you real things that happened to real people. You'd know about it if you ever paid any attention to anything but MTV. The Green River Killer. Ted Bundy. The Zodiac Killer—"

"What about Jeffrey Dahmer?" LizaAnne said. "I've heard about him. He killed a lot of boys because he was gay. That's why people do those things. They're gay. Arthur Heydreich isn't gay."

Actually, if LizaAnne were completely honest, she had to admit that she didn't know if Arthur Heydreich was gay or not. She hadn't really thought about it. She just hated it when Heather got that way, and Heather got that way more and more often every day. It was a good thing they would all be going off to college soon, and she and Heather wouldn't be going to the same place. Heather's parents would never be able to afford a really good college unless Heather got scholarships. Heather wasn't going to get a scholarship unless they gave one out for being retarded.

Now LizaAnne sat on the bench at the edge of the green nearest to Arthur Heydreich's house and waited. She drove her own car to school, so she didn't have to worry about how she would get there if she missed the bus. Usually she drove Heather into school, too, but today she'd told Heather she was sick. That way, if Heather was asked at school, she would say LizaAnne was sick, and LizaAnne would get lots of Brownie points when she showed up later and said she'd felt better and decided to come in.

If anybody in the world was really, really retarded, it was teachers. Teachers believed anything you said to them.

LizaAnne was sitting on the bench because she didn't think it made sense to skulk around. When you skulked around, you looked conspicuous. She had a magazine with her. As soon as she saw Fanny Bullman come out of her house, she picked it up and pretended to be reading it. She couldn't help feeling a little self-satisfied. She had had to pick the route—green or road—and she'd picked right. That was because all adults were retarded. They thought they were staying out of sight by going by the route that passed only the backs of the houses. Instead, they were just where everybody could see them. That was a big selling point of Waldorf Pines. Every house had lots of rooms with a view to the green. That was because older people thought golf was really important.

Fanny Bullman wasn't even looking out to make sure she wasn't seen. She didn't glance in LizaAnne's direction even once. She cut across the green, right in the open, as if she didn't care what anybody said to her. Even if you weren't on a clandestine mission to commit illegal sex, it was a bad idea to cut across the green because it was forbidden. The green was raked and seeded and tended and cared for every minute of every day. If it wasn't, the golfers complained, and this was supposed to be a place for golfers.

Fanny Bullman got just two houses down from Arthur Heydreich's and slowed down. She looked around as if she were surprised to find herself where she was. Then she moved slowly over the edge of the green, to the pathway where people were allowed to walk.

LizaAnne wondered what was wrong with the woman. She wasn't dressed up to see somebody and impress them. She was wearing old jeans and a long-sleeved T-shirt and a cardigan sweater that looked like it had been through the washing machine a hundred and fifty times. She was wearing her hair tied back in a ponytail that looked like it had been put up first thing in the morning, with a rubber band, and without looking in a mirror.

There were people out this morning, moving around near the pool house. LizaAnne only recognized Horace Wingard. The other two men just looked old and probably retarded. Fanny Bullman saw them and hesitated. The pool house was not near Arthur Heydreich's house. It wasn't really near Fanny Bullman's, either. Fanny Bullman hesitated anyway, as if she were afraid the people there were going to take notes and ask her to explain.

The men at the pool house were not looking at Fanny Bullman. They were not looking at LizaAnne Marsh, either. Fanny Bullman shuddered slightly and turned away from them, making her way straight to Arthur Heydreich's house now. She had a hitchy little limp in her step. She looked like she didn't care at all what she looked like.

Fanny Bullman climbed onto Arthur Heydreich's deck and knocked on the sliding glass doors. LizaAnne saw that shadow that was the evidence of curtains being pulled back and then saw the sliding glass doors open. It seemed to LizaAnne that it would make sense if Arthur Heydreich would come out and look at people, but he didn't. There was no sign of a person inside the glass doors. Fanny Bullman just went through them, and they closed behind her.

LizaAnne was sure she would never behave like that if she was in Arthur Heydreich's position. She would make a point of being seen right out in public and everything. If you skulked around and tried to hide, you looked guilty.

The magazine she had was *Vogue,* and she was bored with it. The only really good things about magazines were the ads, and *Vogue* had very good ads. Someday, LizaAnne wanted to have a diamond-paveéd spiral snake bracelet like the one in the ad for Harry Winston, the one she knew better than to ask her father for. She was pretty sure her father could afford it, but she also knew how he felt about snakes. He had had the Bible read to him a lot when he was a child.

LizaAnne was very glad that nobody read the Bible to her, ever. She didn't think she could stand it if she was supposed to take church seriously, instead of a place you went a couple of times a year to wear clothes you bought for the holidays.

The curtain had been pulled across Arthur Heydreich's plate-glass windows. LizaAnne left the magazine on the bench and got up to go over there. She did not worry about crossing the green. She did not care if somebody in the houses saw her. She was not the one doing something she shouldn't.

She got to Arthur Heydreich's house and considered the possibilities. They could have gone upstairs to one of the bedrooms. She had a hunch that that was not what they would do. It would be gross to have sex in the same bed you had sex with your wife, and now she was dead, or she wasn't. LizaAnne hadn't quite worked it through in her head. First Arthur Heydreich was supposed to have killed Michael Platte and Martha. Then he wasn't supposed to have killed anybody because Martha wasn't dead. Then it was Martha—

It made no sense. It was retarded.

LizaAnne climbed carefully up on the deck, to make sure she wasn't heard. She walked slowly over to the plate-glass windows. The curtains were closed tight. She couldn't see a thing. She could hear something, though. There was a lot of panting and grunting. There was a lot of shuffling of feet.

Was it really possible that Arthur Heydreich had had sex with his wife in this house, or anywhere? LizaAnne couldn't imagine anybody having sex with Martha Heydreich.

She moved along the deck until she got to the second set of windows. These were higher on the wall, and by the time she was half-way there, she could tell there were no curtains pulled across them. That was because they were small windows, meant to sit about the television set. You'd have to be right up against the house and standing on tiptoe to see anything through them.

LizaAnne got right up next to the house. She stood on tiptoe. She was reasonably tall, but she wasn't very flexible. It took her a couple of tries. On the third try, she made it all the way to where she wanting to go, but she was out of breath.

She looked through the window and saw Fanny Bullman, naked except for her little white socks against the beige leather of the family room sofa. One of Fanny's legs was high in the air, arching over the curve of Arthur Heydreich's back. Arthur Heydreich was not as naked as Fanny was. His shirt was off, but his trousers were still on. They were just puddled around his ankles, as if he were using the toilet.

It's just so retarded, LizaAnne thought, and then, in a movement so fast, she almost didn't believe it was real, Arthur Heydreich turned around and stared directly into her eyes.

FIVE

1

The hard thing about consulting—the thing you did not have to put up with if you were a regular part of the investigative team—was not knowing what you could and couldn't trust about the reports you had been given. When you were part of a team, you knew the other players. You knew that Bob was color blind, and that Sherrie tended to oversympathize with witnesses. You knew that lab reports from Melanie were first rate on poisons but unsure on gunshot residue. You knew which coroner had an obsession with which cause of death, and which one didn't see murder even when it slapped him in the face.

In this case the investigative team was limited, and switching out among them would not have been an option. But he still didn't know what to think of the reports he'd been given, and he was not made confident by the problem with the key.

Right now, what concerned him most was the state of the pool house. He had asked to stop by to see it on their way across the complex to the Platte house, and Horace Wingard had allowed the visit with the kind of grudging condescension that told Gregor he was scared to death. There were, of course, obvious reasons for Horace

Wingard to be scared to death. This was probably a very good job. It would not only pay well, but it would leave a lot of room for Wingard's autonomy. He could run his own show as he saw fit as long as everything was going along well. He could make his own hours, although he probably made brutal ones. He could order around the staff. He could even bully the residents. And in this economy, this would be a hard job to replace.

Still, Gregor was only half convinced. People didn't usually get the deep willies about losing a job unless there was a lot going on behind the scenes—a house, a mortgage, children to support, debts. Gregor revised this. Just a house and a mortgage and children, on its own, wouldn't produce that kind of underlying panic. For that, you needed some serious overextension. Gregor thought he was guessing right that Horace Wingard wasn't married and that he didn't have children. He also thought he was guessing right that Wingard probably lived on the grounds. It was interesting. The man was as twitchy as if he had mob money behind him. It was one of those things that might be worth it to check out.

It would explain, as well, why Ken Bairn was so jumpy about upsetting the management at Waldorf Pines.

Horace Wingard took them along a back path from the clubhouse proper to the pool house. Gregor found himself looking at the brushed flagstone walk and kicking against it to see if the stones came loose. They didn't. There might be a few corners being cut on the maintenance of the pool house during repairs, but they weren't being cut on anything a resident might be able to see for himself.

When they got to the pool house, Gregor turned around and looked back at the clubhouse. It wasn't very far away.

"There are security cameras on this walk?" he asked.

"Of course there are," Horace Wingard said. "There are security cameras everywhere."

"I just want to be absolutely clear," Gregor said. "There are cameras all along this walk? Or just at one end?"

Horace Wingard stepped up and pointed into the trees above them. "There's one at the clubhouse end, pointing out toward the walk. On the other side of it is one pointing into the door of the club- house. Then there's another in the center here. Then there are two more at the pool house door itself, one pointing back up the walk and one pointing in at the door. Of course, residents are not sup- posed to use this door. It's a convenience for the maintenance staff. However—" Horace Wingard fluttered his hands.

Gregor nodded. "And given what security tape you do have of the night in question, there was nobody on this walk?"

"No. Of course—"

"There's an hour and three-quarters missing," Gregor said, before Horace Wingard could. "I know. But from what I understand, there isn't any tape missing from the morning of the fire."

"That's right," Horace Wingard said.

"And the missing time," Gregor said, "that was because the tape was—what? Malfunctioning? I thought I heard somebody say it had been turned off."

Horace Wingard looked uncomfortable. "That seems to be the best explanation anybody can give me," he said. "That somehow somebody or something just turned off the master switch in my office and then turned it back on again later. It sounds ridiculous to me. I'm in my office most of the time. I wouldn't have allowed somebody to walk in and just—"

"Are you in the office all the time?" Gregor asked.

"No," Horace admitted.

"And is your office locked when you're not in it?"

"It is if the club is open when I'm gone," Horace said.

"Were you gone on the night of the murders?"

"No," Horace said.

"Were you in your office the entire time?"

"No," Horace said again.

"Was Miss Vaile in her office?"

"Miss Vaile had gone home," Horace Wingard said. "But—"

"Where is the master switch for the security system in your office?"

Horace Wingard looked about ready to spit. "It's just inside the inner door," he said, "and yes, please, don't tell me. Anybody could have gone in there while I was walking around on my own that night. But it would have been taking a chance. It would have been taking a very big chance."

"It seems to me that we have somebody who murdered two people on a night when there were any number of other people wandering around. Whoever it is doesn't sound to me like somebody who would be averse to taking chances," Gregor said. "Let's get back to where we were. On the day after the murders, the day when the bodies were discovered, there wasn't anybody on this walk?"

"I was on this walk," Horace Wingard said. "I came out this way when I was first informed there was a fire. As you must have noticed, this door is very close to my office. I came out to see what was going on."

"All right," Gregor said.

They went into the pool house by the back way, through a tangle of wires and repair material and past large machines that probably did things like run the lights and power the heat in the pool. They came out at the pool itself, a great concrete mass painted blue and now drained entirely of water. There was no sign that there had ever been a body in it. The sight of it made Horace Wingard fuss.

"The police drained the water," he said. "I don't know what that's going to mean with the repair people, because of course we haven't been able to get anything done. We thought we'd have access back by now, of course, but then there was that terrible mistake, and now we're back to having a crime scene on the premises. I think it's ridiculous, if you want to know the truth. Why do you have to close off an area for months at a time, just because a crime was committed there?

You wouldn't do it with the Grand Concourse at Grand Central Station. You wouldn't do it with a street corner. And yet, here we are."

"We were just being careful," Larry Farmer said. "And you should be glad we were. Think what a mess we'd be in now if we weren't."

"You're already in a mess," Horace Wingard said acidly.

Gregor walked around the pool, very slowly. "It was full of water," he said, "regular pool water? Chlorine? That kind of thing."

"Of course," Horace Wingard said. "If you don't put chlorine in the water, you get . . . scum."

"And Michael Platte drowned," Gregor said. "He was alive when he went into the water. We know that because there was blood in the water, and water in his lungs. Those things are in the reports."

"We went over all this before," Larry Farmer said. He sounded exasperated.

Gregor shook his head. "I'm just trying to get some things straight in my mind. Michael Platte was hit on the back of the head hard enough to at least potentially kill him. What with? Have you any idea?"

"There are a lot of ideas," Larry Farmer said, "but you know the kind of thing we're talking about. A shovel. A rock. We haven't found anything with blood on it yet, if that's what you mean."

It wasn't quite what Gregor meant, but he let it go. The pool was an ordinary pool, "Olympic-sized" as the saying went, but without the bells and whistles you'd find in a more expensive place. There were no waterfalls. There were no side pools with hotter water.

Gregor walked the length of the pool to what had to be the "front" of the room, the doors leading out to the foyer and the place where residents would enter if they wanted to swim. He looked around the ceiling.

"There are cameras here?" he said.

"Yes." Horace Wingard was hurrying to catch up. "In three places, including one aimed at the door to the outside, one aimed at the pool room door, and one aimed at that door that leads to the locker rooms.

There is also a camera inside the men's locker room, but not one inside the women's because—because women—"

"And these cameras were running on the day of the fire?" Gregor asked.

"They were," Horace Wingard said. "And before you ask, there was virtually nothing to see on them. We do have footage of Arthur Heydreich entering the building, and of Arthur Heydreich going to the door of the locker rooms and opening them. He stepped inside the women's locker room briefly, but he was out again in no time at all. It's hard to tell what he was doing, really, but he seems to be just standing there."

Gregor went to the little entry to the locker rooms. He found himself staring at a small wedge-shaped space. On the left was the door to the women's locker room. On the right was the door to the men's. The space itself was tiny. The doors were propped open with wooden door wedges.

"Were the doors open like this on the day of the fire?"

"I don't know," Horace Wingard said. "I suppose they must have been. We've been keeping them open to make Michael Platte's job easier. There's no point in keeping them closed if nobody's using them, and if they're open it's easier for a watchman to hear sounds."

Gregor nodded. That made as much sense as anything else. "What about the method of setting the fire?" he asked. "The report I saw said that the accelerant was basically nail polish, but it doesn't say anything about the catalyst. I take it that means nobody found one. There wasn't debris with the remnants of a timer, a clock, some wires—"

"It wasn't an explosion," Larry Farmer said. "It was a fire."

"Fires can be rigged just like explosions can," Gregor said.

"If I'd heard anything like an explosion, I'd have come running without hesitation," Horace Wingard said. "There was nothing like an explosion. Arthur Heydreich said he smelled smoke, and I didn't believe him, because of course I thought he was just saying what he had to say now that he'd been arrested. But if you think about it, that's not really implausible. I mean, if the fire had been started much earlier, say half an hour or so before Arthur Heydreich noticed it, well that's just the way it would happen. It would take a fire a little time to get going."

"Not if the place had been doused with nail polish," Gregor said. "And the smell should have been overwhelming. Arthur Heydreich didn't say anything about a smell?"

"Just the smell of smoke," Larry Farmer said.

"But the cameras were running here all the time," Gregor said. "Nobody could have gotten in after Arthur Heydreich to throw nail polish around and set a fire. Unless there's a back door?"

"There's the same back door we came through," Horace Wingard said. "But there are cameras there, as well. Of course, the locker rooms were dark. And there was no camera in the women's locker room. So if somebody stayed in there all night, and if nobody put on a light—"

"Yes," Gregor said. "I got that part. But whoever came to the locker room should have been caught on the security cameras outside when he left, and nobody was. Which brings us back to what started the fire, because if there was nobody inside to throw a match, and no evidence of a timer device to set the thing off—"

"That's right," Larry Farmer said. "I mean, you've got to see our point, Mr. Demarkian. We weren't being sloppy. Nothing else made sense except—"

"Don't start that again," Horace Wingard said. "Really, Mr. Farmer, don't start that again."

Gregor left them to it and walked out into the cool of the morning air. The little parking lot in front of the pool house was empty and an old man was walking up the road in their direction, looking put out on general principles. Gregor had met old men like that before. He wasn't interested in meeting another one this morning.

Horace Wingard went off to talk to the old man, and Gregor looked at the arrangement of parking spaces and small paths that surrounded the pool house's front door.

"Who lives directly there?" he asked Larry Farmer, pointing to the first house on his left. It was the only house right at hand, actually, because to his right was the clubhouse, and it was only beyond that, on the other side of the curve, that houses started on that side.

"That's the Dunbar house," Larry Farmer said, making eye movements in the direction of the man talking to Horace Wingard. "He was right on our tails as soon as the first police cars showed up. He likes to contribute."

Gregor let that one pass. "I'll have to talk to him eventually," he said. "You're sure he didn't see someone tromping up the green in the middle of the night or something else that might be useful?"

"He complained that somebody had thrown a garden hose on his deck on the night in question," Larry Farmer said, "but our guys looked at it, and I think they even took it into evidence just in case, and I don't think there was anything remarkable about it. It was a garden hose. There are dozens of them around here. They use a lot of them on the green."

"In October?"

Larry Farmer shrugged. "They're coiled up around the spigots, that's all. Maybe somebody threw it and maybe they didn't. It wouldn't surprise me if somebody did. He's a pain in the ass, Walter Dunbar. Somebody ought to do something about him."

Gregor went back to looking at the front of the pool house.

He could think of at least one way for that fire to have been set, but it wasn't an explanation that made a lot of sense.

2

They could have driven from the pool house to the Platte house, but the more Gregor looked at Waldorf Pines, the more he wanted to see of it. It was an interesting arrangement of buildings. The clubhouse was situated at the front gate not only because it could then be seen from the road, but because it was the single most impressive building of the bunch. The pool house, being hidden, was much less so. Both were more flash and splash than substance.

But it was the houses themselves that Gregor found most interesting, and especially the way they were arranged around the green. Gregor didn't know a lot about golf, but he was fairly sure that most first-class golf courses were more expansive than this, with rolling meadows and little copses of trees and bumps and water among the grass. This was a more or less flat space, with little flags where the holes were supposed to be, but small enough that Gregor could see across the whole thing from where he was standing. The houses sat strung out along the edge of it like so many hulking bogeymen under the bed. They looked both massive and oppressive, as if they had been built to make people feel insecure about themselves.

Horace Wingard came up to where Gregor was standing and looked proud of himself. "It's a wonderful design, don't you agree? It's not the kind of course that would do for professionals, of course, but we don't want professionals here. This is supposed to be a place for people to relax."

Gregor thought he'd be better able to relax on the New York City subway at rush hour than he could in a place like this, but he didn't say so. He looked down the green past the house he now knew was Walter Dunbar's.

"Where's Arthur Heydreich's house?" he asked.

Horace Wingard pointed almost directly across the green. The Heydreich house was not the first one next to the clubhouse, and it wasn't the second. It was about a third of the way down the road. It had a big deck that snaked around both sides of it, complete with Adirondak chairs.

"It's a one-way road," Horace Wingard explained. "You come in at the gate and you go right, which would take you past Arthur Heydreich's house immediately. Then, if you want to go out again, you have to come all the way round here and exit to the left. We discussed making the thoroughfare two-way, but we thought it would result in much too much confusion in the mornings. Our residents work, you understand, in jobs that make very heavy requirements of them. Most of them are up and out long before they'd have to be with ordinary nine-to-five routines."

"And Arthur Heydreich was up and out that morning? The morning of the fire?"

"He was on his way to work when he discovered it, yes," Horace Wingard said.

Gregor shook his head. "Where is Michael Platte's house?"

Horace Wingard counted down from Arthur Heydreich's and stopped on one nearly in the middle of the opposite line. There was a curve in the green. Gregor was fairly sure that nobody could get from Michael Platte's house to Arthur Heydreich's house, or vice versa, without being in full view of other surrounding houses. Getting from Arthur Heydreich's house to the pool house was something else. The big problem would be the clubhouse. If that was shut up for the night, you could go by the path at the edge of the green and stay close to the buildings and be in and out without anybody being able to see anything.

But would anybody want to do that? Assuming your objective was to kill two people in the pool house, why would you necessarily go around that way to begin with? Especially since the security cameras were off. And they were off from . . . Gregor reached into the pocket of his jacket and pulled out his notes. Ten forty-five and twelve thirty. That was the middle of the evening, a time when there would be lots of people out and around, even on a work night. There would be people in the clubhouse. There would be people on decks, even in this weather. There would be people on the road. Why go through all the trouble of sneaking around on the edge of the green when sneaking could not keep you from being seen no matter what you did?

Gregor looked up and saw that Horace Wingard and Larry Farmer were looking at him anxiously. He'd spent a lot of his life with people looking at him anxiously. He straightened his shoulders.

"Let's go over to the Platte house," he said. "And let's walk. I want to see how this place plays out."

"We can go by the road or by the green," Horace Wingard said. "It is forbidden to walk across the green itself, of course, but there's a path—"

"Do many people walk across the green anyway?" Gregor asked.

Horace Wingard went red again. "Of course they do. It becomes a matter of pride to let people know that you're not following orders, or that you're above the rules. Of course, they expect other people to follow the rules. They think the world is coming to an end if some- body cuts across their lawn."

Gregor nodded. He was sure they did.

He stepped out onto the green anyway, looking up and down the circle of houses that surrounded it. All of those houses had huge walls of windows looking onto the course, and big decks where people could sit and watch the action. Gregor assumed they were set back far enough not to endanger residents and their windows from flying golf balls, but he might be wrong about that. Maybe people liked the idea of being close enough to the action to really feel it, at least every once in a while.

He looked from Arthur Heydreich's house to Michael Platte's house and back again. There was some kind of activity going on at Arthur Heydreich's that he couldn't quite make out.

"All right," he said. "If we do a direct run across the green, we'd get to the Platte house fairly quickly, and that's what I suppose he did when he went to work at the pool house. He should have shown up for work at what time that night?"

"Six," Horace Wingard said. "But I told you. Michael didn't keep schedules. Not really. He—"

Gregor waved this away. "He spent a lot of time screwing around, I know. Ten forty-five to twelve thirty. That's the problem. From the way this shapes up, everything would have had to be done between ten forty-five and twelve thirty. There would have been people in the clubhouse then. There would have been people around. Your gate is always manned? There isn't a time at night when the guards are off and residents use a key or a code or something like that?"

"Certainly not," Horace Wingard said. "Our gates are manned all day every day. It's one of our premier claims to distinction."

"But that back gate you mentioned," Gregor said. "For that, people have keys."

"They're not supposed to use the back gate," Horace Wingard said. "It's a service gate. It's only a few families who have children. There's a school bus stop on the road there. They use that gate. No-body else ever goes in or out of it."

"It doesn't matter," Gregor said. "That won't work, either. If the second man had come in by the back gate, he'd have had to cross the green to get to the pool house, or use the road or the path. But in any case, if he did that between ten forty-five and twelve thirty, it would be nearly impossible for him not to be seen."

"Well, it should have been impossible for Martha Heydreich not to have been seen," Horace Wingard said, "and Michael Platte and whoever else was here, but nobody seems to have seen anything. It's as if the security cameras went off and everybody went blind and deaf."

"But Martha Heydreich and Michael Platte were seen. It's in the notes I have. Several people saw them walking across the green to-gether. And they saw other people walking across the green. But Martha Heydreich and Michael Platte lived here," Gregor said ab-sently. "People wouldn't have been surprised to see them. They'd have been much more likely to notice a stranger, especially if he was a stranger on his own. Of course, he might not have been on his own. There's that."

They were coming up on the Platte house, and he wished he could say he could determine something from the way it looked. People's houses came to reflect them after a while. There were lawn ornaments and decorations, choices in the color of paint, repairs that were done well or done badly or not done at all. All the houses at

Waldorf Pines looked like they'd been cloned from the world's least interesting architecture.

Gregor came up to the back of the Platte house. He went past the green and over the path and directly into the backyard. The yard was empty. There was no lawn furniture. There were no toys the way there would be if the children here had been small. There were no ornaments. Gregor looked at one side of the house and then went around the deck to look at the other. It was all completely blank, and the odd thing was that the lawns of the houses on either side looked completely blank, too.

Gregor went around again to the center of the deck. It had a small staircase leading down to the path and the green, to make it possible for the people who lived there to get to the golf course without having to go around by the road. He looked around and saw that all the other houses had small staircases on their decks, too.

The standardization made his head ache.

He looked up at the deck. It seemed to be empty, but that might be the angle he was looking at it from. He went to the little staircase and opened the gate. He could see without having to work at it that the gate was for cosmetic purposes only. It would never keep anybody out. He climbed the short half-flight of stairs and came out on the deck proper. It really was bare of everything. There wasn't even a chair.

"I don't think you should be doing that," Horace Wingard called up to him. "You're on the Plattes' private property. You can't do that without a warrant, can you? You should come around and ring the bell at the front door."

Gregor was sure he should come around and ring the bell at the front door. He wasn't entirely sure why he wasn't doing it. What he was doing instead was pacing along the edges of the deck, looking back up the green, looking around the deck again, and feeling entirely without purpose or direction.

He stopped at the very center of the deck and contemplated the drawn curtains across the big sliding plate-glass doors. He remembered when sliding glass doors had been an important badge of status in the suburban world, but he was pretty sure that was a long time ago.

He walked across the deck and stood directly in front of the windows. He leaned in toward the glass to see if he could make anything out through the curtains.

Then he stepped back hurriedly and stared.

A second later, he made the best attempt he ever had at kicking in a door.

PART III

ONE

1

If Bennis had been there, she would have told him, in no uncertain terms, that he should have known better. He was not now, and he had never been, the kind of person who could kick through windows and jump off cliffs. Even at the Bureau, he had spent most of his time in front of a desk. He was good at thinking, and once he'd learned how to use the computer, he was also good at finding things and putting them together. It did him no good to wish he was Indiana Jones.

It was not Gregor Demarkian's finest hour. His feet hit the glass just as they were supposed to, flat on, but it didn't matter. The glass didn't break. He just bounced off it and landed on the deck on his side. He felt a sharp pain go up the side of his left leg. He had a sudden flash of insight that told him just what Bennis would say if he'd done something elderly, like broken his hip. Then he put his hands flat on the wooden decking and forced himself up. It worked.

Gregor was just thinking that he'd dodged a bullet there, and a big one, when he saw Larry Farmer peering through the curtains that covered the plate glass windows.

"Jesus Christ," Farmer said. Then he began hammering on the plate glass. "Mrs. Platte! Mrs. Platte! What are you doing?"

"Have you both gone crazy?" Horace Wingard demanded. "You can't break into a house. You can't break the windows. You need a warrant just to get onto this property, and now you're doing God only knows what."

Neither Gregor nor Larry Farmer was listening to him. Gregor, on his feet again, was looking through the plate glass and curtains another time. Mrs. Platte—if the woman inside was Mrs. Platte—was still standing on the chair Gregor had first seen her on, but she was no longer holding the noosed rope in her hands. Instead, it swung as if there were a breeze, its shadow clocking back and forth across the kitchen floor like some kind of manic pendulum.

"Jesus Christ," Larry Farmer said again.

Gregor Demarkian found himself wishing that Larry Farmer could say anything at all besides the cliché of the moment.

Larry Farmer pounded on the plate glass again. "Mrs. Platte," he yelled. "Come on now, Mrs. Platte. Open up."

Horace Wingard charged at the sliding glass doors, got a look himself at what was going on inside, and then backed away.

"Oh, my God," he said.

Inside the house, Eileen Platte had turned to look at them, or at least to look at the sounds coming from her deck. To Gregor, she looked dazed and unsure of herself, as if she'd forgotten what she set out to do.

Eileen Platte steadied herself on the cabinets. The chair she'd set up for herself was right next to the longest of the kitchen counters. The rope was wrapped around the kitchen chandelier. It was not the most coherent suicide plan Gregor had ever seen.

Larry Farmer started to move as if he were going to try breaking down the glass doors just as Gregor had, but Gregor held him off. In the kitchen, Mrs. Platte was still moving, very slowly, very slowly, but moving.

She leaned down and hopped a little to get back onto the kitchen floor. She picked up the chair and walked it back to the breakfast nook table from where it had come. Gregor watched her look over the table, straightening a place mat and then another one, moving the basket of nuts in their shells that served as a centerpiece. Horace Wingard was still fussing.

"We can't stay out here," he said. "We really do have to go around to the front door. There are legalities involved."

"If we leave here to go to the front door," Gregor said, "she might think we've gone away, and get back on that chair. We could stand on the front porch for a year while she was in here—"

"Yes, yes," Horace Wingard said. "I understand that. I understand that. But there are legalities. . . ."

A moment later, the legalities became moot. Eileen Platte had shuffled her way across the kitchen to the sliding glass doors. She pulled one of these back without pulling back the curtains. There was a low wind. The curtains blew back against her body and made her look like a ghost from a Thirties movie.

"I didn't hear the doorbell," she said, through the cloth that covered her mouth.

Gregor leaned forward and pulled the curtain away. He'd meant to be gentle about it, but the curtain was heavy, and there was a lot of it. He had to struggle to get it aside. While he fought with fabric, Eileen Platte stayed perfectly still. She was like a windup doll that had wound down.

Gregor got the curtain pulled back, and the three of them stared at a middle-aged woman in a blue sprigged house coat. She looked at them as if she found nothing at all odd about having three men on her deck in the middle of a morning.

"I didn't hear the doorbell," she said again. "I would have answered the doorbell. I'm supposed to answer the doorbell when it rings."

"I'm sure you are," Gregor said.

Eileen Platte looked away from them. "I was tidying up the kitchen," she said. "It always needs a great deal of tidying. I used to think it was Michael who made the mess, but now of course it couldn't be. It's a mess all the same. Maybe I make it myself. Stephen thinks I make it myself."

Gregor stepped into the kitchen and looked around. It was a big space, with cabinets going all the way up to a ceiling that it would take a ladder to reach. There was a big center island with a gas cooktop and a grill. Above it hung densely packed copper cookware, all shiny and looking as if it had never been used. The breakfast nook was a smallish octagonal space with a ceiling even higher than that of the rest of the kitchen. There were windows in the six angled walls that looked out, of course, on the green.

Eileen Platte sat down at the table there and looked at the three of them. "Am I supposed to be giving you something?" she asked. "Am I supposed to be making coffee?"

Gregor looked at Larry Farmer. "You'd better call an ambulance," he said. "She should be on suicide watch."

"But not with sirens," Horace Wingard said hastily. "We don't need sirens. There isn't any rush."

Gregor ignored him. Eileen Platte was sitting quietly, her hands folded on the table. She was looking at everything and nothing. Gregor couldn't help wondering if she were drugged.

"I'll call the ambulance," Horace Wingard said. "They won't be able to get in if I don't okay it anyway. I'll call them and then I'll be right back."

Gregor let him go without bothering to watch him leave. Then he sat down at the table opposite Eileen Platte. Her face was as white as if it had been made of plaster. Her eyes were dead.

"It doesn't matter anymore about Michael," she said. "There's nothing I can do for him. There's no way I can keep him safe."

"No," Gregor admitted. "There isn't."

"That was what I always tried to do," Eileen said. "Keep him safe. Even when he was little. Because he was always that way, you know. He was always like that. It wasn't the drugs."

"All right," Gregor said.

"I only said it was because that way, if Stephen believed it, I thought I could . . . he would . . . that he wouldn't be so sure of it. Wouldn't be so sure that Michael was . . . wrong. I don't think it mattered, really. I don't think he believed me. I don't think Stephen believed me. Sometimes I think Stephen hated Michael from the very beginning, from the first day we brought him home from the hospital. But that can't be true, can it? Fathers don't hate their sons that early, do they? They wait."

Gregor did not know what to say to this, but behind him, Larry Farmer was getting restless.

"Here's the thing," Larry Farmer said. "Mr. Demarkian? We can't talk to her like this. It won't be admissable. We haven't even read her her rights."

"We aren't going to arrest her," Gregor said.

"Yes, well, I know," Larry Farmer said. "But maybe that's just the way it looks now, you know. Maybe later it will be different."

Gregor didn't want to say that things would never be so different that Eileen Platte would be arrested for the murder of her son, because things did change. There was always the chance that he was wrong about some of the conclusions he'd already come to. He said nothing.

Eileen Platte was looking out the breakfast nook windows now. "I remember when we bought this house," she said. "I remember coming to look at it and thinking how much I like this, this octagonal thing. I thought it would be like living in a castle. That was my ambition growing up. I wanted to live in a castle. I wanted to be a fairy princess. I thought that if I could have a wand, I could make all the noise go away. All the noise and all the alcohol."

"Ah," Gregor said.

Eileen looked at her hands. "It's the same old thing. It's always the same old thing. But that wasn't what was wrong with Michael. I knew that from the beginning. I could see into him all along. I just kept hoping it would go away."

"What's she talking about?" Larry Farmer demanded. "Do you know what she's talking about?"

Gregor knew what she was talking about. It gave him the answer to a question he had been asking himself for a long time. Did anybody ever see a sociopath for what he was before he really got started? So many people didn't. Maybe their mothers did.

"I should get work done," Eileen Platte said, moving to get up.

Gregor put a hand on her arm. "Answer a couple of questions for me before you go," he said. "Some questions about Michael."

"There aren't any more questions to answer about Michael," she said. "Michael is dead."

"I know," Gregor said, "but there are some things I still don't understand. Like the safe-deposit box key. Did Michael have a safe-deposit box that you know of?"

Eileen looked startled. "A safe-deposit box? Do you mean in a bank? Of course he didn't have anything like that. If he'd had something like that, he would have used it, don't you think? He'd have put things in it. Valuable things in it."

"I don't know what he would have kept in it," Gregor said. "There was a key to a safe-deposit box in his clothes when he was found—found—"

"Dead," Eileen said.

"That's right, dead. There was the key, but there was no way to tell what bank it was from. We can't go to look in it if we don't know where to look."

"He didn't have a safe-deposit box," Eileen Platte said. "I know he didn't. If he'd had it, he'd have kept his money in it, and he didn't. He kept it upstairs. He kept it in his closet."

"A safe-deposit box isn't a convenient place to put cash," Gregor said. "It's usually used for things like important papers."

"Michael didn't have any important papers," Eileen said. "He had a passport, but that's upstairs on his bureau. Everything is upstairs just the way he left it, except for the shoe box, and I'm not supposed to talk about that. Stephen took it with him to work today. He said if I said anything about it, he would say it never existed, it would be just my word against his, and everybody would believe him. But I was the one who found it. I found it. And I knew where it came from, too."

"The shoe box?"

"What was in the shoe box. She didn't bring it in a shoe box. She had a big envelope, a big manila envelope. I saw her. She brought the envelope to the pool house when he was working one night, and I was just coming down to bring him something to eat. Not that he ate anything. He ate less than any other person I'd ever met. I made sandwiches with cream cheese and pimento olives the way he liked them and I took them down there and she was there first. And he took the money out of the envelope and counted it."

"Money," Gregor said. "You're talking about cash? How much cash?"

Eileen bent over and began to pick at the place mat in front of her. "I should have said something at the time," she said. "I should at least have told Stephen. What was she doing, giving him money like that, and in an envelope? But then, you know, I was just—I wasn't really sure. Because I saw them there and I didn't go in. I tried to listen, but I didn't really hear very much. And he counted and I thought I heard, but then maybe I didn't hear right. It was hard to know what to do, do you see that? And I thought about it and I thought about it and I thought about it, and the more I thought about it, the less I was sure."

"But you're sure now?" Gregor asked. "You're sure because you found the money in a shoe box?"

"In his closet upstairs," Eileen said. She leaned far over the table and whispered, "Twenty-five thousand dollars. In tens and twenties. When I found it in the closet, I took it down and counted it. I counted it over and over again. Then I put it back. I didn't know what to do with it. Then later I told Stephen about it. But that was the wrong thing to do."

Eileen sat back. She looked oddly satisfied, but at the same time she still looked blank. It was as if something inside her had broken down for good.

"The ambulance is on the grounds," Horace Wingard said, rushing in from wherever he had been for the last ten minutes. "They'll be at the door in an instant. Let's try to get her out of here without too much fuss."

Gregor didn't care about the fuss, but he thought getting Eileen Platte into a medical facility as quickly as possible was the best idea in the room. She was staring at the wall now as if she'd never seen one before. It wasn't clear that she was seeing it now.

"Let me just ask you one more thing," Gregor said, hearing the air brakes on the road. "Just to make sure I have this straight. You saw Martha Heydreich give your son a manila envelope with twenty-five thousand dollars in cash in it, when was this? Just before he died, months ago, last year?"

Eileen Platte was staring at him "It was just the week before he died," she said. "But Martha Heydreich didn't give him the money. She did. The one who thinks she's so perfect. I knew there was something wrong there. She isn't who she says she is. She really isn't. And Michael knew all about it."

"All about who?" Gregor asked.

"Caroline Stanford-Pyrie," Eileen said. Then she made a face, the kind of face children make when they think something is "yucky." Then she leaned very close to Gregor and said, "She thinks nobody suspects anything, but it isn't true. We all suspect something, even if we don't know what it is. Her and the other one. They're always walking around, making like the rest of us don't know anything. But we know enough to tell."

"Tell what?" Gregor asked.

"Tell that they're gay," Eileen said. "What else would two old biddies like them have to hide that anybody would care about? They're both gay and Michael knew it and then they killed him for it. I've been watching them ever since."

Eileen sat back, looking suddenly very happy and amused. Just then, there were the sounds of a door opening and the ambulance team coming in, ushered about by Horace Wingard speaking in hushed but very insistent tones.

"I will not have a fuss," he kept saying. "I will not have one."

Gregor was willing to bet almost anything that if he stepped out of the house and onto the road right this minute, he'd catch half a dozen people staring out their windows, ready to observe and report on whatever was going on.

2

It was Horace Wingard's job to "do something" about Eileen Platte's attempted suicide—or maybe not quite attempted suicide—and what he did was to run around looking important and barking directions into his cell phone. Gregor had no way of knowing if all the bustling was necessary. He did know that he and Larry Farmer should not stay in the house. Eileen Platte's husband was called. Various members of the ambulance team got to work checking blood pressure, heart rate, pupil dilation, mental responsiveness. Gregor listened to Eileen Platte cheerfully answer the question about who was president of the United States with "Dwight David Eisenhower!" and wondered again about drugs.

Out on the road, he caught up with Larry Farmer and took the man's arm. "Let's go do something on our own while Horace Wingard is distracted," he said. "Do you have somebody in your notes named Caroline Stanford-Pyrie?"

"Of course I do," Larry Farmer said. "We interviewed everybody, we really did. We interviewed every single resident of Waldorf Pines. We've got notes on all of them."

"Then let's go over there and find out if she's home."

"There are two of them," Larry Farmer said. "Two ladies, both widows, I think. The other one is Susan Carstairs. They're refined."

"What?"

"They're refined," Larry Farmer repeated. "You know what I'm talking about. They have really good manners. Their manners are so good, they make people nervous."

"All right," Gregor said. He had a sudden flash of a woman he had seen through the window of Horace Wingard's office, the woman he had recognized.

But Larry Farmer was just getting going. "I think it defeats the purpose, don't you? Having manners like that, I mean. What's the point in being all polite like that, if nobody will talk to you because you scare them? I don't know, Mr. Demarkian. I don't know what to say to people like that."

Gregor let this slide. "Which one is her house?" he asked. "Maybe we should go back towards the green."

He turned around and headed to the backyard, going by the side of the house where Horace Wingard was least likely to see him. When he got to the green, he stopped and waited for Larry Farmer to come through.

"I don't suppose I have any luck, and these women live in the house directly to the right of the clubhouse," he said.

Larry Farmer panted a little and shook his head. "I don't remember off the top of my head who lives in that house, but it's not them. They're over there."

Larry pointed across the green, so close to where they were it was almost next door. Gregor sighed. "I don't suppose the people who do live in the house next to the clubhouse have some secret to hide that Michael Platte might have found out about."

"They might have," Larry Farmer said, "but they didn't kill him. They've been in Florida since right after Labor Day."

Gregor let it go, and started across the green again, this time in a very small cut, toward the house that belonged to Caroline Stanford-Pyrie and Susan Carstairs. The route they would have had to take to get to the pool house to kill Michael Platte was plain enough, but at the time of night it would have been necessary to get there, it also would have been easily seen. It was as if these people lived on a stage set and kept track of each other with score cards.

Of course, if Eileen Platte had been telling the truth, Caroline Stanford-Pyrie had made that trek at least once at night, and early enough at night for Eileen to think it was a good time for sandwiches. Gregor wondered how many of the neighbors had witnessed that little jaunt, and what they had thought of it. Given the things people said about Michael Platte, they'd probably thought he was screwing another old lady.

Gregor started off toward the Stanford-Pyrie house, going a little farther out into the green this time, so that he could get a better look at the possible routes. The only one who really had a good shot at getting to the pool house without being seen was Walter Dunbar, and Walter Dunbar was the one person Gregor had seen only for a second, and only in passing. Even so, it had been a strong first impression. It wasn't hard to see what kind of a person Walter Dunbar was. Anybody who had ever worked in a large organization had met men like him. Gregor could certainly envision Walter Dunbar committing a murder, but he thought the murder would be much more brutal and direct than finding some esoteric way to light a fire from a distance.

Gregor corrected himself. That assumed that the murders were connected, and that there was only one murderer. It also left out the whole problem of Martha Heydreich. Still, it bothered his sense of proportion to think that there had been two, or maybe even three, murders in the same night, and in the same place, and more than one murderer.

He made his way a little farther out into the green. He looked around for 360 degrees. The problem remained intractable. He did another 360-degree turn, and realized that there was a teenaged girl sitting on a bench, staring at him. He stopped for a moment to stare back. The girl was blond and chunky, too heavy for fashion and wearing both too much jewelry and too much makeup. For a moment, Gregor wondered if he was seeing Martha Heydreich herself, complete with clown mask. Then the girl got up and walked toward him, and he could see she was much too young.

Larry Farmer was getting more nervous by the minute. "We ought to get out of here," he said. "Horace Wingard is going to have a cow."

The girl kept coming. Gregor waited for her. When she got close enough for Gregor to smell her perfume, she stopped. The perfume was Joy. Gregor recognized it because he'd bought it for Elizabeth half a dozen times, special gifts for anniversaries, because it was billed as the most expensive perfume in the world.

The girl was not chewing gum, but there was something about her that made her seem as if she was. Close up, she was even more outlandishly made-up than she'd appeared to be from afar. She sized Gregor up and down and shrugged her shoulders.

"Are you that guy," she asked, "the detective? I heard somebody say the police were bringing in this great detective because they didn't know who did the crimes."

"I'm Gregor Demarkian," Gregor said. "I am a detective, yes. I don't know how great."

The girl shrugged again. "I just thought I'd tell you," she said. "It's just retarded, what everybody is saying now. That Arthur Heydreich didn't kill Michael, I mean. Of course he killed Michael. I practically saw him do it."

"What?" Gregor said.

"Well," the girl said. "Okay. I didn't actually see him. I mean, I saw him, but I didn't see him kill Michael. Michael was out walking on the green, and Mrs. Heydreich was with him. I could see them from my window. And he came out of the house and sat on his deck. Then he went inside again."

"Do you even know if he saw them?" Gregor asked.

"Of course he saw them," the girl said. "Everybody saw them. It's so retarded, the way everybody acts like they didn't see anything that night, just because they're afraid the police will talk to them. It was a lie that Michael had an affair with her. He would never have had an affair with her. I mean, for God's sake, she was practically a gargoyle. He's having an affair with the other one though, that Mrs. Bullman. Did anybody ever tell you that?"

"No," Gregor said.

"She lives in that house over there," the girl pointed vaguely across the green. She could have been pointing at any house or none of them. "She came out of the house and watched them, and then she went across to the clubhouse. I saw her. She left her kids alone and everything. She was trying to see if Mr. Heydreich was having a drink at the bar."

"You know that—how?" Gregor asked.

The girl made a face. "I know that because I know what's going on around here," she said. "Mrs. Bullman and Mr. Heydreich have been screwing each other like rabbits ever since he got out of jail. I've seen them. Actually seen them. That's who the other body is, in the pool house. It's Mrs. Bullman's husband. They had to get rid of him, just like they had to get rid of Mrs. Heydreich, who's probably buried in the basement or something, or they took her out and dumped her in a river. There are rivers around here. And they had to kill Michael because he knew all about it, and he would never have just let them get away with it."

"Yes," Gregor said. "I see."

"You don't have to listen to me if you don't want to," the girl said. "I think it's just retarded the way everybody around here just does whatever and doesn't think about it at all. You tell me where Mr. Bullman is. You just tell me. I haven't seen him around since the murders. The two of them got together and killed them, and you're going to let them get away with it."

The girl turned on her heel and marched off, her exit made a little less impressive by the fact that the high heels on her impractical shoes kept sinking into the grass of the green.

"Who was that?" Gregor asked Larry Farmer.

Larry Farmer produced one of his signature sighs. "That," he said, "was LizaAnne Marsh. I think the usual term is 'piece of work.'"

TWO

1

Susan lost her head. This was not surprising, because Susan always lost her head. Back in the worst of it, when everything was coming apart, when the only thing keeping them alive was being able to think straight—well, Susan hadn't been able to think straight. Caroline wondered now, as she had wondered then, why she had taken the woman along with her. She could have made her exit on her own with a great deal more ease.

Ah, well, it wasn't hard to answer that one, Caroline thought. She'd always had her principles. And if they were, as her sons put it, the principles of the Mafia—so be it.

Gregor Demarkian and that idiotic man from the local police department were coming across the golf green. It was getting late in the day for that. The green was raked, and people still played on it well into the fall. Any minute now there would be a couple of old men with their bellies hanging over the waists of their golf shorts, done up in caps with little balls on them, teeing up. Caroline had a sudden shuddering moment of self-awareness. She lived among these people now. She would live among these people—or people just like them—for the rest of her life. It was the one thing she would never be able to forgive Henry for.

Gregor Demarkian and the Keystone Kop were climbing up to the deck. Susan gave a strangled sob and dashed out of the kitchen. Caroline heard her racing upstairs, and then the pounding of feet in the upstairs hall, and then the slamming of a door. She sighed. It was always the same. Time after time. Once, one of the lawyers had suggested that it would be better for everybody if they just drugged Susan into insensibility and stashed her in a closet somewhere until the publicity had died down.

Except, of course, that Susan hadn't been Susan then, any more than Caroline had been Caroline.

The two men made it all the way up to the deck itself, and Caroline made up her mind. She stepped out to where they were and waited until they were close enough to her so that she wouldn't have to shout, even out here in the wind.

"Mr. Demarkian," she said. "You may come inside."

"Inside would be good," the other man said.

Caroline turned to him. "I said Mr. Demarkian could come inside. I did not say you could. You can wait out here, if you like, or you can go back to where you came from, but you're not going to enter my house without a warrant. Am I clear?"

"Oh, wait," the other man said.

"I'm glad I'm clear," Caroline said. She turned to Gregor Demarkian. "If you could come through here," she said, stepping away from the sliding glass doors. "I'm afraid it's a bit of a step. They're a nuisance, these kinds of doors. I've never liked them."

"See here," the other man said.

"A warrant," Caroline said, not bothering to look at him.

Gregor Demarkian stepped into the kitchen. Caroline stepped in after him and pulled the sliding glass door shut. Then, just to make sure, she locked it.

"We should go into the family room," she said, waving to her left at the other end of the vast open space. "They were designed for young families, these houses. I'm sorry about your friend out there. I can never remember his name. Do you know mine?"

"I know both of them," Gregor Demarkian said. "At the moment, you're calling yourself Caroline Stanford-Pyrie. I think it's an interesting name. Very distinctive. It's not what I would have chosen under your circumstances."

"Susan thinks like you," Caroline said. "That's why she calls herself Susan Carstairs. But I thought it would be counterproductive. One of my sons studied film in college. He says that what you call this, what you call what I'm doing with my name, is 'hanging a lantern on it.' If you want to get away with something very outrageous, something everybody is going to pick up on right away, then you call attention to it, and sometimes they don't pick up on it. I don't talk to my children anymore, of course. But I remember that."

"Is that your decision or theirs?"

"Mine," Caroline said. "I know who I am, Mr. Demarkian, in spite of going under a false name. I know who I am and I know what I believe. And one of the things I believe is that loyalty to family and then loyalty to friends must outweigh any other considerations of any kind whatsoever. Legal considerations. Moral considerations. My sons didn't agree with me."

"I think you're being a little hard on them," Gregor said. "It was the biggest con in history, the biggest financial scandal in history. They must have known that as soon as they discovered it was going on. It wasn't going to stay hidden forever."

"It had stayed hidden for nearly thirty years," Caroline said. "Did you ever wonder how that happened, Mr. Demarkian? There was my husband, the great Henry Carlson Land, running this enormous business, with fifteen hundred employees, with trading partners all over the world. And he wasn't being shy about being seen, or being quoted, either. I have a scrapbook full of pictures somewhere, of the two of us. Charity balls. Opera first nights. Movie premieres. Alison and Henry, Mr. and Mrs. Carlson Land. I liked being Mrs. Carlson Land. Did you know that?"

"No," Gregor Demarkian said. "But I could have guessed."

"I was arrogant about it, too," Caroline said. "Part of it was just—well, when I was growing up. Everybody was always saying it was impossible. With the tax laws the way they were, and inflation, and people having so many other options for work rather than going into domestic service. The world I was born into was dead as a dodo, nobody could live that way anymore. Or, if you wanted to, you had to marry one of these new people, who didn't care about any of the things we thought were important. And then there was Henry, one of our own and still able to—well, able to."

"I think there are lot of people who would be surprised to find that you think Wall Street bankers are doing all that badly in this economy," Gregor said.

Caroline snorted. "Don't be ridiculous. It's not that they're doing badly. It's that they're thugs. That's what you have to be to get along in the market these days. And Henry was a thug. I should have realized it. I should have realized that it was impossible for somebody to be, these days, what Henry appeared to be. Well bred as well as well heeled. Operating in the old way, in a gentlemanly way. Do you know he never went into the office until ten o'clock?"

"Really?"

"Bankers hours, we used to call them when we were growing up," Caroline said. "Bankers worked less than other people because they were bankers. They didn't get out of bed at four and into the office by five-thirty. They had lives, real lives. We sat down to dinner at eight. We went to the opera and the symphony. We sponsored art exhibitions. We did all that kind of thing. You know the kind of thing, because you married one of us. You married Bennis Hannaford."

"She doesn't do much of that kind of thing anymore."

"It's the way people were supposed to live," Caroline said. "It's the way people of good family were supposed to live. And we were people of good family. I'm a descendant of travelers on the *Mayflower* on both sides of my family. Henry's great-grandfather gave a library wing at Yale, and his father gave the sports complex at Hotchkiss."

"Mrs. Land," Gregor said faintly, "or Mrs. Stanford-Pyrie, or whatever you want to call yourself. Your husband bilked investors and banks out of sixty *billion* dollars. Billion, with a 'B.' He ruined countless midlevel investors. Took their entire life savings. He brought down two international banks. And the last I heard, he was in jail for the next two hundred and twelve years."

"He's seventy-two," Caroline said. "I rather think he's going to cut that sentence short by a bit. The scam of the century," Caroline said. And then she laughed.

Up to then, they had been standing in the middle of the open space that was designated as a "family room"—Caroline preferred rooms with doors, thank you very much—and now she dropped down into a chair and stretched out her legs. Gregor Demarkian looked at her for a bit and then sat down himself, on the very edge of a love seat.

"The Susan you refer to," he said.

"She calls herself Susan Carstairs now," Caroline said. "It's Marilyn Falstaff, of course. Poor Neddy Falstaff. He was like Susan, really. He didn't have the stamina it takes to get through something like this. As soon as Henry decided to spill it all to the police and the FCC, Neddy couldn't take it, and there he went, right out a twentieth-story window. I was surprised he could get it open. Anyway, Susan needed somewhere to hide just as much as I did, so I took her along with me."

"And that was—"

"About two and a half years ago," Caroline said. "It's amazing how much time has passed, isn't it? It's been nearly seven years now since the smashup. And then, of course, there were lawsuits everywhere. Everybody was convinced I must have known all about it. I didn't. I wasn't brought up to stick my nose into my husband's business affairs. And I had money of my own, from my own family. I didn't see the justice in allowing a lot of—well, people, let's say. I didn't see why Henry's investors should be allowed to take my money."

"What have the courts had to say to that?"

"That I'm right," Caroline said. "My money is my money. Are you surprised?"

"No."

"The only problem left after that was the publicity," Caroline said. "And there was a lot of it. People yelling at me on the street. Henry's investors following me from place to place. And the reporters, of course. And the stories in the magazines and the newspapers and on television. And the books. My grandmother used to say that a lady never got her name in the papers except when she was born, when she married, and when she died. I should have listened to her. There were so many photographs of Henry and me at one thing or another, in society columns, in *Town & Country*. They just get dredged up and reprinted wholesale when anybody wants to write a story."

"So you changed your name and came out here," Gregor Demarkian said. "And then Michael Platte found out who you were."

"It bothered me, that business of his finding out who I was," Caroline said. "Who Susan and I were, I should say. You never met Michael Platte, of course. He was dead before you were brought in on this thing. But he wasn't a bright boy. He was a sociopath, that was certain. But he wasn't bright. And he was not curious. He didn't paw through old newspapers and magazines. I doubt if he ever listened to any news at all. That's why I always thought it must have been her who figured it out, and not him."

"Her?"

"Martha Heydreich," Caroline said. "She was a sociopath, too, if you want to know the truth. And absolutely the creepiest human being I've ever met."

"That's something I hadn't heard before," Gregor Demarkian said. "That she was creepy. What does that mean, exactly?"

Caroline shrugged. "It was uncomfortable to be around her. She was just—off, somehow. I don't mean all the silly exaggeration, the makeup, the endless piles of pink everything. I mean she just felt like she oozed. And I never believed all that stuff about her having an affair with Michael. I'm fairly sure Michael was more gay than not, if he ever got around to sex in the middle of all the drugs he took. And he took a lot of drugs."

"And you gave him twenty-five thousand dollars in cash," Gregor Demarkian said.

Caroline stared up at the family room ceiling. It had patterns in it. She had never known why. "I did give him twenty-five thousand dollars in cash," she said. "I suppose it was LizaAnne who knew about it. He told her, or she found out somehow. She was always chasing Michael around, stalking him. I'm old enough to know how those things work, of course. It was supposed to be a single one-time payment to keep his mouth shut, but it wouldn't have been that. He'd have been back for more. He had too big a habit not to be back for more. And I could never have counted on his not telling anybody. He was drugged too much of the time."

"It makes a good motive for murder," Gregor said.

"It does," Caroline agreed, "but I didn't murder him. All I did was buy a little time, time enough to get off somewhere else where nobody would know who we were. And I will guarantee you Susan didn't murder him. I could see her bashing somebody on the back of the head and then taking off, but not all the rest of this nonsense, fires starting with nothing to start them and then only after hours and hours. Susan, like Michael Platte, is not very bright."

"You're bright enough," Gregor Demarkian said. "And at the moment, you're really the only one with a motive I have."

"Well, blackmail is certainly a motive," Caroline said, "but if that's what you're looking at, you must realize it wasn't only me. There's Fanny Bullman, for one thing. By now that woman must have slept with nearly everybody at Waldorf Pines. It's really quite amazing. She's sleeping with Arthur Heydreich now. I think that's because he's become something of a celebrity. I marvel at the innocence of somebody who thinks that being arrested makes somebody a celebrity. Did you know that Henry is giving press conferences from prison? I don't know how he gets away with it, but he is."

Gregor Demarkian didn't look interested. "So Michael Platte was blackmailing you, and you think he might have been blackmailing Fanny Bullman."

"We could go on," Caroline said. "There's our esteemed manager, Horace Wingard."

"He has something to be blackmailed about?"

"It depends," Caroline said. "I don't know if he cares or not. It's nothing criminal. It's just that he wasn't born Horace Wingard, and the background he implies for himself is completely bogus. His name was something impossible to pronounce, Testeverde, something like that, and his father was an immigrant from somewhere in the Soviet Bloc. He went to public schools and some godforsaken community college, and then he just sort of reinvented himself as Mrs. Vanderbilt's private bouncer. I suppose it depends on whether or not the people who hired him here care or not. If they don't care, then Horace Wingard probably doesn't care, either."

"But you had him followed? You hired a private detective."

"Oh, no, Mr. Demarkian. I wouldn't bother to do that. I knew he was fake from the moment I met him, but I wouldn't do anything like that. No, I recognized him. Once, about twenty years ago, he got caught in the same police sweep in Fort Lauderdale during spring break as my son Jack. I went to rescue Jack so Henry wouldn't have a fit, and while I was taking care of that they were processing other people out, and one of them is now Horace Wingard. It's impossible to mistake him. He's such a peculiar-looking person."

"If you recognized him, maybe he recognized you."

"And gave Michael the information to blackmail me?" Caroline said. "Yes, I suppose it's possible. And, of course, if you wanted to go in for blackmail, Horace has the perfect position for it. Maybe Martha Heydreich had something to be blackmailed about. It wouldn't surprise me. I wish Walter Dunbar did."

"Why Walter Dunbar?"

"He's one of those people," Caroline said. "Complains about everything. Butts into everybody's business. Has a new petition for the residents' association every single meeting, and they're all vile. Ever since the bodies were found, he's been going on and on about how the murderer came right past his house and threw a garden hose on his deck, and he wants somebody to do something about it. What's anybody supposed to do about it? And what does a garden hose have to do with anything? You probably think it's a clue."

"It could be," Gregor Demarkian said.

"Well, maybe the murderer will come back and kill him because he knows too much," Caroline said. "At least that would get him out of my hair."

"What about the other body?" Gregor Demarkian asked. "I was thinking, earlier this morning, that we spend all our time thinking about Michael Platte, because we know who he is and we have some insight into what an investigation into his murder would look like. But we also have another body, and we don't know who it belongs to. We don't even know why it was where it was. I had someone suggest to me that it might be somebody named Mr. Bullman."

"That would be LizaAnne again," Caroline said. "Talk about sociopaths. Do you ever wonder why everybody in the world seems to be a sociopath lately? My sons are both sociopaths. They'd have to be to turn their own father over to the police. LizaAnne is Fanny Bullman's biggest competition for whore of Waldorf Pines. I think it drives her crazy that somebody as 'old' as Fanny Bullman can be sleeping with all these men. Of course, if she'd just take off about thirty pounds, there might be some more interest, but that's LizaAnne. She ought to get whatever she wants because she's LizaAnne. God, I've known Rockefellers without that kind of attitude."

"Do you think she could be right?" Gregor asked. "Do you think the unidentified body could belong to Mr. Bullman?"

"No," Caroline said. "You might as well check it out, of course, but Charlie Bullman is away on business a lot, which is when Fanny manages to do most of her damage. And this time it's been a while. Almost two weeks, I think. There might be something there. But there might not. It's hard to tell with Charlie and his trips. Even when he's home, he's not home. Mind you, she can do it most weekdays anyway, because Charlie works almost constantly. But I think if you check into things, you'll find that he's just off in Houston or somewhere on some kind of business trip. I find other people's marriages fascinating, to tell you the truth. They have two children, those two do, and that seems to be all there is to it. They can't have much time to talk to each other, and I don't see how she could possibly have the energy to sleep with him after all the sleeping around she's doing. And now Arthur Heydreich. She'd better watch it. There are news camera crews watching Arthur Heydreich. She could get caught."

"One more thing," Gregor Demarkian said.

"Fire away," Caroline said.

"On the night before the bodies were discovered," Gregor said, "on the night that the murders were actually committed. Were you out and around between ten forty-five and twelve thirty?"

"For goodness sake," Caroline said. "Of course I was. Everybody was. Susan and I went to dinner at the club and then we stayed to play bridge. A lot of people do. The club is always full to bursting until at least eleven thirty, and after that there are stragglers at the bar. I don't think Susan and I came home until midnight."

"And did you see anybody, in all that time, on the green, or going to the pool house?"

"Anybody at the clubhouse could have been going to the pool house. They're right next door to each other. And if you mean did I see Michael Platte and Martha Heydreich taking their walk across the green, of course I did. Everybody did, even if they tell you they didn't. We were all talking about it. You're not supposed to walk on the green at all, and those two—well, those two. You'd have had to see them together to understand."

"Were they fighting? Were they holding hands? Was anything memorable about them at all?"

"Not a thing," Caroline said. "And they never held hands, and Martha only had screaming fights when she had an audience. They were just walking across the green. They could have been going to the pool house. Michael was supposed to be working there. They

222

could have been coming into the club. They could have been doing anything. It wasn't as if it was the first time, Mr. Demarkian."

"Ah," Gregor Demarkian said.

Caroline stood up. "Do you know why I let you in here and not your friend? Because I do not expect you to tell anybody outside this room that you know who I am. Oh, I know you might have to if you want me arrested for the murder of Michael Platte and whoever else that was, but I didn't murder Michael Platte. And I don't welcome the prospect of having to change names and move to God only knows where yet again. I did not kill Michael Platte. I did not help my husband steal sixty billion dollars. And I want to be left alone."

2

Back in his office at the clubhouse, Horace Wingard was working out—mentally, with nothing on paper—just what it was that could go wrong from the way things were working out now. Horace Wingard did not like the idea of things going wrong that could not be anticipated. He had lived his life heading trouble off at the pass, and he wasn't about to stop now.

Miss Vaile was out there, sitting at her desk, doing work on the computer while she waited for him. She always waited for him. It was one of the things he had hired her for.

The introduction of Gregor Demarkian into this thing was good on a number of levels, Horace decided. It was especially good because, in the cleanup that was going to have to come after somebody had been arrested, he'd be able to tell new people interested in Waldorf Pines that Waldorf Pines had enough weight in the local community to require them to hire a high-priced consultant in case anything went wrong on the premises. Dealing with the kind of people who wanted to live at Waldorf Pines, it was never a bad move to associate yourself with celebrities. Gregor Demarkian was a bona fide celebrity, even if only a minor one. He had even been on television.

In another way, though, the introduction of Gregor Demarkian was a problem. He was not local. He was not Larry Farmer or Ken Bairn. Horace had known from the moment he was first introduced to the man that Gregor Demarkian was not about to allow himself to be ordered around, and not about to focus his investigation in the direction that was most likely to be good for Waldorf Pines.

Horace didn't give a flying damn if Michael Platte was dead. He'd wanted the boy off the premises for months. He didn't care about the identity of the unidentified body, either, because that was likely to be something he would not want associated with Waldorf Pines. He didn't even care about the strange disappearance of Martha Heydreich. The woman had been an embarrassment to have around.

All that mattered, in the end, was making sure that Waldorf Pines was safe, and that he himself was safe. And that was going to take planning.

He opened the big, deep drawer on the left side of his desk and got out his old-fashioned Rolodex. Everybody else in the universe had given them up, but he still found his useful. He looked through the entries he had for private detectives and discarded each one. He didn't want to know if a resident's daughter was having an affair with the son of a Mafia boss or if one of the women was shoplifting at every store from here to Philadelphia. He tried his professional contact list, but he had the feeling that if he asked his man at the FBI about Gregor Demarkian, he'd be told to take a long jump off a short pier. It was difficult, knowing how to approach this.

He drew his phone close to him and called out to Miss Vaile at her desk.

"Miss Vaile," he said. "That woman Mr. Demarkian is married to. She was, she is—"

"Bennis Hannaford," Miss Vaile said. "Engine House, on the Main Line. Those Hannafords."

"Ah."

"There was a scandal a few years ago," Miss Vaile said. "One of her siblings, I don't remember if it was a sister or a brother, anyway, whoever it was, committed a murder. And was executed for it, I believe."

"And was Miss Hannaford involved?"

"I don't think so, no."

"Ah," Horace Wingard said again.

"I could get some more information for you, if you'd like," Miss Vail said.

"Yes, please," Horace said. "Yes, I'd like that very much. Are Mr. Demarkian and Mr. Farmer still on the grounds?"

"I just saw them come out of the Stanford-Pyrie house. Or, Mr. Demarkian did. Mr. Farmer seemed to be standing on the porch."

"Fine," Horace said, although he didn't feel fine about that at all. "Tell me when they leave, will you? I want to talk to them before they go."

"Of course, Mr. Wingard."

Horace put down the phone. There had to be something, somewhere, to get this thing moving in the direction he wanted it to go.

Because the bottom line was simply this: Once the initial shock of the publicity was over, the deaths of those two people in the pool house and the disappearance of Martha Heydreich were not necessarily a bad thing. He was rid of two people he hadn't wanted around anyway, and the publicity was already fading into legend.

Horace Wingard could handle a legend.

What he couldn't handle was round two of a world-class scandal.

THREE

1

Larry Farmer was waiting on the deck when Gregor came out, feeling a little stunned by the entire conversation—or maybe by the entire situation. It didn't help that Larry was jumping around like a six-year-old who hasn't been allowed to play recess games.

"You really shouldn't do that," he kept saying, as Gregor began to walk across the golf green.

"I shouldn't walk on the golf green?"

"You shouldn't talk to suspects like I'm not here. That's not part of the agreement. You're supposed to be consulting. I need to know things."

"You don't need to know that," Gregor said. "Caroline Stanford-Pyrie isn't your murderer."

"You know that for sure? How can you know that for sure? And she's done something. I can tell. I may be a hick town sheriff, but I can tell."

"I want to see Arthur Heydreich," Gregor said.

He looked up and down the length of the golf course. The houses were not the same and yet the same all at once. It made him crazy.

Larry hurried up from behind—somehow, Larry was always hurrying up from behind—and pointed at a house that was nearly all the way around the circle from the clubhouse. Gregor nodded and headed for it.

"You can't just go barging in there," Larry said. "You need a warrant."

Gregor was about to say he didn't have time for a warrant, but it felt like a waste of breath. He cut across the green to Arthur Heydreich's house and rang the doorbell. The sound that came from inside was out of tune and echoing.

"Suspects won't just talk to anybody," Larry Farmer said. "It's not like television."

Arthur Heydreich opened the door and looked Gregor Demarkian straight in the face. He looked—untidy. His hair was uncombed. His shirt was twisted on his body. He looked like a man who just didn't care anymore. Or wouldn't, when he had a chance to think about it.

"Ah," Arthur Heydreich said. He did not bother to notice Larry Farmer.

"I'd thought I'd ask if I could talk to you," Gregor Demarkian said.

Arthur Heydreich made a face. "I didn't think there was anything to talk about," he said. "The police arrested me. They were wrong. Now I'm not arrested anymore."

"Well," Gregor said. "Your wife is still missing. There's that."

"Is there?" Arthur Heydreich said.

Gregor knew the signs. Heydreich's lawyer might have been a public defender, but he obviously wasn't one of the violently stupid ones you sometimes read about in cases that went to appeal. He must have told Arthur Heydreich not to talk to the police, and not to talk to reporters.

Gregor cleared his throat. "I can stand here forever. Or I can stand in the road. We could probably work up an audience if I stayed here long enough."

Arthur Heydreich shrugged. Then he looked straight at Larry Farmer and said, "Not you. And don't tell me it can't be done. I don't have to talk to the police if I don't want to. I never did have to talk to you."

"This can't happen," Larry Farmer said.

But it was the same here as it had been at Caroline Stanford-Pyrie. Maybe, Gregor thought, it was part of the Waldorf Pines mystique. Maybe all these people thought they were too important to talk to the local hick town fuzz.

"It's not like the neighbors don't know what's going on," he said, leading Gregor back through the house down a central hall. "Everybody knows what's going on. While I was in jail, the Pineville Station Police Department made themselves famous all over the county telling people I was the only person who could have committed two murders. The place is a mess. I don't care if you mind or not."

The place was indeed a mess, the kind of mess that happens when nobody bothers to so much as pick up a dropped napkin off the floor for days on end. Gregor was fairly sure this was not the way the house could have looked before Arthur Heydreich was arrested. He was also a little surprised to think it could have gotten into this state in only two days. Under the debris, it was more or less the same open space as the one Gregor had just seen in Caroline Stanford-Pyrie's house. The houses, then, were only dissimilar in their cosmetics.

Arthur Heydreich looked at the pile of dishes in the sink and the boxes from frozen food on the floor and said, "The maid left while I was in jail. Not that you can blame her. She'd been hearing for weeks that her boss was a vicious homicidal maniac who killed people wholesale and then burned them up. I wonder what they would have done if I hadn't seen that smoke and gone to investigate."

Gregor leaned up against the counter. It looked like the only clean space in the room. "They probably would have done the same," he said. "It's standard procedure. The husband is always going to be the first suspect."

Arthur Heydreich shrugged. "So I'm the first suspect. That's very nice. I'm on paid suspension at work. I think they were just going to fire me, but the lawyer I've got ran interference with that. I think Horace Wingard was going to invoke the no-bad publicity clause, or whatever it is, but he backed off from that, too. So now I'm here, and if you don't find out who did this, it won't matter what my lawyer does. I'll be the man who murdered his wife and got away with it."

"Did you murder your wife?" Gregor asked.

"As far as I know, my wife hasn't been murdered," Arthur Heydreich said. "At least, that was the last news I got. That's why they let me out of jail and let me come back home. The other body in the pool house was a man. Have they changed their minds about that now?"

"No," Gregor said.

"The lab results could be faulty," Arthur Heydreich said, "but if they were going to be, I'd think they'd make them faulty to their own advantage. I used to hear all kinds of things I didn't believe about police departments using any means necessary to get a conviction, but I didn't believe it before now."

"You don't know where your wife has gone?"

"No," Arthur Heydreich said.

"Do you think it's possible that she was involved in a scheme for blackmailing her neighbors?"

Arthur Heydreich blinked. "What are you talking about? Martha wouldn't blackmail anybody. And she wouldn't know anything to blackmail anybody about anyway. People around here did not tell Martha secrets. She didn't fit in that way. She didn't fit in at all. Maybe if I had realized it before we moved here, things would have been different."

"Things?"

Arthur Heydreich shrugged.

Gregor had not made anything like a promise to keep Caroline Stanford-Pyrie's secrets, but he didn't see any point in giving out information for no good reason at all. He found a way to phrase it that at least didn't lead to identifications.

"At least one of the people at Waldorf Pines," he said, "was being blackmailed—heavily blackmailed—by Michael Platte. This person is of the opinion that Michael Platte was not intelligent enough to have thought up such a scheme on his own. This person has also suggested that the person who did think up the scheme, the brains of the outfit, so to speak, was your wife."

"Ah," Arthur Heydreich said. "For God's sake."

"You don't think that's true?"

"I don't think it's true that Michael Platte was too stupid to come up with a blackmail scheme on his own," Arthur Heydreich said. "That's the kind of mistake people make about people who take drugs. They're so out of it when they're high, you think they're like that no matter what state their minds are in. But Michael Platte wasn't drugged all the time. He wasn't drugged even most of the time. And a right little shit he was, too."

"What kind of a right little shit?"

Arthur Heydreich shrugged, again. "My guess is he knew who was sleeping with who everywhere in Waldorf Pines, for one. I don't know what Horace Wingard thought was going to happen when he had the pool house closed up for the winter, but I could have told him in advance. Everybody and his sister-in-law was screwing like rabbits over there, and I don't mean just the teenagers. You wouldn't believe this place for sex."

"I might believe it," Gregor said. "The rumors around are that your wife was having an affair with Michael Platte."

"I know what the rumors are. That was supposed to be my motive. It wasn't true. My wife was not having an affair with Michael Platte."

"Can you really be sure?"

"Yes," Arthur said. "I know it for a fact."

"You're very definite."

"I have a lot to be definite about," Arthur said. "Martha was not having an affair with Michael Platte."

"Was she in partnership with him in a blackmail scheme?"

"No."

"You're definite about that, too."

"Yes," Arthur Heydreich said, "I am."

Gregor considered this. Arthur Heydreich was standing in the middle of the breakfast nook. He had been standing there the entire time he and Gregor had been talking. He did not look like he needed to sit down.

"Most people," Gregor said carefully, "in situations like yours, are more tentative about what they did and did not know before the murder."

"Are they? Maybe most people are guilty."

Gregor thought about that, too. In point of fact, he wasn't sure that there was any one way people behaved when they were guilty. There wasn't one way that they behaved when they were innocent.

"There are several people," he said, "who say they saw your wife taking a walk with Michael Platte on the golf course fairly late on the night of the murders. Do you believe that?"

"I don't believe she was taking a walk with him. She didn't like him. Maybe they met up on the green and they were going in the same direction. Michael Platte was an oozer. He oozed."

"Do you mind telling me what you were doing on the night of the murders?"

"I already told it to the police," Arthur Heydreich said. "I was up at the clubhouse for a while. I played some bridge. I had a couple of drinks. I left around eleven."

"And?"

"And I came back here," Arthur Heydreich said. "There isn't much else to do at Waldorf Pines. Golf, bridge, and sex, the upper-crust suburban dream."

Gregor thought about it. "You say you came back at eleven."

"That's right. Around eleven."

"That would have been during the time the security cameras were not turned on."

"That's not my fault," Arthur Heydreich said. "I can hardly be held responsible for whatever little incompetencies Horace Wingard has managed to commit now. And trust me. It's going to turn out to be incompetence. The man is an idiot."

"Did anybody see you leave the clubhouse at eleven?"

"I don't know."

"Did you talk to anybody going in or going out?"

"I don't know."

"Do you remember anybody remark on the time who might remember your being there?"

"No, of course I don't," Arthur Heydreich said. "Why should I? I wasn't on my way to commit a murder. I wasn't trying to establish an alibi. I was just spending a little down time at the club and when I got tired, I went home. Do you really think that everybody who isn't intent on slaughter goes around making sure other people remember when and where he comes and goes so they can testify to it afterwards?"

Gregor did not think that, but he didn't think Arthur Heydreich thought he thought it, either.

Gregor weighed his options. "A couple of people I've talked to," he said, "have suggested that you yourself were having an affair, with a woman named Mrs. Bullman."

Arthur Heydreich grimaced. "That'll be our LizaAnne," he said. "Now, there's somebody who could blackmail the entire population of Waldorf Pines and make a good job of it. If you think Michael Platte had brains behind his blackmail operation, that's where to look. LizaAnne Marsh. Our resident cunt."

"That's not an answer," Gregor pointed out.

Arthur Heydreich stood up. Gregor began to think he was not going to answer, and it struck him again that there was no reason why Arthur Heydreich should answer any questions at all.

Then Arthur Heydreich turned away. "I never," he said, "not even once, in all the time that Martha was here and with me, in all that time I never once had sex with anybody else. What I've been doing since I got out of jail is none of your business."

2

On the way back to the police station, Larry Farmer was in a snit.

"This isn't the way I thought it was going to work," he said. "I mean, as a consultant, I thought you'd consult. We'd do the regular police work, and then we'd talk about it with you. Talk about it. You know. We'd gather the evidence and then we'd show it to you and we'd talk about it. I didn't realize you were going to go around questioning suspects."

"You couldn't have questioned this particular suspect if you wanted to," Gregor said. "He was under lawyers orders not to talk. It's a good thing I was there and that he'd talk to me."

"But it doesn't matter if he talked to you," Larry said. "It's not official. You couldn't testify to it in court. Or could you? I can never get it straight, those rules of hearsay evidence straight. We need evidence, Mr. Demarkian. We need something solid we can bring in to court so we don't look like jerks. And we do look like jerks. Let me tell you."

"I need a map of Waldorf Pines," Gregor said.

"A map of it? Why?"

"So I can keep straight who lives in which house," Gregor said. "I've got notes, and I tried to draw my own map, but I need something more stable, I guess you'd call it. Did you do what I told you to? Did you call the Bureau?"

"Yeah," Larry Farmer sounded depressed. "God, those guys are badass. Even the women are badass."

"Did you put out an all-points bulletin? If we're going to find Martha Heydreich, we're going to have to make sure we look everywhere."

"Yeah, yeah," Larry Farmer said. "We've got them putting out notices and I don't know what, and we're going to be featured on *America's Most Wanted*. I'd never have thought of that. I gave them six different pictures, and I gave even more to the FBI. I don't understand why she isn't the easiest person to spot in the world. She's weird enough looking."

"And she probably doesn't look like that now," Gregor said. "And there's no real way, from those photographs, to tell what she actually looked like when she was at Waldorf Pines. She might as well have been wearing clown makeup."

"Yeah," Larry Farmer said. "Do you think that's the solution? Martha Heydreich murdered Michael Platte and the other guy and then took off? I guess it would make sense, you know, if we knew who that other guy was."

"I think the key to solving this problem is finding Martha Heydreich," Gregor said, "and beyond that, I'm not going to go. Not yet. Right now, I need to find my driver and get myself home."

"Home?" Larry Farmer said. "Home? Now? But you just got here. We haven't got anything done!"

"It's five thirty," Gregor said, "and I haven't even had lunch."

"Okay," Larry Farmer said, "it got late, but you don't understand. Ken Bairn is going to have a complete fit. I mean it. He went to all the trouble to get you out here, and—"

"And he's going to get exactly what he says he wants," Gregor said. "A solution to this mess. We've been out at Waldorf Pines all day. We've talked to everybody we could conceivably talk to. Did you send somebody out to talk to Stephen Platte?"

"Yeah," Larry Farmer said. "I sent Sue Connolly, if you want to know the truth. We don't have the staff for this kind of thing, Mr. Demarkian. That's another reason we got you out here. It was you or the state police, and Ken hates it when the state police are brought in. They treat us all like a bunch of hicks. They don't treat you like any kind of hick. You scare the shit out of them."

"That's fine," Gregor said, "but I'm going home, and I'm going to get something to eat. And I'm going to think for a while. Have a report for me on Stephen Platte when I get in tomorrow morning, and I'll be early. Oh, and the safe-deposit box."

"Right," Larry Farmer sat up. "I forgot about that. I forgot about the safe-deposit box."

"It belonged to Martha Heydreich," Gregor Demarkian said. "And

I'm pretty sure that when we find it, it will still be full. She couldn't have gone to empty it after the murders, and I don't think she emptied it beforehand. We're going to have to discover the name of the bank. It's going to matter."

"The name of the bank?"

"What's in the safe-deposit box," Gregor said.

They were coming up on the police station now. Gregor looked out of the car and thought that the entire place seemed to him to be forlorn. He understood Ken Bairn, in an odd way. He understood the need to keep and preserve something that had been yours from childhood. But the days of Pineville Station weren't numbered. They were over. They had been over long before Waldorf Pines was built. Waldorf Pines was like those machines that kept a body pumping blood and sucking in air long after the body itself had ceased to function. There would be no more places like Waldorf Pines built in Pineville Station. There would be no Pineville Station resurrected into a haven for the not-quite-upper-middle-class.

Gregor's car was parked in the police station's parking lot. Gregor got out of Larry Farmer's police car as soon as it glided to a halt.

"Do the things I told you to do, and I'll be back," Gregor said. "I'll be here first thing in the morning, and I promise you, you'll be able to arrest somebody this time, and it will be the right person, and it will stick."

"I don't see how you can know that," Larry Farmer said. "I've been with you all day. Have people been telling you secrets? I bet they have. I think you ought to tell me everything they said, so that I can at least know what's going on and report to Ken and Buck. We're the ones with our asses on the line here. You're supposed to work for us."

"I know," Gregor said.

His driver must have been waiting right inside the police station's door. He came hurrying out as soon as Gregor was on the asphalt. Gregor got into his car as quickly as he could, nearly desperate not to have to go on with this conversation. He tried to think of what to say to mollify Larry Farmer for an instant. All he could come up with was, "You should check into the background of Horace Wingard. His name isn't really Horace Wingard, and I think there might be something in his background."

"Horace Wingard? You think the killer is Horace Wingard? Ken will have a cow."

Gregor thought Ken Bairn probably had a cow every week, but that was one of those things better left unsaid, and so he left it.

3

For some reason, the trip to Philadelphia this time seemed to take forever. Gregor sat in the backseat of the sedan and went through his notes and the notes the police had given him. He understood how the police had felt about this one. Larry Farmer was not a good police officer. He was barely an adequate police officer. His "department" was not so much a department as an instant replay of Andy Taylor's Mayberry.

Still, Gregor thought, he could see why they had thought what they had thought. It was what he had thought. It was what anybody would have thought. And that, he had finally realized, had to be the key.

He shuffled through the folders and found the pictures of Martha Heydreich the police had given him, the copies of which they had presumably given the FBI and *America's Most Wanted*. The pictures were as impossible as they had ever been. The woman looked less like a human being than a piece of modern art. Her makeup was so thick, it practically had topography. Her clothes looked decent enough when they were viewed in black and white, but in any color picture they became immediately extreme. There was all that blinding, uncompromising pink. Nobody wore pink like that. This was a woman who was dressing to disguise herself in plain sight. She had meant to be unrecognizable.

He found the report from the lab again. There was really nothing more to read. The body had been so thoroughly burned there was almost nothing left of it. It was a miracle that they'd been able to get DNA. And it had burned fast. There was security tape of that room during the early hours of the morning, the hours before Arthur Heydreich had stopped because he thought he saw a fire. If there had been fire in there before he said he saw it, it would have showed up on the tape. The fire had to have started when Arthur Heydreich said it had, or close to it.

And that, of course, was impossible.

The driver pulled through the drive-through at some godforsaken fast-food place, and Gregor got a hamburger and a little bag of French fries. The stuff was so awful, he couldn't even feel any satisfaction in the fact that Bennis and Donna wouldn't approve.

He went back to his examination of documents, but the examination always came out the same. There should be the remains of a remote timer mechanism to start the fire, or there should be security tape of somebody entering the pool house just before or after Arthur Heydreich did on the morning the fire started. There was neither of those things.

The car got him back to Cavanaugh Street, and Gregor got out just as people began wandering out of the Ararat in little clumps. With his luck, Bennis would already have eaten. He did not count what he had done as eating, and he didn't think anybody else should, either.

He paid the driver and made arrangements for the morning. Then he walked down the street toward the restaurant. Donna had been active while he'd been out and around. Her own house was neatly done up as a gigantic Thanksgiving turkey. Most of the other houses on the block had little dangly things of turkeys and pilgrims and Indian corn. Whatever had happened to Indian corn? It had been a staple of public school Thanksgiving decorations when he'd been growing up. He couldn't remember seeing it for years.

He got to the Ararat and walked in, looking around the tables to see if he recognized anyone. In the morning and for most of the afternoon, the Ararat was the special province of the people who lived on Cavanaugh Street, but in the evenings they got a tourist trade, and they were very happy with it. Tourists meant money, and money meant a family restaurant that was not going out of business anytime soon.

Tibor and Bennis were sitting at a small table against the wall. Gregor almost missed them because he didn't expect to see them outside the window booth. There they were, though, Bennis leaning against the wall at her side, having coffee.

Gregor made his way to the back and looked around for a chair. There wasn't a single empty chair anywhere.

"Ah," he said, when Linda Melajian came running out to him. She had a chair in her hand, and she looked flustered.

"It's because it's for you," she said, "but you know how my mother is. There are fire regulations for capacity—"

"Oh, I'll take him home if you're going to have a problem," Bennis said. "I feel like I've been here all night as it is."

"No, no, we're just going to have to pull a chair from one of the tables when somebody leaves. With any luck, there won't be a line, or there'll be a couple in the line, or something. Gregor, do you know what you want to eat? Should I give you a menu?"

Gregor considered the hamburger from earlier in the evening. There were very few things in the world that could make him want to eat green vegetables. That hamburger was one of them.

"You could get me an Armenian salad and a cup of coffee," he said. "Unless that's too complicated."

"Don't be ridiculous," Linda said. "It's been an incredible day, let me tell you. And you've been on the news."

Gregor looked at Bennis and Tibor. Tibor said, "It was not you per se, Krekor, it was that woman who is missing. They had a picture of her and then a little story about the investigation. And you were mentioned."

"Well," Gregor said. "I suppose that's good news. Larry Farmer was telling me the truth about getting out an all-points bulletin. I've had an incredible day, too. I've been lied to, yelled at, accused of almost everything you can think of, and I've only just reached the conclusion that Sherlock Holmes was right. I want you to look at this."

He took his own homemade map of Waldorf Pines out of his briefcase and put it on the table.

"Who lied to you?" Bennis asked.

"A woman who calls herself Caroline Stanford-Pyrie told me that she recognized the manager of Waldorf Pines, a man who calls himself Horace Wingard, because she'd seen him once being processed at a police station in Fort Lauderdale, Florida, during spring break. She was there getting her own son out of jail."

"And you knew that was a lie?" Bennis said.

"Of course I did," Gregor said, "and if you don't, you've never been at spring break. But whether you've been or not, you'd know that they don't take down the information about what your father does for a living when you're being arrested for being drunk and disorderly. I do not as yet know where she recognized him from, but since she gave me that story while trying to divert suspicion from herself after she'd been discovered to have paid one of the murder victims twenty-five thousand dollars in cash in blackmail money, I'm going to find out."

"Right," Bennis said. "Are you going to be okay?"

"I'm fine," Gregor said.

Linda was back with his salad. He took it from her and shoved it over to the side of the table so that he was able to look at his map.

"Take a look at this," he said. "This is Waldorf Pines. On the night of the murders, the security camera system went down between ten forty-five and half past twelve. They didn't break, you understand. After twelve thirty, they were operating normally. They were operating when Arthur Heydreich went into the pool house the next morning. They just stopped working for that particular period."

"Well," Bennis said.

"There's no 'well' about it," Gregor said. "The cameras are not secure. The master switch that turns them on and off is right inside the door of Horace Wingard's office. Horace was there late and alone, but he went in and out often, and he never bothers to lock that door. Well, he wouldn't, of course, if he was in and working."

"And that means?"

"That means," Gregor said, "that somebody who was in the clubhouse that night walked into Horace Wingard's office when he wasn't there and turned the cameras off. And then, an hour and forty-five minutes later, that person came back and turned the cameras on again."

"And nobody saw this person? Ever?"

"Everybody saw this person. It just didn't matter, because there was nothing out of the ordinary in seeing him. Or her. Nobody saw this person going in or out of Horace Wingard's office, or actually throwing the switch, but the chances that that would happen are small anyway."

"All right," Bennis said.

"During that two-hour period," Gregor said, "somebody saw Martha Heydreich walking with Michael Platte on the golf green. Other people were wandering around. But that's not the kicker. The kicker is this: On the morning Arthur Heydreich found the bodies, the security cameras trained on the green show nobody else going into the pool house. What do you think of that?"

"Maybe whoever committed the murders stayed in the pool house all night," Bennis said. "Then, you know, the next morning—"

Gregor took the coffee cup and half drained it. "I suppose that's just possible, but that's not what happened."

"What happened?"

"Exactly what was supposed to," Gregor said. "And that's what makes me so angry."

FOUR

1

Martha Heydreich's picture was all over the news. This was not so surprising. It had already been all over the news, on the days after the murders were discovered, when everybody was convinced that the second body had to be hers. Fanny Bullman still found it hard to watch. The news stories were so different now. And there was something that just felt so . . . wrong about the whole thing. Fanny tried to think of Martha Out There, Somewhere. She came up blank. She'd never been able to understand Martha at the best of times. Now, the woman just seemed bizarre. Characters in books did the kinds of things Martha was supposed to have done. Characters in movies did them. People who lived in places like Waldorf Pines just got up and went to work and did the chores and thought about sex.

There were no chores to do in the house now. Everything was quiet. Dinner had been made and eaten and the dishes put away. Homework had been done at the dining room table and carefully checked. Clothes had been chosen and fought over and laid out in the bedrooms upstairs for tomorrow morning. Debris had been picked up in the family room. Three dropped socks had been picked up from the stairs. The children were settled in for the night in their beds, even if they weren't asleep. The lunch boxes were set out on the counter in the kitchen, waiting to be filled in the morning. No matter what happened, or when it happened, or how it happened, life in a place like Waldorf Pines was always the same.

Fanny went to the sliding glass doors of the family room and stepped out onto her deck. Across the way, she could see lights in Arthur Heydreich's family room. He had the curtains open over there. It could have been any night anytime anywhere. It could have been last July, except that it was definitely getting colder, and Fanny felt a little frozen standing on the deck in her bare feet.

She went back into the house and locked up. She went to the front door and made sure that was locked, too. She thought about all the things that could possibly go wrong. There were a lot of them.

Fanny looked around her foyer. There was nothing there. There was nothing anywhere. She went up the stairs and into the hall and down the hall to the master bedroom. Josh was sleeping. She could hear him breathing. Mindy was humming something to herself.

Fanny closed the master bedroom door behind her and looked around. Her parents had never had a master bedroom like this, even though they had always had much more money than she and Charlie did. Her father always said a house like this was not worth the trouble it caused. Fanny did not think it was the house that had caused the trouble.

She went to the back of the master suite and into the little hall with the walk-in closets on both sides. She opened Charlie's closet and stared at the things inside. There were clothes there. There were shoes there. There were belts and ties and cuff links and handkerchiefs and a little stack of pajamas that Charlie never wore. There was a built-in drawer full of boxer shorts. Three times a week, Fanny washed all the clothes and ironed them and folded them and put them up here in their proper places in their proper closets. If she opened the closet on the other side of the hall, there would be clothes like these in stacks there, too.

Fanny walked farther into the closet and looked around. She reached out for the suit jackets on the hangers and pulled at them. Suit jackets fell to the ground. She pulled at more. More fell to the ground. Suit pants were still hanging, still folded over the hanger arm where they had been hidden under the jackets. Fanny pulled and pulled and pulled some more. She pulled until all the suits, the pants as well as the jackets, were on the floor.

The heap of clothes at her feet looked awful. They looked like the aftermath of a fire. She reached out for the ties and pulled half a dozen of them at once. The ties fell to the floor on top of the suits. She opened the built-in drawer and took out the boxer shorts in big stacks. She put her hands on the handkerchiefs and tipped them over. They cascaded past empty hanger rods and landed on top of everything else, spilling out, being somehow too white next to everything else that was around them.

I could light a fire here, Fanny thought. *I could take a match and drop it on these clothes, and they would burn. Nobody would see me do it. There are no security cameras here. I wouldn't need kerosene or gasoline or any of that stuff. I wouldn't need anything but an ordinary kitchen match.*

And nobody would be able to tell.

Fanny thought about the fire in the pool house. She hadn't seen the aftermath of it, of course. Nobody had been allowed inside once the firemen and the police got there. Still, she could imagine it. Nail polish, the news had said—it was nail polish that had made that fire burn so brightly. Maybe no fire burned that hotly unless there was something to make it worse than just an ordinary fire would be.

Fanny looked down at the pile of clothes on the closet floor. Then she turned away and headed out of the master bedroom again. She went down the hall—Josh still snoring, Mindy still singing—and down the front stairs. She went back into the kitchen and opened the cabinet under the sink. There was a big box of garbage bags in the cabinet, the kind of garbage bags that came in rolls of a hundred or more. She took one out. She thought about it. She took another. Then she headed back upstairs.

Back in the master bedroom, Fanny threw one of the bags on the floor and kept the other. She went into the closet and opened the bag as widely as she could. She knelt down and started stuffing clothes into the bag, one handful of them after the other.

When the bag was full there were still clothes on the floor, and there were the shoes. She had forgotten about the shoes. She was out of breath, and no matter how hard she worked at it, she couldn't stop herself from shaking. People did things like this all the time. They did them in real life and they did them in movies. How did they get through it without dying?

She got the other bag and started throwing shoes into it, one pair after the other. They fell into the back and hit the floor beneath it with a *thud*. Fanny wished she could just breathe, just a little. She wished she had the courage to start a fire. She could throw a match on all this and then get the children and get out.

She tried to visualize the world made perfect, the world with all her problems erased. She saw only the memory of a bumper sticker: FORGET WORLD PEACE, VISUALIZE USING YOUR TURN SIGNAL.

The bag was full and the clothes were almost all gone. The clothes that were left on the floor were not important enough to pick up.

She had no idea what to do next, or why she would want to do anything.

There was a noise in the room and she looked up to see Mindy standing in the doorway.

Mindy was wearing Strawberry Shortcake pajamas. She should have been carrying a Teddy bear, but she wasn't. Mindy didn't go in for teddy bears. She only wore Strawberry Shortcake because she liked the color.

Mindy looked down at the two enormous black trash bags full of clothes and said, "Everybody at school says Daddy is dead."

2

Eileen Platte had been in the hospital most of the day, and most of the day she had been in this room, which was very carefully designed to have nothing in it that she could use to try to kill herself again. She had tried to tell the psychiatrist they had sent in to see her that she hadn't really been intending to kill herself, no matter what it looked like. Yes, she had stood on the chair. And yes, she had made a noose from a rope she had found in the garage, a rope Stephen and Michael had both used at one time or the other, to lash things to the roof rack of the bigger car. Of course, they weren't cars anymore. That wasn't what you called them. They were SUVs, or trucks, or "recreational vehicles." Eileen couldn't keep track of it all anymore. It made her tired.

For a while this afternoon, she had been able to hear Stephen, his harsh, booming voice traveling down the hall, saying things that should have embarrassed her.

"Always been a little off her nut," was one of the things he said, and "telling the police crazy stories that are likely to get me arrested."

It was obvious, though, that he hadn't been arrested. She didn't see why he ought to be. If they were going to arrest somebody, they should arrest her. Wasn't it always the mother's fault if the child turned out badly?

That was what she had been thinking about, sitting here all these hours. Michael had turned out badly. That was the conclusion she had reached this morning. But if Michael had turned out badly, it had to be for a reason. People were not just born bad. She must have done something. She must have said the wrong thing at the wrong time and turned some switch in his head, and now she ought to be grateful that it hadn't been worse.

"He's going to say I imagined it," she told the psychiatrist. "He's going to tell the police that I just made it all up, that it never existed, that the shoe box never existed, that the money never existed. I think he wants to keep the money. I think that's what that's about. He kept the money he found before."

The psychiatrist hadn't said anything. Eileen had read enough women's magazines to know that he wasn't supposed to. She wasn't sure what he was supposed to do.

"The other money wasn't so much," she said. "It wasn't any huge amount. It was just a couple of thousand dollars. And there was a key. Gregor Demarkian asked me about the key, but I didn't tell him. I didn't lie, but I didn't tell him. It was Martha Heydreich's key. Stephen didn't find it."

The psychiatrist still said nothing, and Eileen found herself drifting off. It was very peaceful, sitting in the chair the way she was. She felt as if she were floating in a vast ocean, and nothing and nobody would ever be able to find her. She would float away, and when she had floated away far enough, there would be mermaids singing. There were mermaids in the *Odyssey*. There were mermaids in "The Love Song of J. Alfred Prufrock." She had never paid enough attention in school.

When she got back to her room, the sun was shining. There were birds making fretful noises outside her window. They had given her a pill. It had made her sleep. She lay down in her bed and drifted off again.

Here was something she liked more than any of the rest of it. She liked the way this made her feel that she could sleep and sleep, sleep and sleep, forever, without anybody being able to wake her up. She would be like a princess in a tower, and some day a prince would come to kiss her awake. What she really wanted was for no prince to come at all. She would just sleep. And if a fairy godmother ever asked to know where she was, people could say that she'd left on vacation, and never come back.

Stephen's voice at the end of the hall had been strident, insistent, a little panicked.

"She tells all these stories," it said. "She tells them and she has no idea whether they're true or not. She tells them and then she can't remember if she made them up or not, and then everything goes to hell."

A little while after that, Stephen came down to the room and sat in its one, hard-backed visitor's chair. He had his jacket unzipped. His hair was very mussed. He sat with his legs apart and his forearms on his knees and watched her for a while, as if it would be useless to talk to her. The light in the window came and went and came again. There were clouds out there. Eileen could tell.

"I don't know what you said to them," he said, "but they had a warrant when they came to my office. A warrant when they came to my office. Can you imagine? It will be all over town before you know it. I could have been arrested."

Eileen reminded herself that she was on a deep sea. The law of the sea said she did not have to answer questions. She would never answer questions again.

"They found the money," Stephen said. "It was sitting right there in my desk drawer. I hadn't had time to do anything with it yet. Do you think when you do these things? Do you ever think at all?"

Eileen almost said that she was thinking right then, right that minute, but if she'd done that, it would have started a conversation. She didn't want a conversation.

"There's all kinds of shit hitting the fan at the moment," Stephen said. "I hope you're satisfied. I hope this is what you wanted."

What Eileen wanted was Michael back. Michael just the way he always was. Michael as she had loved him from the very first moment she had seen him in the flesh. Sometimes she thought she could still feel him moving around in her body, the ebb and flow of him that last two months or so before he was born. Sometimes she thought she could see him in his playpen the very first year, slamming soft toys one against the other as if his life depended on tearing them apart.

Stephen had gotten up and gone after a while, and then there had been nothing but the bare empty room and the silence that choked it. The day had gone on without incident, except that a nurse had come in to bring her lunch, and a nurse had come in to bring her dinner, and yet another nurse had come in to bring her pills to swallow. Of course, there was a nurse always on watch just outside the door, because they were all afraid she would make another attempt to kill herself.

She had known, stringing the rope up this morning over the beam, that the beam was only decorative. It would not hold. She would not die. She would step off the stool and into the air and then she would fall, creating a mess in the kitchen, making a noise. When Stephen came home, he would find her lying there, and she would give him no explanation.

She had no explanation for anybody now, either, except the obvious one. She had seen Michael with Martha Heydreich on the night he was murdered. That was it. Everybody at Waldorf Pines had seen the two of them together. She had stood on her own deck and watched them walking across the green, far away, almost at the pool house, and for a moment she hadn't recognized them.

It was one of the odder things about Martha Heydreich that if you saw her unexpectedly, and couldn't get a clear look at the color of her clothes, you almost wouldn't know who it was.

3

Horace Wingard was getting ready to shut up the office. He'd stayed late tonight, because he always stayed late, and because tonight was not a good night to seem to be ignoring the finer details of his job. The announcements about the search for Martha Heydreich were everywhere. He'd had three or four people stop in to comment on them tonight. Miss Vaile was still at her desk, typing away at the computer. He wasn't sure why she hadn't gone home. He wouldn't keep her this late unless he was in the middle of a true emergency, and this was not really an emergency. It was, he thought, the difference between acute and chronic disease. Acute disease was an emergency. Chronic disease was just something you put up with, because you had to. Because it was there.

Most of what Horace had been doing for the past several hours was just make work and unnecessary. He had gone over the figures for the maintenance of the golf green. Keeping the turf in shape was getting more expensive every day. He took out the folder with the specs for repairing the pool and went over that yet again, although there was nothing he could do about it anytime soon. The pool was a big selling point at Waldorf Pines. It was heated, and supposed to be open and ready fifty-two weeks a year. They were going to have to rethink the club dues soon, no matter what kind of fuss it was going to cause.

When he finished with the figures, he went to the computer and looked up the data on the new people asking to buy houses at Waldorf Pines. There were not very many houses for sale. Even when the complex had first opened up, there had been nice long waiting lists of people who had wanted a house here. People were afraid of themselves and each other these days. That's why they wanted the gates and the locks and the security cameras. He was a little surprised that none of the three couples with applications in had dropped out of the process.

You had to at least pretend to be exclusive, Horace thought. That was one of those things he had learned on his way up. People always cared most about who was being kept out. That was why Horace didn't mind LizaAnne Marsh. LizaAnne was crude about it, and she was rude about it, but she was not dishonest. People could complain about her all they wanted to, but she was only saying what all of them thought.

Horace put everything away and looked around the room. Everything was in its place. All the issues were resolved for the night. He got up and started turning off lights, going from one to the next like an old-fashioned lamplighter on a street that had just been fitted for gas.

When the office was dark, he turned back to look at it. People at Waldorf Pines thought they had secrets, but they didn't really. Horace Wingard knew all about them. He had made it his point to know all about them. He went out into the anteroom and closed the door behind him. Miss Vaile looked up from her computer.

"Are you going home now, Mr. Wingard?"

"I thought I might as well," Horace said. "There isn't anything to do around here any more tonight. Although we might look ahead to problems for tomorrow."

"Tomorrow?"

"Figuratively speaking," Horace said. "Over the next few days, perhaps. Or the next few weeks."

Miss Vaile cocked her head. "Do you really think he has the answer, then? Gregor Demarkian? Do you really think he knows what happened in the pool house?"

"I have no idea," Horace said. "But it wasn't that I was thinking about. I was thinking about other things."

"I'll admit," Miss Vaile said, "I've been worried. First the murders, then the mistake about the murders, then Mrs. Platte trying to commit suicide. It feels like everything's out of control. It's not a feeling I like."

"It's not a feeling I like, either, but I think that it is under control, as best it can be. As long as there is a solution of some sort, I don't think we have to worry about that in the long run. No, it's something else, something I've been expecting for some time. I have notified upper management. They are prepared for it coming."

"Are they?" Miss Vaile said. She looked momentarily confused. "Should I be? Is this something I'm going to have to contend with?"

"We'll all have to contend with it for a while," Horace said. "But I'm not sure that, in spite of the bad publicity, well, I'm not sure that the bad publicity will be all that bad. People are very odd that way, these days. Fifty years ago, it would have mattered outside the bounds of its real importance. It would have been a matter of principle. But these days, the only principle is money, and there is certainly enough money."

"I don't think I understand you," Miss Vaile said.

Horace smiled, and went to the coat rack to get his coat. Except for the very top of the summer, he always wore a coat, and the coat he always wore was a Chesterfield. He always wore gloves, too.

"Do you remember a man named Henry Carlson Land?"

"Do I remember him?" Miss Vaile said. "He's still in all the papers. He gives press conferences from prison. You have to wonder how so many people could be so fooled so much of the time."

"They weren't fooled," Horace said. "At least, a lot of them weren't. The small fry were, I suppose. They didn't know who they were dealing with. It's the great vice of most small investors. They don't really want to be bothered with their money. But the rest of them, the banks, and the brokerages—well, those people knew. They were just trusting to their ability to make it out in time. And most of them were wrong."

"I still don't understand," Miss Vaile said. "Did Henry Carlson Land—was Waldorf Pines one of his properties? Are we about to go bankrupt? Is that what the problem is?"

"Absolutely not," Horace said. "Henry Carlson Land didn't own properties. He just pushed money around. Until it all disappeared, of course. That's what you must never forget, Miss Vaile. Don't ever rely on the appearance of wealth. The appearance of wealth Is easy enough to fake."

"You're making me very nervous," Miss Vaile said. "I wish you wouldn't."

"Then I'll stop," Horace said. "It's about time I got home, at any rate. I'll see you in the morning, Miss Vaile."

Horace left the building, but he did not go home. Home was, after all, still Waldorf Pines, and he had no intention of being caught on Waldorf Pines's security cameras making a phone call in the middle of the night.

Instead, he left the clubhouse and went right across the parking lot to the front gate. He said hello to the night guard and kept on walking. He walked down the long, curved road that led away into Pineville Station. The night was cold and his shoes were hard. There was a slight wind blowing against his face as he went.

He went down the road and down the road and down the road. At about a fifth of a mile from the gate, the road curved sharply to the right. He went all the way around the curve until he came to a small copse of trees that he knew could not be seen from the entry to Waldorf Pines. He went into the trees and made sure he was well away from the road.

When he was sure he could not be seen by anybody, he pulled a cell phone out of his coat pocket and turned it on. It was not his usual cell phone. He had bought this one, prepaid and anonymous, the day after the bodies had been discovered, just in case.

All it would have taken to ruin the entire plan, of course, would have been to find that there was no cell phone reception in the copse. Fortunately, the reception was just fine. It was better than it was at Waldorf Pines, and Waldorf Pines did a lot to make sure its reception was as good as money could buy.

Horace flipped to the little address book. There was only one number there. He had programmed it into the phone on the day he bought the phone. He had been wearing his gloves on that day, too, and he was fairly sure that nobody he knew was watching him.

Of course, that had been in the King of Prussia Mall, so there was no reason to worry that somebody he knew would be watching him.

Horace punched in the call and waited. The phone rang and rang and rang, and he felt suddenly irritated that he couldn't know if the person on the other end was also hearing the ringing. He wondered what he would do, and when, if the person he wanted didn't answer. He'd gone to some trouble to find out the best time to call.

A moment later, the phone was picked up, and a man said, "*Philadelphia Inquirer*. Martin Roark."

"Mr. Roark?" Horace said.

"Who's this?" Martin Roark asked.

"It doesn't matter who this is," Horace said. "It matters that I have information you want. About, let's call them 'the malefactors of great wealth.'"

"Who *is* this?" Martin Roark asked again.

Horace sighed. "I'm the person who can tell you how to find Mrs. Henry Carlson Land."

FIVE

1

It was rare that Gregor Demarkian had one of those nights when he just couldn't sleep. On most nights, he didn't even toss and turn. Bennis said she was fascinated with the way he could just lie back still and drift off without so much as a crossword puzzle to relax him. Gregor said that he didn't need to relax, because he was usually so tired that the chance to sleep was like being hit over the head with a two-by-four.

That night, however, there was no two-by-four, and it was well after two when he was repeating the same message over and over again.

"There's a sort of protocol to these things," he kept saying. "You go out to wherever it is that has a problem and you look into it, and there's usually something so complicated that it takes a week or ten days to figure it out. You feel like you've earned your fee. They feel like you've earned your fee. *The Philadelphia Inquirer* starts getting ridiculous with its commentary. There it is."

"You keep saying 'you,'" Bennis said. "You mean 'I.'"

"The whole thing is perfectly ridiculous," Gregor said. "I knew what was going on within hours of looking into it—well, no, I didn't exactly. But I knew who the murderer was. And then yesterday. Well, yesterday."

"If you mean earlier today, you should say that," Bennis said.

"Earlier today then. A garden hose. I mean, for God's sake. Who would use a garden hose?"

"Who would use a garden hose for what?"

"And the guy was perfect," Gregor said. "They could have gotten him out of central casting. You should have seen him. It was like that comedian's dummy come to life. I don't remember the comedian's name. Don't ask me. He uses dummies. And then—do you know what it is? It's television. And crime novels. That's what it is."

"That's what what is?"

"This idea everybody has that it's perfectly rational that a murderer will do all sorts of weird things just to disguise the murder, or for fun, or something or the other. He'll put the corpse in a Santa Claus suit to make a statement. Or she hated the victim so much, she dressed him up in garlic to show that he was an emotional vampire. Or something. And do you know why murderers don't really do things like that? Do you know why?"

"They don't have the time?" Bennis suggested.

"They don't do that kind of thing," Gregor said, "because when they do that kind of thing, they're likely to get caught. And they know it. Assuming that you're an intelligent murderer, you know, and not the kind of person who thinks it makes sense to slam a baby against a wall until its skull breaks just because it won't stop crying—"

"Gregor."

"You know what I'm talking about. Assuming you're an intelligent murderer and not one of the tribe of congenital idiots, you don't do anything out of the ordinary unless you absolutely have to. And that's why, when you find something out of the ordinary, you have to pay attention to it. Do you see what I mean?"

"I might see it a little better if I was awake," Bennis said. "What time is it? What are we doing up?"

"I'll talk to you in the morning," Gregor said. "I want to leave early."

It was true that Gregor wanted to leave early, but not true that he was getting up to get ready. It was much too early for that.

He just couldn't stop pacing.

2

He did call ahead, to Pineville Station, just to make sure he didn't arrive to find the town and its officials all asleep. Then he sat back in his hired car and worked out the logistics of it on a legal pad. There were logistics here that had nothing to do with what the murderer had and hadn't done. There were things that had to do with what Waldorf Pines was and what it wasn't, and those kinds of things always interfered with an investigation. Who was sleeping with whom. Who was not sleeping with whom. Who had a drug problem. Who was stealing small sums of money from the company till. It was always necessary to contend with that kind of thing. It took a while to sort it out and know what was irrelevant.

The car passed out of the solid core of Philadelphia suburbs and began to move through territory that was more rural. It was easy, living in Philadelphia, to forget just how rural most of Pennsylvania was. There were the Amish, of course, but there were always hundreds of small family farms, truck farms and dairy farms and even some horse farms. There were dozens of small townships just like Pineville Station, and all of them had one thing in common: all of them were dying.

Gregor had never understood how, if the country as a whole had nearly twice as many people now as when he was born, so much of that country seemed to be emptying out of people. There had been thriving towns in these places for generations, towns that hadn't needed a big-box store or a massive corporate employer to survive. Now it was as if all the people in them had forgotten whatever it was they were supposed to do to keep a town going without help from outside.

There was something fundamentally illogical about all that that Gregor's brain couldn't process this early in the morning.

The car bumped down into Pineville Station itself. The brick buildings looked uninhabited at this hour of the morning.

The driver started to turn in to the Pineville Station Police Department parking lot, but Gregor waved him off to the other side of the street. He had arranged to meet everybody in Ken Bairn's office, because getting the explanations out once was easier than getting them out a dozen times. Here was something he didn't like about consulting: The need to get permission to do whatever it was you needed to do next to make sure the case was solved and solved in such a way that it could be prosecuted. He would have been happier this morning if he could just have gone out to Waldorf Pines himself.

He was getting out of the car in front of the municipal building when its front door opened and Buck Monaghan came out. He looked only half dressed for work, although by now it was close enough to the start of the real day that Gregor thought he should have been perfectly professional.

Buck reached out and took Gregor's briefcase and his copy of *The Philadelphia Inquirer*, which was still unread.

"You were in a hurry," he said.

Gregor got his briefcase back. "There's always the chance that the murderer may do something stupid," he said, "although this one hasn't been stupid yet. Well, in perhaps one point. Is everybody upstairs?"

"In Ken's office, yes," Buck said. "Are you going to do a Hercule Poirot and give us the solution? Don't you need all the suspects together in one room in order to do that?"

"I'm not sure anybody ever really does do that," Gregor said. "No, this morning, I'm not giving out solutions. This morning, I'm asking for what I need and for some force beyond poor Larry Farmer to help make an arrest. You do have other police officers in Pineville Station besides Larry Farmer?"

"Two, I think," Buck Monaghan said.

They went up the steps and into the building. Gregor marveled again at what towns had found possible in his childhood and before that they no longer found possible now. They went up to Ken Bairn's office and found the doors wide open and Delores Martin and Sue Connolly sitting together near the anteroom desk.

Delores looked up and said, "We're just hoping you're going to tell us that those people at Waldorf Pines are all murderers and we should lock them up."

Gregor shook his head and headed back to Ken Bairn's inner office.

Ken was sitting behind his desk, the chair turned so that he could look out the window into town. Even from here, Gregor thought, it didn't look like much of a town.

Ken turned around. "Are you going to tell me that everybody at Waldorf Pines is a murderer?" he asked. "I knew when this started that it wasn't going to do us any good."

"Everybody at Waldorf Pines isn't a murderer," Gregor said. "Only one person is. But that was inevitable. I can tell you one thing that might help your relations with Horace Wingard."

"What's that?"

"As I told Larry Farmer last night, he's operating under an assumed name," Gregor said. "Not that there's anything illegal about that, because there isn't. In the United States, you're within your rights to use any name you want to as long as you do not do so with an intent to defraud. I don't think Horace Wingard intends to defraud anybody. He just wants very desperately to be anybody else but who he was born to be."

"And who was he born to be?" Buck Monaghan asked.

"The son of a working-class father," Gregor said. "But you do realize, he isn't the only one. There's Caroline Stanford-Pyrie and Susan Carstairs. They're operating under assumed names, too."

"I knew there was something like that going on," Larry Farmer said. "That's why she wouldn't let me into the house yesterday. I still say you had no right to do what you did there, Mr. Demarkian. Suspects have no right to refuse to talk to the police—"

"Of course they do," Gregor said. "And you should know that. Anyway, she talked to me when she wouldn't talk to you, and that worked. And I'd have said nothing about it, except that it isn't going to matter much in the next day or two. If Horace Wingard hasn't called the papers to tip them off yet, he will as soon as we've made an arrest."

"Tip them off about what?" Ken Bairn said.

"About the fact that Waldorf Pines is harboring the wife of Henry Carlson Land, the same wife that half of Land's investors think is hiding most of the money that Land bilked out of investors in his Ponzi scheme. And in case you're wondering, he's known pretty much from the day Alison Land showed up. He's probably been keeping the knowledge in reserve for an emergency, and this is beginning to look like an emergency."

"Beginning to?" Buck Monaghan said.

"Alison Land," Larry Farmer said. "My God. That must mean the other one is Marilyn what's-her-name. There have to be a million lawyers looking for those two. But how did you find that out? They've been hiding for over two years."

"They weren't doing much of anything to disguise themselves except living at Waldorf Pines, which is a place where they wouldn't be expected to be," Gregor said. "But then it's the nature of Waldorf Pines that matters, too, as much as the identity thing. All through this thing, there are too many people pretending to be somebody they aren't. That's true of Horace Wingard. It's true of Caroline Stanford-Pyrie and Susan Carstairs. And, of course, it's true of Martha Heydreich."

"All that makeup," Larry Farmer said. "I kept thinking that must be hiding something. I suppose now she's wandering around Waldorf Pines, being somebody else, and we haven't either noticed her."

"Well," Gregor said, "the last time she was at Waldorf Pines, she was definitely being somebody else, and you could say that the entire time she was at Waldorf Pines she was somebody else, or at least, like Horace Wingard, somebody other than she had started out to be. But she's not at Waldorf Pines now. By the way, speaking of people who are or are not at Waldorf Pines, when you did your initial investigation, did you look into the whereabouts of somebody named Charles or Charlie Bullman?"

"I suppose I ought to have," Larry Farmer said.

"The notes I have from you say that Charles Bullman was away on a business trip on the day you first went to Waldorf Pines to investigate," Gregor said. "And you were told that by his wife. After that, there isn't anything at all, which sounds to me like you didn't follow up. I've been told by several people, however, that not only was Charles Bullman not at Waldorf Pines on the day the bodies were discovered, but he hasn't been there since. At all."

"Wait," Buck said. "Do you mean that's the answer? The other body in the pool house belongs to this Charles Bullman?"

"No," Gregor said. "Do you remember that I said there were several things that mattered? Let me spell them out. First, nobody in this case is what he or she seems to be, and that includes most of the people we've met at Waldorf Pines. That's true in the usual sense, meaning that people put up a good front for the public, but it's also true in that a fair number of people there are hiding their real, or at least original, identities. So there's that, yes."

"Yes," Buck Monaghan said.

"Good," Gregor said. "The second thing to remember is that Waldorf Pines itself is not what it pretends to be. It is not an upper-class gated community. It's gated, all right, but in fact it's aimed at the high end of small town and the low end of corporate success. It is not a place for aristocrats. It is a place for people who like pretending to be aristocrats. And that means something very important. It means that the people of Waldorf Pines are not independent. Reputation matters to them in a very real and unequivocal way. Being suspected of a murder, for instance, can get these people fired, or destroy their businesses. So can a lot of other scandals that might not affect them if they were actually what they pretend to be. Michael Platte had a nice little line of blackmail going at Waldorf Pines and that blackmailing is why Michael Platte is dead."

"The blackmail," Ken Bairn said. "Not because he was having an affair with Arthur Heydreich's wife."

"This was how I was trying to explain it to Larry yesterday. Michael Platte is the key to all of this because Michael Platte's behavior is the catalyst for what everybody else is doing here. And I don't mean that it's the catalyst for the murderer, although it is that. There's a lot of seriously strange behavior going on at Waldorf Pines, and most of it has nothing to do with who was murdered or why. But it all has to do with Michael Platte."

"It's incredible that somebody who was that much of a total screwup could be that effective," Buck said.

"He was effective because he paid attention, and because he knew what people like his parents cared about. But even so, I'm fairly sure he wasn't having an affair with Arthur Heydreich's wife," Gregor said. "Although I'd be willing to bet anything that it was Martha Heydreich's safe-deposit box key we found on his body. You'll have to look into that later. But there's a third principle here, and you can't forget it, because it matters. Murderers do not do strange and outlandish things for the hell of it. The real world is not a murder mystery. It's not even an episode of *Law & Order*. If there's some aspect of your case that seems particularly unnecessary and bizarre, the chances are good that there was some need for it to be particularly unnecessary and bizarre. And this case had something particularly unnecessary and bizarre from the beginning. One of the bodies was in the pool, whacked on the back of the head in the standard manner for that kind of thing, dead of drowning because he was alive when he went into the pool. That's fine. But the other body was burned until it was unrecognizable."

"But you don't know that that was what the guy intended," Larry Farmer said. "He could have meant the whole pool house to have burned up. Or she could have. You know what I mean. You start the fire meaning for it all to go up in flames, and then somebody comes along and calls the fire department too early, and there you are."

"Possible," Gregor admitted, "except for the fact that in order for that body to have been in the condition in which you found it, the murderer would have had to start the fire directly on the body to begin with. He'd have had to douse that body with enough accelerant to make sure it went up and went up good, and he'd have had to light the match almost directly under it. That's a lot more forethought than you would have put into it if you'd wanted the entire pool house to go up, and not at all what you would have done if you'd wanted to disguise both of the bodies. The swimming pool was full. Michael Platte's body was floating in water. No fire would have disguised what happened there under any circumstances. There's only one reason for that fire to have been started where and how it was, and do you know what that reason is?"

"No," Larry Farmer said.

"That reason," Gregor said, "is the fact that the identity of the second body is the most important point. If you know the identity of the second body, you know who committed the murder, and you can figure out why without working too hard for it. The second body was the key, because the second body was the reason there was a murder at all. And that brings us to the stupid thing,"

"Nothing seems all that stupid so far," Buck Monaghan said. "In fact, this whole thing is beginning to sound like something out of one of those detective novels you've been complaining about."

"No, no," Gregor said. "The whole thing is incredibly simple. It was so simple, I almost missed it. But here's the thing. Two things in this case happened because the murderer knew that the first thing you were going to do when you discovered the bodies was to arrest Arthur Heydreich for the murders. The first thing was the burning of the bodies. The second thing was the depositing of a small garden hose on Walter Dunbar's porch."

"Walter Dunbar?" Larry Farmer exploded. "I can't believe it.

Walter Dunbar is an ass. He's a prick. He's one of those guys who runs around making himself important any way he can. We don't even know somebody put that garden hose on his porch. He could have made it all up. It could have been his own garden hose. He just wants to act like he knows everything and have an excuse to call us all hicks and idiots."

"Exactly," Gregor said. "That's exactly why that garden hose was thrown onto his deck. It was, in case you can't see it, nearly perfect. Anything that happened, no matter how trivial, would have gotten Walter Dunbar up in arms and telling the world, but something that happened on a night when murders were being committed—well, it was the perfect thing. Walter Dunbar is Walter Dunbar. He'd be sure to tell everybody he met about it, his neighbors, the police, the newspapers if they asked. That was exactly the point."

"I don't know what you're talking about," Larry Farmer said.

"I think you ought to get those two police officers and take me out to Waldorf Pines," Gregor said. "I don't believe in murderers who run around doing extra murders to keep people quiet, or whatever the reason's supposed to be, but I don't like the idea of letting this person run around loose. He's entirely too good at this."

3

The drive out to Waldorf Pines felt as if it took forever, and it took longer because Larry Farmer spent it talking to Horace Wingard on his cell phone.

"Nobody's trying to ruin your life," Larry kept saying. "Nobody's trying to ruin anybody's life. We're just trying to do our jobs . . . yes, I know what my job is . . . yes, I know what Waldorf Pines means to Pineville Station . . . well, why do you have six news vans parked in front of your gate?"

The news vans were, most definitely, parked in front of the gate. There were so many of them that Gregor was afraid they wouldn't be able to get inside. And it wasn't only the news vans that were causing the problem. There were also sightseers, people who had shown up in their cars for no good reason Gregor could tell, plus sightseers from Waldorf Pines itself on the other side of the gate. Reporters were trying to climb Waldorf Pines's low stone wall. People with phone cameras were climbing trees and taking pictures of the people milling around in the clubhouse parking lot.

One of the young officers in the front of the car flipped the siren on, and people began to move back and away. The car inched forward, more and more slowly, more and more insistent. The officer started leaning on the horn as well as blowing the siren. He got them all the way to the gate when there was another obstruction. It was Horace Wingard. He was standing athwart the passage as if he could physically protect it with his own body.

It was an act, but Gregor Demarkian had to admit it was a very good act.

Gregor tapped the young officer on the shoulder and asked him to stop. "I might be able to help with this a little," he said, "and it's something we need, anyway."

"Something we need?" the officer asked.

"Yes," Gregor said. "I should have thought of it. But I don't think it will matter. It will only waste time."

Gregor didn't know if the officer was naturally uncurious, or if the situation was just too tense to allow for questions and conversation. The officer stopped the car. Men and women swarmed around it, including many reporters with microphones. Gregor opened his door and stepped out, getting it closed just in time to keep a young woman reporter from landing on Larry Farmer's lap.

"Jesus Christ," Larry said from inside the car, and then the door was closed.

Reporters closed in around Gregor now, and he had to back up all the way against the police car to keep from getting run over.

"Mr. Demarkian," one of them yelled, "are you here about the Land financial scandal? Is that really why you were called in by the Pineville Station Police Department?"

This was so ridiculous, Gregor didn't even try to answer it. If he had been here looking for Alison Land, he wouldn't have come on the request of the Pineville Station Police Department. That would have been an FBI operation, and they wouldn't be looking at retired agents to help with it.

"Mr. Demarkian," another reporter yelled, "do you think Alison Land should be required to pay back the money her husband stole? What about the small individual investors who lost everything they had?"

"Mr. Demarkian! What do you think of Alison Land living in luxury in a place like Waldorf Pines when many of the investors her husband ruined are looking forward to a retirement eating dog food?"

"Mr. Demarkian! When did you first suspect that Alison Land was hiding out in Waldorf Pines, and why didn't you immediately inform the public of her whereabouts?"

Did they go to journalism school for this? Gregor wondered. *Did they really?* Tommy Moradanyan Donahue could think of better questions to ask in this situation, and he wasn't out of elementary school.

He also knew something about jurisdiction, too.

Gregor edged his way toward the gate and Horace Wingard.

"There's something you've forgotten," Gregor told Horace when he got up next to him.

"What's that?" Horace said.

"This isn't the only entrance to Waldorf Pines."

Horace Wingard looked momentarily appalled. Then he turned his back to the reporters and ran off through the clubhouse gates.

Gregor Demarkian turned back to the mob. A dozen microphones were suddenly shoved into his face.

"Ladies and gentlemen," he said, "if you'll take the road you came in on just a little farther along the curve, you'll find the back entrance to Waldorf Pines. You might want to go and check there. If he's got any sense, Arthur Heydreich is right now trying to get out that way in an attempt to avoid being arrested for the murder of his wife."

EPILOGUE

1

It was cold on the day the call came from the National Surgery Registry Database, cold enough so that Gregor didn't have time to be annoyed about institutions that refused to name themselves anything anybody could recognize. Maybe annoyed was not the word he was looking for. He had only been finished with this case and Pineville Station for three days, and in those days Bennis had said "but I still don't understand" at least forty times. Bennis did not usually have a problem understanding things. In fact, for Gregor, her usual problem was understanding things far too well. Gregor was not the kind of person who would cheat on a wife, but if he had been, he truly hoped he'd have the sense to know that Bennis was not the kind of wife you cheated on. She'd know you were doing it before you did.

The call came in on his cell phone as they were walking back from the Ararat on a clear November morning. Donna Moradanyan Donahue had managed to get at least half the buildings on the four-block stretch that was the neighborhood decorated to look like something having to do with Thanksgiving. When Donna decorated, it was not a minor thing. Entire buildings were encased in crepe paper.

Roofs sprouted gigantic papier-maîché Indian corn crowns. Streetlamp poles were encased until they looked like actual candy corn, monstrously enlarged by a nuclear accident. Gregor had never understood why the city of Philadelphia didn't complain about the streetlamp poles, but it never did.

Surely, he thought, there had to be a bureaucratic Death Star somewhere, or a division, or an agency, that had to have six different kinds of paper to allow anyone to decorate a lamppost, and then had to have those six kinds of paper filed for each post and then had to have them all filed again for each new use at each new holiday. That was the way these things worked.

The call came and he fished his phone out of his pocket while Bennis was still talking.

"It's all well and good to tell me I ought to think," she said, "but I've been thinking, and so has everybody else. You'll note they aren't saying anything about this on the news. And you know why they're not. They're not saying it because they're not getting it. And they're not getting it for the same reason I'm not getting it. Because it doesn't make any sense—"

"It makes perfect sense," Gregor said over the top of his phone. Then he asked a question into it, and another one, and said, "Thank you." He put the phone back into his pocket. "They do get it," he said. "They just haven't had the proof they needed to announce it. I do understand their reluctance to announce anything until they were sure they were covered. They're now covered, and they'll probably announce sometime tonight."

"They announced that they arrested Arthur Heydreich," Bennis said. "Nothing stopped them from announcing that."

"Nothing could stop them," Gregor said, "the man was arrested in full sight of half the mobile news vans in the greater Philadelphia area. The arrest made CNN."

"I did notice. But I don't see why they were willing to arrest him when they didn't have whatever it is that you think they've got now.

I mean, they'd already arrested him before, and they had had to let him go and drop the charges, so why did they arrest him again when they didn't have—what is it you think they're supposed to have had?"

"What I just got in that phone call," Gregor said.

"Which tells me nothing," Bennis said. "You're being very annoying."

"I'm not being annoying," Gregor said, "I just want you to think like an intelligent human being. The first thing Larry Farmer ever told me, the one thing both Buck Monaghan and Ken Bairn kept repeating, over and over and over again, is that they couldn't be blamed for arresting Arthur Heydreich because it looked like it was impossible for anybody else to have committed the murder. And they were right. They were more right than they knew. Just studying the notes, and looking over the site, there really was nobody else who could have committed those two murders. The security cameras were off from ten forty-five to twelve thirty, but that just kept somebody from being caught on tape. That isn't a quiet time at Waldorf Pines. There were people on the green and there were people in the clubhouse. Arthur Heydreich was in the clubhouse himself. He was seen by half a dozen people. Martha Heydreich and Michael Platte were seen by more than that walking together on the green. Technically, I suppose, the murder could have been committed by anybody who was in the clubhouse between those two times, because the clubhouse is right next to the pool house. But none of those people had any reason I could see for committing two murders. And none of them was completely blank on the time between ten forty-five and twelve thirty. Arthur Heydreich tried to tell me he'd left the club at eleven, and that nobody had seen him, but it's his unsubstantiated word. And the fact is that people did see him, on and off, just not going from the clubhouse to his own house. He was out and about in all the right places during the time that matters. He was in the club when the cameras must have been turned off. There's no reason why he shouldn't have been in the club when the cameras were turned on again. Granted, it's not the kind of thing I like. I like solid, hard evidence. I wish somebody had seen him go into that pool house. But I don't think the prosecutor is going to need that."

"It sounds on the news like everybody had enough reason to kill everybody in that place," Bennis said. "Alison Land. Who would have thought it? I don't see what good hiding was going to do her, though. Those lawsuits were going to go through whether they could find her or not. If she gave Michael Platte twenty-five thousand dollars, I don't see why she didn't kill him."

"She didn't need to," Gregor said. "This is Henry Carlson Land's wife. She has lots of money stashed somewhere. She paid him off to buy herself time. She was going to disappear again. She had the resources to disappear. Why kill somebody and risk being caught if you don't have to?"

"And Arthur Heydreich had to?"

"He thought so," Gregor said. "He had a job he liked and did well enough at, but it was at a very conservative firm, conservative in more ways than one. So he couldn't have a serious scandal, and he also couldn't be perpetually suspected of having murdered someone, never mind two someones. And yet he knew that if he committed those murders, he'd be the first to be suspected, and he'd probably be arrested. So he needed a way to make sure that once arrested, he would have to be released. And the best way to do that was to let the police think what they would think automatically, let the police arrest him for it, and then make sure that they couldn't make the charge stick. And the way to make sure that they couldn't make the charge stick was to make sure there was no way to identify Martha Heydreich's body as Martha Heydreich. And if you know that much, you ought to know enough to be getting on with."

"You're saying that Martha Heydreich was actually a man," Bennis said, "and either Arthur Heydreich never figured that out, or they were both gay."

"If Arthur Heydreich and Martha Heydreich were a gay couple with Martha in drag, there would have been no reason to murder

Martha Heydreich in the first place. And yes, I do know that there have been cases where one spouse has kept her gender identity secret from the other over the course of a very long marriage, but if you look at those cases what you'll find is that nearly all of them involve a woman pretending to be a man. It would be a lot harder for a man to be pretending to be a woman. If Martha Heydreich was gay and in drag, Arthur Heydreich would have known she was gay and in drag, and there would have been some kind of arrangement. Or, for that matter, Martha could just have come out. Arthur wouldn't have much trouble finding a job in Philadelphia as a gay man with a partner. And if he wanted to stay at his present firm without being uncomfortable, he and Martha could have murdered Michael Platte and gone on as before. Obviously, then, Martha Heydreich could not be a gay man in some sort of permanent version of cross-dressing."

"So that means Martha Heydreich was a woman," Bennis said, "and that means Arthur Heydreich must have done something to tamper with the DNA evidence. But could he do that? Could anybody do that? And how did he light that fire, anyway?"

"He lit the fire by walking into the locker room, lighting a match, and throwing the match on the body, which was already covered with nail polish. He'd done that the night before. Covered it with nail polish. He could light the match because the lights in the locker room were out—he'd broken the bulbs the night before—and because the security cameras in that room were very carefully set not to catch residents without their clothes on. There'd been a flap about that. So all he had to do was to walk in there and toss the match. The cameras wouldn't have caught anything. And, in fact, given that the cameras caught nothing else and there was no sign of a timer in the debris, that's the only way the fire could have been started. He killed them both the night before and just left the bodies where he wanted them."

"Somebody could have come in and found them before he got the fire started," Bennis said.

"That's true," Gregor said, "and if that had happened, he'd have been largely doomed. But it wasn't too likely. The pool house was undergoing repairs. Michael Platte was supposed to be there guarding it and it was the middle of the night. He did get there first thing in the morning just in case Horace Wingard took it into his head to check the place."

"And the DNA? How did he tamper with the DNA?"

"He didn't," Gregor said.

"But I thought you just said Martha Heydreich was a woman."

"She was," Gregor said. Then he stopped in the middle of the sidewalk. "Look at that," he said, pointing up the street at the brownstone house they lived in. "I think that's Marty Tekemanian and the nephew. The one who's coming to be a graduate student at Penn and needs an apartment. Did I tell you that Marty was bringing a nephew?"

"Yes," Bennis said. "You did tell me that. But I want you to tell me about Martha Heydreich. I want to know—"

But Gregor was already on his way up the street, moving as fast as he could without actually running. He was painfully aware that there was a time, and it wasn't that long ago, when he had been able to move much faster.

Behind him, Bennis was hurrying, too. She was also muttering.

2

For some reason that was not immediately apparent, Marty Tekemanian was nervous about showing this apartment to what turned out to be his cousin.

"It's a beautiful place," he was saying as Gregor pulled up. "It's a little musty, but we've had somebody in to clean, and we're having a real do up this coming week. And you can't ask for a better location. This has to be the safest street in the city of Philadelphia proper. And you're not all that far from Penn."

"I'm sure it'll be fine," the cousin said. "I mean, considering the rat holes I've been looking at lately, it would have to be the pit of hell for me to hate it. You should stop worrying about it."

"Oh," Marty said. He looked at Gregor. "Mr. Demarkian. This is my cousin, Steve Tekemanian. Steve, this is Gregor Demarkian. He's—"

"I know who Gregor Demarkian is," Steve said, grabbing Gregor's hand and pumping it. "He's been all over the news for the past three days. And before that, too. Do you live here? Right in this building?"

"For the moment," Gregor said.

"Mr. Demarkian and his wife bought a town house at the other end of the neighborhood," Marty said. "They're renovating it. When they renovations are done, they're supposed to move."

"Assuming the renovations are ever done," Gregor said.

Bennis reached them. "The renovations will be done," she said, coming to a halt. "I'm Bennis Hannaford Demarkian. Who are you?"

"That's polite," Gregor said. "Aren't you the one who went to dancing class?"

"I'm Steve Tekemanian," Steve said. "I've read all your books. I think you're fantastic."

"I like him already," Bennis said. "I've been thinking. It must have to do with the garden hose."

"What has to do with the garden hose?" Marty asked.

"The solution to the murder," Bennis said, "which, apparently, everybody in the entire world knows except me, and Gregor won't tell me. It must have to do with whatever it was he used the garden hose for. Because he used the garden hose. He threw it on that man Walter Dunbar's deck. And you haven't said anything about it."

"I haven't said anything about it," Gregor said, "because it wasn't that kind of important. The garden hose was a deliberate red herring, an anomalous occurrence that he hoped would make law enforcement think twice about any automatic assumption of his guilt. He threw the thing on the deck of the one person in the entire complex who could actually have gotten from his house to the pool house while the security cameras were on without being caught on camera. And by a very nice coincidence, it also happened to be the house of the man most likely to broadcast the event to the world at large.

Sometimes, it really is the case that people just get lucky. And it wasn't necessary for Arthur Heydreich to make his red herring a serious clue. In fact, the less sensible it seemed, the better off he was. That way, he'd have people running around trying to explain something that had no explanation."

Marty Tekemanian looked pained. Steve Tekemanian looked delighted.

"Are we doing this? Really?" Steve said. "Do people do this around here all the time? That would be great. I mean, it would really be great."

"Steve is studying to be a forensic pathologist," Marty said. He looked pained, again. Gregor thought that Marty looked pained far too often.

Bennis just looked exasperated. "This really is annoying of you," she said. "I get the picture. Arthur Heydreich wanted to murder his wife and Michael Platte because—wait, was it because they were having an affair? Didn't you say they weren't having an affair?"

"That's right," Gregor said. "They weren't having an affair. Michael Platte was blackmailing Martha Heydreich the way he was blackmailing a good third of the people at Waldorf Pines."

"But that doesn't make sense, either," Bennis said. "Why kill his wife if she was the one being blackmailed?"

"Oh, I've got that," Steve said, "it's because he hated whatever it was she was being blackmailed for."

"Exactly," Gregor said. "You really are letting this get out of hand, you know. He's beginning to look smarter than you are."

"I'm trying," Bennis said. "Arthur Heydreich killed them both because of whatever his wife was being blackmailed for, and then he left the bodies in the pool house over night and then he went into the pool house in the morning and lit a match and threw it on Martha Heydreich's body in the locker room because he didn't want anybody to be able to identify the body as Martha's because if they did they'd know immediately that he was the one who killed them. And then somehow he switched the DNA—"

"No," Gregor said patiently. "He didn't. Didn't I just get a phone call? And isn't it the one I've been waiting for? And the one I've been waiting for was coming from where?"

"Some agency thing with a name that makes no sense whatso-ever," Bennis said. "You said that yesterday."

"Wait," Steve Tekemanian said. "I'll bet I can guess. The National Surgery Registry Database."

"He is smarter than you are," Gregor said.

"Maybe he just reads different magazines," Bennis said.

"The National Surgery Registry Database is a registry of informa-tion on people in the United States who've had sex change surgery," Steve Tekemanian said. "It's very—I don't know the word we want here. Very careful about what information it gives out. The registry is needed because people who have had sex change surgery can be more liable than people who haven't to run into certain medical problems in the long term, and almost all of them are taking hor-mone therapy. So it would be dangerous to do something like blank out all the records of the surgery or of their treatment, but at the same time—"

"At the same time," Gregor said, "there's still an enormous amount of negative feeling about people who are transgendered, and espe-cially about people who have had the surgery. Not all transsexuals want people to know they're transsexuals. That's why, when the po-lice ran the DNA, they came up blank on an identification. The regis-try will give out information when they deem it appropriate, but their files aren't available for the kind of global database search done in a criminal investigation. I've been wondering this whole time if Arthur Heydreich knew that, or if he even considered the possibility that there might be medical records out there about his wife. My guess is that he committed the murders too soon after finding out about his wife to have thought it all that far through. And yet he did think it through remarkably well."

"And if all you have is DNA," Steve Tekemanian said, "you can't tell if the person was transgendered or not. A transgendered male's

DNA is just male DNA. There aren't any genetic markers for trans-gendering that we know of."

"You mean Arthur Heydreich married his wife without knowing she'd had a sex change operation?" Bennis said. "Is that really possible?"

"Sure," Steve Tekemanian said. "The results of the surgery and the therapy are mixed, of course, but she might just have been a very successful case. And I've seen pictures of her. The usual things that give a transsexual away are the hands and the waist. She had very delicate hands and the kind of figure you see on *Playboy* centerfolds. And then there were the, you know, the chest. She must have had that done. I don't think they come that big naturally."

"Although I would have started wondering if some woman I knew were as fanatic as Martha Heydreich appeared to be about broadcasting her femininity," Gregor said. "There was the pink car, the pink clothes, the pink everything. Larry Farmer told me that her ring tone for her phone was 'I Enjoy Being a Girl.' Martha Heydreich seems to have spent half her time letting everybody on the planet know how female she was. And then she made herself up to the point where she could have looked like Attila the Hun without anybody knowing it."

"Didn't Arthur Heydreich see her without makeup?" Bennis said.

Gregor shrugged. "He might just have thought she was a homely woman. Or maybe she didn't take the makeup off. At any rate, I think it's absolutely the case that he didn't know until very close to the end that she had had a sex change operation. I think if he'd have known earlier, he would just have divorced her, and that would have been that. It was only after she got caught in Michael Platte's blackmail that it became necessary to deal with the issue as an issue. It's one thing to ditch your wife through no fault and just chalk it up to irreconcilable differences. It's another not to know when the other shoe is going to drop, when Michael Platte or somebody else like him was going to get into things and make trouble. Once Arthur Heydreich realized that Martha Heydreich was recognizable as a transsexual, or at least as more masculine than she should have been, to people in the general public, he'd have had to worry for the rest of his life that somebody else would make the same discovery Michael Platte had. Since nobody else had made the discovery yet, now was a good time to end the entire problem. And he did end it."

"Wasn't there some kind of mysterious safe-deposit key?" Steve asked. "That was on the news a few days ago."

"It was Martha Heydreich's safe-deposit key," Gregor said. "They did find the box eventually. It contained the records of Martha's surgery, and a few other things. Diaries going back to her childhood. The journal she kept when she first started the hormone therapy leading up to the surgery. I don't suppose we'll ever know how Michael Platte got that key or if he ever looked into that safe-deposit box. Arthur Heydreich says he didn't know about the box, and I believe him. If he had, he'd have taken that key off Michael Platte's body. Instead, he didn't even go looking for it."

"Do we know how he killed her?" Steve Tekemanian asked.

Gregor shook his head. "This time, he's got a serious lawyer, and he isn't talking. I suppose I can't really blame him for that. I wouldn't talk either if I was in his position. But I do wonder about it. It isn't as easy to kill somebody as you'd think. He whacked Michael Platte on the back of the head hard enough to give Michael a skull bone collapse across the back of the head and it didn't kill him. Michael Platte went into the water alive and drowned. Part of me has to wonder if the same sort of thing didn't happen with Martha Heydreich, if she didn't spent the last hours of her life alone in that locker room, unable to speak or move but still living. Part of me has to wonder if she was alive when he lit that match."

Steve Tekemanian coughed. "She might have been alive," he said, "but she wouldn't have been conscious. If she had the same kind of hole in the back of her head the papers said Michael Platte had, she wouldn't have been aware of anything at all."

"Maybe," Gregor said. "But I've read too many stories of supposedly unconscious coma victims waking up and describing everything that's gone on around them for the last thirty years to be all that sure about that."

"This is really depressing," Bennis said. "I mean, this is really, really depressing. And it's such a nice day."

"And I've got a new apartment," Steve Tekemanian said, "right on practicum central and everything. Do you do a lot of these cases, Mr. Demarkian, or just a couple a year?"

Marty Tekemanian made a strangled noise. "I don't think that's very fair, Steve. Mr. Demarkian just came back from breakfast. And you can't expect him to tell you everything about his clients, he's got professional ethics to consider and—"

"Keep your shirt on, Marty," Steve said. "I won't compromise Gregor Demarkian's professional ethics. But let's be real here. You can't learn real forensics out of a textbook. You've got to know how real murders happen in the real world."

Marty Tekemanian made another strangled noise.

Gregor started up the long flight of stone steps to the front door, thinking it might be a good idea to speed up work on those renovations.

3

Fifteen minutes later, Gregor was standing at the window of the living room of the apartment he shared with Bennis, looking down on Cavanaugh Street and seeing nothing. Somewhere underneath him, there were noises. Marty and Steve were cleaning out old George's apartment for the last time, picking up odds and ends, making sure the place was clean. Gregor had looked in on the place for a moment on his way upstairs, and the sight of it had made his stomach clench. He had calmed down a little in the time since old George had died, but he hadn't moved on. Not really.

He heard the door open in the foyer and the sound of Bennis's clogs on the foyer floor. He didn't understand how she could wear those things. He and Tibor had tried them on once when Bennis was out, and they'd both felt as if somebody was cutting off their feet.

Bennis came into the living room. He heard her drop down onto his overused couch.

"Well," she said.

"Well, what?"

"Tibor says you're obsessing about why anybody has to die," Bennis said. "I wouldn't have put it that way, but I think I know what he's talking about. He's right, you know, Gregor. Dying is a part of life."

"Did you ever ask yourself why?"

Bennis made a strangled noise. "Everybody asks themselves why. Usually while they're taking Introduction to Philosophy freshman year."

Gregor shook his head. "I'm not being juvenile, and I'm not being an idiot, I deal with death all the time. I understand why murder victims die. Somebody blows a hole in their heads, or knifes a gash in their hearts, and the organs stop functioning. I understand why cancer victims die. I understand why heart attack victims die. I'm not complaining about death. I'm complaining about—"

"What?"

Across the street, Lida Arkmanian was coming out of her own front door, carrying something in a covered tray. That would be food for Steve.

"In Norse mythology," Gregor said, "the gods were eternal, but they weren't immortal. You could kill them, but if you didn't kill them, they never died. Do you see what I mean?"

"Not exactly," Bennis said.

"I think I could handle the idea of human beings as eternal but not immortal," Gregor said, "what bothers me is the idea that people can die for no reason. That some day, we all just stop. Just because we do. We stop."

"He was a hundred years old," Bennis said. "Maybe his body just wore out."

"Precisely," Gregor said. "And that's the problem. I can't get rid of the idea that it's just wrong. Age isn't a disease. Most of my life, I've thought it was a blessing. Seriously. Consider the alternative."

"Right," Bennis said.

"It's not a disease and it's not a fault and it's perfectly natural," Gregor said, "and there's something fundamentally wrong with the fact that it ends you up dead. I don't know how to say it any better than that."

"It's all a little mushy," Bennis said.

"It's a little mushy to me, too. I'm sorry that I'm being so— adolescent."

"That's all right," Bennis said. "I get adolescent all the time. Usually about handbags."

Gregor sighed.

Down below him, Lida and Marty and Steve were standing in the street, as if they would never have to worry about traffic. Marty was holding the covered dish. Lida was saying something emphatically, with lots of hand waving and foot stomping and general body language. Down the street a ways, Gregor could see the bits and pieces of Donna's latest decorating project, which seemed to be taking up the majority of the U.S. supply of Indian corn.

It was an ordinary day on Cavanaugh Street, and as long as there were ordinary days on Cavanaugh Street, old George Tekemanian would never really be gone.